P9-DEU-398

The Great Harvard Robbery

BOOKS BY JOHN MINAHAN

A Sudden Silence
The Passing Strange
The Dream Collector
Jeremy
Sorcerer
Nine/Thirty/Fifty-five
Almost Summer
Nunzio
Complete American Graffiti
Eyewitness
The Great Hotel Robbery
The Great Diamond Robbery
Mask
The Face Behind the Mask
The Great Pyramid Robbery
The Great Harvard Robbery

TRANSLATION
The Fabulous Onassis

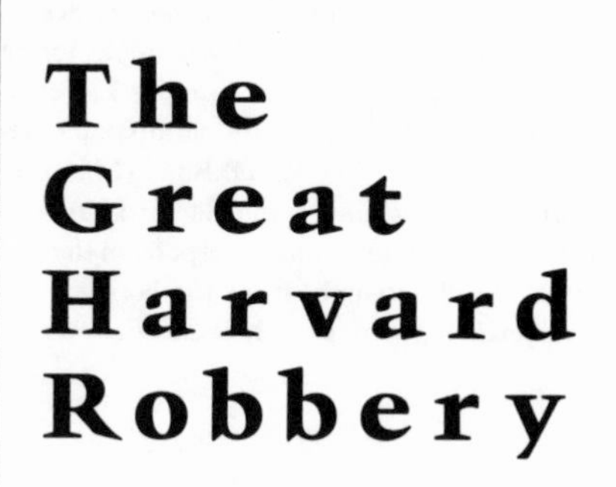

The Great Harvard Robbery

John Minahan

W · W · Norton & Company
New York · London

Grateful acknowledgment is made to Cornell University Press for permission to reprint five excerpts from *Satan: The Early Christian Tradition* by Jeffrey Burton Russell, copyright © 1981 by Cornell University Press; to Avon Books for permission to reprint two excerpts from *The Satanic Bible* by Anton Szandor LaVey, copyright © 1969 by Anton Szandor LaVey; to *Harvard Magazine* for permission to reprint one excerpt from the article "The Gutenberg Caper" by W. H. Bond (March-April 1986 issue), copyright © 1986 by *Harvard Magazine;* and to the Harvard University Office of News and Public Affairs for permission to reprint one excerpt from the article "The Black Presence at Harvard" by Caldwell Titcomb, from the booklet "350 Years: Historical Notes on Harvard," copyright © 1986, President and Fellows of Harvard College.

Published simultaneously in Canada by Penguin Books Canada Ltd., 2801 John Street, Markham, Ontario L3R 1B4
Printed in the United States of America

The text of this book is composed in Times Roman, with display type set in Trump Bold. Composition and manufacturing by The Haddon Craftsmen, Inc.

First Edition

Library of Congress Cataloging in Publication Data
Minahan, John
The great Harvard robbery / John Minahan.
p. cm.
I. Title.
PS3563.I4616G69 1988
813'.54—dc19 88-5872

ISBN 0-393-02605-1

W. W. Norton & Company, Inc., 500 Fifth Avenue, New York, N. Y. 10110
W. W. Norton & Company, Ltd., 37 Great Russell Street, London WC1B 3NU

1 2 3 4 5 6 7 8 9 0

Acknowledgments

I want to express my appreciation for the technical advice of Lt. William F. McCarthy, commanding officer of the Bomb Squad, New York Police Department, and Deputy Chief Jack W. Morse of the Harvard University Police Department. A special note of gratitude goes to John F. Adams, assistant dean of the Harvard University Extension School, who read the manuscript to ensure factual accuracy about Harvard, thereby saving my tail on quite a few occasions.

To Joan Davis

and

Connie Weber,

who know I'm not
irreverent
in my heart.

Falling in love with Harvard is like falling in love with the Statue of Liberty. You can never put your arm around it.

—JOHN FINLEY
Professor *Emeritus*
of Greek Literature,
Harvard University

The Great Harvard Robbery

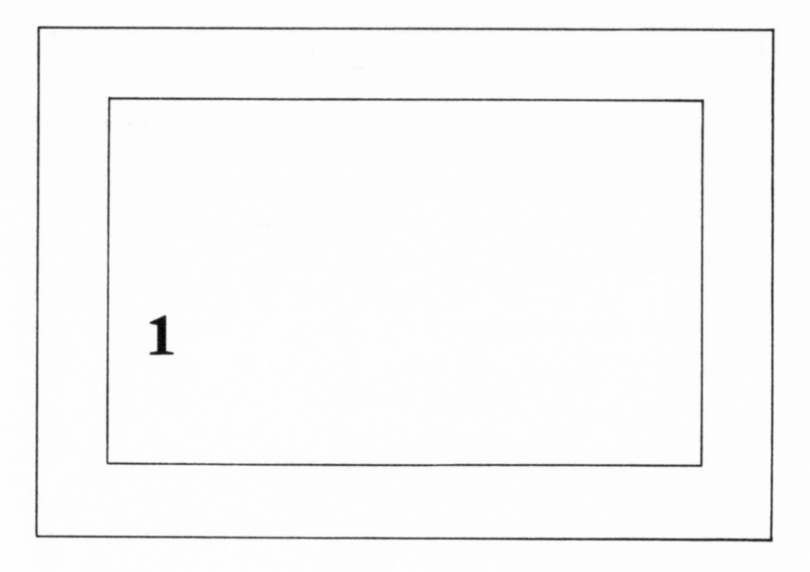

1

NOTHING IS SACRED in New York, everybody knows that, but when I read about this particular theft, it gave me a strange feeling. It was in the *Daily News,* Sunday, August 24, 1986, just a humorous little piece with a picture. Thing that caught my eye was the headline: "Holy Mike! He's gone!" Then there was a subhead: "Saints preserve us, is nothing sacred?" What happened, some clown stole a four-foot-high bronze statue of St. Michael, the archangel, from its pedestal outside St. Michael's High School, Thirty-third Street and Tenth Avenue, where it'd been since the late nineteenth century. School's principal, a Catholic nun, said the police believe someone took it to melt it down. It was welded to a platform about eight feet above the sidewalk. Apparently, the crook stood on a wooden box and used a wrench to unbolt the statue itself, leaving behind its inscribed stand. According to the inscription, it was donated to the school in 1896 by Mr. and Mrs. James Fitzgerald. Photo that ran with the story showed the classic old statue, St. Michael with his wings and all, strong right arm raised in victory, and he's stomping on the ugliest Satan I ever saw, complete with horns and bat-like wings, cringing on the ground in defeat. What St. Michael's doing, of course, he's throwing the rebellious Lucifer into hell. It's in the Bible.

Anyhow, that afternoon, Sunday afternoon, I get a call at home from Chief Vadney. Very unusual. Conversation goes like so:

"Rawlings, y'read today's *News?*"

"Yeah."

"Y'read that story about the statue of St. Michael?"

"Matter of fact, I did, yeah."

"There's more to it than we told the press, Little John. The guy who stole the statue left a note."

"A note?"

"Yeah, he taped an envelope to the empty pedestal. Addressed to Commissioner Reilly."

"Holy shit."

"Yeah. I'm afraid we're dealing with a real sicko here."

"What'd the note say?"

"It's weird, Little John, I can't—I really can't discuss it on the phone, know what I mean? Sorry to pull you away on a Sunday, but there's a time element involved here, we need you in here."

"Where?"

"Headquarters. Reilly's office."

"What time?"

"Soon as possible. It's now one-forty-five. How's the Sunday train schedule out there?"

"Not good, Chief. I'll have to drive."

"Make it by two-thirty?"

"I'll try."

We live in Bellmore, Long Island, just twenty-four miles from Manhattan, so it's not that big a deal. Besides, I don't get to drive my new car that often, I take the train every day, and I enjoy driving this thing. I call it "new," but it's twenty months old now, first sports car I ever had, a 1984 Nissan 300-ZX Turbo, white, with a thin black trim. Bought it December 1, 1984. Turbo makes all the difference, never had a car with this much pep, 200 horsepower maximum at 5200 rpm, and it averages nineteen to the gallon. Truth is, I never really enjoyed driving before I got this thing. All right, okay, I know the cliché about how older guys buy sports cars because it makes them feel young, but I don't care. I mean, it's probably true, what can I tell you? Only important thing, I like driving it, it makes me happy. I'm fifty-three years old, for Christ's sake, I've been a cop for thirty-one years, I can afford the payments (sixty-month plan), so why shouldn't I have it? I figure I've earned it, I deserve it.

Only thing that bothers me about driving to Manhattan, it means I'll have to skip my workout routine this afternoon, and I haven't missed a day in over two months. Jogging? No way. Me, I play basketball every day. Not in competition, I'm not ready for that yet, not even one-on-one. I play alone. Started to get a little potbelly last June, even my wife made a few subtle comments about it. That did it. Out I went, bought a good basketball, a Wilson "Grabber," intended for outdoor use, which is where I use it. Play on a regulation asphalt court at the community college near our home. On the job, I work the eight-to-four shift, weekdays, so I try to catch the 4:35 train from Penn Station. That's the local, takes forty-five minutes, but it's not all that crowded, and I get to read the *Post* in relative comfort. Get to the house about 5:30, still plenty of daylight left this time of year. Change to shorts and sneakers, grab my Grabber, drive over to the campus, play hoop for an hour. Work up a good sweat, but I don't overdo it. Get home, I'm soaking wet, which is what I want. Take a shower, come downstairs, feel tired but good. Know what I want to drink? Beefeater martini? Cold beer? No way. Milk. Yeah. Tall glass of cold milk. Not just regular milk. Chocolate milk.

Hate to admit it, but that's the truth. Make it myself with Hershey's syrup. Exact same thing I used to crave when I was a kid, when I got home from high school basketball practice. Big glass of chocolate milk. Dark. If I ever told that to a shrink, he'd have a field day with it, right? Of course, I'll have a few martinis later on, I'm not *that* far gone.

But to get back to this Sunday afternoon, I drive into Manhattan, there's not much traffic until I get in the vicinity of Kennedy Airport, but I'm enjoying it, I got my air conditioner on, I got my good stereo on, and I'm looking forward to the meeting with Commissioner Reilly. He's the third police commissioner we've had since I joined the department and I never got to meet one of them until today. Gives you an idea of what fantastic political clout I've developed over the years. Me, I'm just a robbery detective, Nineteenth Precinct, rarely get an opportunity to rub elbows with the brass. Now, since St. Michael's High School's on West Thirty-third at Tenth, that's the jurisdiction of the Tenth Precinct, down on West Twentieth, which means Vadney's pulling me into this case on a special-assignment basis. At least, that's what I hope he's doing, because I usually enjoy special-assignment duty, particularly under Chief Vadney, never a dull day. Unlimited overtime, unlimited expense account (within reason), unlimited exposure to the Duke's harebrained techniques. Reason we call him Duke, you'd have to know Vadney, he's a John Wayne–type guy, looks like him, talks like him, that's why we hung the moniker on him, fits like his custom boots.

Another reason I hope this is a special-assignment deal, if so, it'll get me out of that rathole of a temporary station house we've been in for over a year now, 312 East Ninety-fourth. Two redesigned floors of a four-story dump that used to be a social services office. Our regular station house, 153 East Sixty-seventh, where I spent half my career, it's being renovated now, job's supposed to take three years. Second oldest precinct in the city, dates back to 1887, it's a New York City Landmark, so they can't change the exterior. What they're doing, they're gutting the inside, transforming it into an ultramodern, computerized, color-coded psycho ward, just like all the others. Change is the price of progress, right?

Driving across the Brooklyn Bridge, first thing that strikes me about the lower Manhattan skyline, there's no smog on Sunday. All the buildings are big and bold in the sun, particularly the towers of the World Trade Center, you can see the top stories today. Refreshing to see the skyline like that once in a while. Air out there looks almost healthy enough to breathe.

At the west end of the bridge, you get into the Civic Center area, which includes a large number of government offices, federal and state as well as municipal, plus six courthouses, and Police Headquarters is just southeast of that complex, One Police Plaza. It's one of the newer buildings (1973), fourteen floors of red brick with deeply recessed windows, looks something like a fortress. Bordered to the north by Park Row, to the east by Pearl Street, to the south by Madison Street, and to the west by—ready for this?—Avenue of the Finest. Yeah. Avenue of the Finest. Meaning "New York's Finest," of course, the NYPD. Ask any New Yorker where Avenue of the Finest is located. Go ahead. Always draws a blank look, then a frown: "Huh? Avenue of the *what?*" Nobody has a clue. Make a good question for Trivial Pursuit, right?

Show my gold to the cop at the entrance to the underground garage, drive down in, place is practically deserted, so I select a parking space near the elevators. Before I get out, I reach down, press the stainless-steel button that arms my car's burglar alarm. Yeah, even in here. You kidding? I've trained myself to push that alarm button every time I get out of the car, doesn't matter where I am, absolutely no exceptions, even do it in my locked garage at home.

Now I take the elevator up to the lobby. Modern, spacious, nobody around but the officer at the security desk. He checks my ID, checks my appointment with Commissioner Reilly, gives me a red plastic visitor's pass to clip to my lapel. Every floor in headquarters is color coded; every visitor, police or civilian, is required to wear a color-coded plastic pass restricting admission to the floor of that color. I clip the pass to my lapel as I walk to the bank of elevators over to the right. In deference to Reilly, I'm wearing my best blue blazer, fresh white button-down shirt, conservative tie, gray trousers, black Guccis that I notice could use a shine, so I give 'em a quick buff on the backs of my trouser legs. My wife hates me to do that, says it's tacky, says I ruin my trousers that way, right? Old habits die hard. Used to do it when I was a bachelor, what can I tell you?

Take the elevator up, Reilly's office is on the fourteenth floor, same as Vadney's, penthouse floor, where else? Step off, check the directory on the wall, turn left, walk down the long, gleaming, hospital-like corridor. Most offices are empty. Commissioner's suite is in the northwest corner. Probably has the best view in the joint.

I enter a gray-carpeted reception area, tasteful decor, soft lamplight instead of the usual fluorescent glare. I'm surprised to see Reilly's secretary at her desk near his closed door, at least I assume it's his secretary. Rank has its perks, this kid's a class act all the way to Cartier and back. Early thirties, chestnut-brown windblown coif frames a flawless oval face dominated by bright blue eyes. Kid's eyes rivet my attention, don't know why. I mean, I'm a trained observer, I pick up on details most people miss, do it almost automatically. Most women, I notice their hair, face, figure, clothes, maybe a few details that set them apart, get a general impression. This kid, she's got all the good stats in spades, but then she's got eyes that tell me something important about her. What is it? That she's very bright? Part of it, no question, but there's more. Savvy? That she's got savvy well beyond her years?

She glances up. “May I help you?”

“Detective Rawlings to see Commissioner Reilly.”

She stands now, smiles, relatively tall, extremely thin, sticks out her hand. “It’s a pleasure to meet you, I’ve heard a lot about you over the years. I’m Samantha Reilly.”

I shake her hand. “Samantha—Reilly?”

“Bill’s wife, yes. I just came along to keep him company. He’s very upset about all this.”

“I see. They haven’t told me much about it yet.”

“He’s inside with Vadney and Mairs. I’ll tell him you’re here.” She leans over, hits a button on the console, speaks into the intercom. Looks smart in a blue-striped boatneck pullover and white cotton slacks. “Detective Rawlings to see you.”

“Please send him in.”

I go to the door. “Pleasure to meet you, Mrs. Reilly.”

Her blue eyes seem transparent in the lamplight. “Nice to meet you, too.”

Reilly’s office, all I can tell you, it’s like a modern corporate president’s office in the sense that it’s designed to look more like a living room than a place of business. Strong sunlight from the west filters through long white curtains, makes patterns on the pale gray carpet, highlights art objects and colorful lamps on glass tables. Off to my left, Reilly, Vadney, and Jim Mairs (commander of the Emergency Service Division) sit on sofas and chairs arranged around a big square glass-and-chrome coffee table. Beyond them, close to the windows, is a conference table that looks more like a dining table. In the far right corner, Reilly’s desk is a graceful wooden table with a low-backed black leather armchair. Only object that spoils the living room atmosphere is the mandatory (I guess) American flag standing vertically in a holder of some kind back near his desk chair.

“Little John, come in, sit down,” Chief says. “Close the door, huh? You know Bill and Jim, right?”

I close the door. "I know Jim, but I've never had the pleasure of meeting Commissioner Reilly."

"Oh, sorry about that," he says, standing. "John Rawlings, like you to meet Bill Reilly."

Reilly gets up, we shake hands, exchange greetings. Man's a little shorter than me, maybe five-nine, well built, looks in good shape, mid-forties, thick dark hair, dark brown eyes, shirt-sleeves rolled to the elbows, tie pulled down, collar open. His right front tooth is chipped off at an angle, not much, but it makes him look almost boyish when he smiles. Don't know what I expected, I'd only seen pictures of him, newspapers mostly, but the way he comes off in person, this guy strikes me as a soft-spoken, well-educated street fighter.

"Let's get you up to speed," Chief tells me. "First off, I want you to read the note this guy left." Sits down, leans forward, shuffles through a stack of papers on the coffee table, frowns, takes a swipe at the cowlick over his forehead. "Where the fuck is it? Jim, you had it last, I saw you with it. Huh? The original, I mean."

Jim Mairs (pronounced "Mars") stands up without a word, goes to Reilly's desk, picks up a white business-sized envelope, comes back. He's in shirt-sleeves too, dark tie pulled down, tall, lean, face with the medium mileage of mid-forties, penetrating green eyes. I worked two other cases with him, I like his style, the guy's a pro's pro. He has his little idiosyncrasies, collects weird objects and that, but nobody's perfect. Dominant impression, my opinion, he comes off like a college professor–type guy, I don't know. We're having a drink one night, I tell him that, he laughs, but he's not exactly wild about the comparison. Also, he dislikes the word "egghead," which I have a tendency to use on occasion. Never used it to describe him, but he's heard me toss it around, he's given me a couple of looks. Now, according to his secretary, I don't know if this is true or not, but according to her, she thinks he's touchy about the word because he happens to have a high forehead.

A high forehead that happens to appear higher nowadays because his hair is receding. But, wait a minute, she bounces back with the observation that lots of women around headquarters consider receding hair on a man to be quite attractive. Actually, the word she uses is "sexy." On the other hand, a detective who knows him well, guy by the name of Hank Smith, old buddy of mine, he puts it another way. "Little John," he says, "on the subject of Jim's forehead, things have progressed since the last time you worked with him." He says, "Jim's forehead now begins at the back of his neck." Not true, of course, but now, as Jim comes back and hands me the envelope, I can't help taking a fast glance at his noggin. Split second, right? Shit, he catches me. Gives me this penetrating green-eyed glare. Absolutely penetrating.

Envelope's got Scotch tape at the ends where it was taped to the pedestal. Feels powdery because the lab dusted for prints. Reilly's full name, title, and headquarters address are typed, looks to my eye like an electric typewriter. Open it up, take out this 8½ × 11 sheet, good quality paper, powdery to the touch. Two even folds, business style, typing is single spaced, very neat and clean:

"There was a war in heaven: Michael and his angels fought against the dragon; and the dragon fought and his angels,

"And prevailed not.

"The great dragon was cast out, that old serpent, called the Devil, and Satan, which deceiveth the whole world."

Revelation
12:7-9

Reilly:

If you want to know who did this, be at the school Sunday, August 24, exactly 11:59 p.m.

Now I hold the paper up to the light, see if there's a watermark. Sure is, big and bold:

PARCHMENT DEED
SOUTHWORTH CO., U.S.A.
100% COTTON FIBER

"It's a very high quality twenty-pound bond," Mairs tells me. "We called a large office-supply store yesterday. It retails for about twenty-two bucks a box, five hundred sheets, and it's sold all over the country."

"Come up with any latents?" I ask.

"Nothing," Reilly says. "The envelope had the school principal's prints, a nun, Sister Mary Garcia. She called the Tenth Precinct. When the detectives picked it up, they dropped it in a plastic evidence bag, so nobody else touched it. As soon as it arrived here, Jim ran it through the X-ray scanner to check for plastic explosives, then he opened it with gloves. After we read it, he had it dusted immediately. Not a single print, not even a partial. Absolutely pristine. Which means the guy had to wear gloves when he was typing it."

"Nothing unusual about the typewriter," Chief adds. "Lab report identified it as an IBM Correcting Selectric Two, with a typeface called Prestige Elite Seventy-two. Very common."

I place the letter back in the envelope, hand it to Reilly. "Why was it addressed to you?"

He shrugs. "I'm a graduate of St. Michael's, class of fifty-nine, I spent four years there. But, I mean, Christ, that was—twenty-seven years ago."

"Make any serious enemies there?" I ask.

"Little John," Chief says, "we've covered all this stuff."

"No, no, Walt," Reilly says. "Rawlings has a right to know firsthand. I mean, if he's going to work this case, he's got to know everything we know. The answer to that question is no, to the best of my knowledge. I mean, I've given it a great deal of thought. And I just can't seem to recall anybody who was a real enemy. I don't think I had *any* real enemies back then. Not in the true sense. I mean, I was a competitive kid, I held class offices, I was president of my senior class. I went out for sports, I played baseball, I ran track. Academically, I finished second in the class, I was salutatorian."

"Who was valedictorian?" Mairs asks.

"Girl by the name of Sherry Young."

"Who finished third?" Chief asks.

He thinks about it. "Jesus, I'm not even sure I can remember who finished third. Good question, but I honestly don't think it's relevant, Walt. Because, as I recall, there was a fairly wide gap between me and whoever finished behind me. Same thing between me and Sherry Young. So there was no race-to-the-wire kind of thing. We all knew pretty much where we'd finish."

"Let's get back to the note," I say. "How about that quote from the Bible? Any special significance to you?"

"No. I mean, I know the quote, it's just—as I'm sure you know, it's just one of many regarding St. Michael. He was—is—the patron saint of the school."

I sit back, take out a cigar, glance at him. "Mind?"

"Not at all." He pushes an ashtray toward me.

I light up. "Did the statue itself have any special significance to you?"

"No. It was just a beautiful old statue. I took it for granted like everybody else."

"Rawlings," Chief says. "Blow that smoke away from me, huh?"

When Reilly smiles, his chin juts out. "Walt, you realize you're the only one who doesn't smoke in this group? You're outnumbered for a change. You're just gonna have to live with it."

Chief gives him a cold fish-eye.

"Commissioner," I say, "mind a few personal questions?"

"No, not at all, John, and please call me Bill."

"Thank you. Are you a practicing Catholic now?"

He hesitates. "We're bringing up the kids as Catholics, but I don't practice the faith anymore, no. I'm an agnostic."

"Are you particularly close to the school?"

"No. In what sense?"

"Do you support the school in any way, financially or—?"

"I've made donations over the years, yes. During fund drives. Very modest donations, John; I'm not a wealthy man."

"Have you attended class reunions?"

"I'm afraid not, no. I just don't go in for that kind of thing."

In the pause, Mairs lights up a Marlboro, clears his throat. "I was thinking last night, maybe we're overlooking the obvious. Every time we mention the statue, we're talking about St. Michael alone. But there's another figure on that statue."

"True," Reilly says. "That's something we haven't addressed, Jim, good point."

"Satan?" Chief asks.

"Satanism," Mairs says. "Satanic cults in this city. Bill, think carefully. Over the years, have you ever had any association with anybody even remotely connected with Satanism or Satanic rituals?"

"No, not to my knowledge. To be honest, I know very little about the subject. Tell us what you know."

"Not all that much," Mairs says, "but I've done some reading on it." He takes a drag on the cigarette, glances at the windows, exhales slowly. "Satanic cults operate underground here, but in San Francisco there's actually a formal religion—that is, a legally incorporated religion—called the Church of Satan. It was founded in the late sixties by a man named Anton Szandor LaVey, and apparently it's grown in popularity, especially among college students. Ceremonies such as baptism, marriage, the Black Mass, and funerals are dedicated to Satan, and there's a well-defined philosophy behind the whole thing. LaVey's published books on the subject, I've read one, *The Satanic Bible,* which is now in its twelfth edition and outsells the Christian Bible on college campuses. He has another book in print, *The Satanic Rituals,* I just browsed through it. There's a third book, can't think of the title, which is out of print now. But, the fact is, you can go into most large bookstores in New York and buy the other two in paperback. They're still in print, so they must be selling. The publisher is Avon, which, as you know, is a very respectable house."

I'm taking notes now, I ask Mairs to spell LaVey's full name and repeat the titles of those two books.

"Jim, tell me this," Chief says. "I mean, just briefly, just the basics. What's this Church of Satan all about anyway, what's it teach these kids?"

"Not what you'd probably expect," Mairs says, "that's the intriguing aspect. This is no wild-eyed occultist outfit. For example, it doesn't depict Satan as the traditional man-like red figure with goat-like horns, hooves, and a tail. Instead, Satan is defined as a dark, hidden force in nature. A real but mysterious force that's beyond the grasp of finite intelligence. At the same time, LaVey recognizes the need for symbols and rituals in any formal religion, so he's devised a complex set of his own, based on various concepts of Satan that go all the way back to pre-biblical roots, then through Hebrew and Christian thought, into the present."

Chief nods, frowns. "I think you lost me there."

"Let's get back to the statue," I suggest. "Let's just suppose, for the sake of argument, that it was stolen by a Satanic cult. Why would they do that? What's the reason, the motive?"

The three of us look to Mairs for an answer.

"Okay, let's approach it logically," he says. "We know it's not a publicity stunt, because the letter wasn't addressed to the press and wasn't even signed—whatever the cult might call itself—to claim credit for the crime. In my judgment, it's logical to assume that whoever wrote the letter was in command of a certain amount of so-called classified intelligence about how this department handles potentially sensitive situations, particularly among its hierarchy. First, there was the commonsense aspect. The individual or group knew this letter would be handled with extreme care, X-rayed, opened with gloves, dusted for prints, the whole nine yards. But, second, whoever did this also knew that it'd be investigated in secret. By a select few. And that not a hint of it would be leaked to the press. Why? Commissioner Reilly is involved and might conceivably be at risk. Whoever did this knew we'd handle it exactly the same way we handle most death threats to public officials and certain civilians. Third, following the same line of logical assumptions, whoever did this has knowledge about Bill's personal background. Knows he's an alumnus of St. Michael's. Knows, or takes an educated guess, how Bill's going to react—with a combination of disgust, anger, and outrage that anybody would steal an old statue that had so much religious and sentimental value to so many people. Bill, is that—? I think that's probably a fairly accurate assessment of how you feel, isn't it?"

Reilly thinks about it, nods slowly.

"And that's what concerns me the most," Mairs continues, tapping his cigarette in the ashtray. "That whoever did this apparently believes he can reach you on an emotional level, manipulate you on an emotional level to get what he wants. In this case, to get you to show up at the school tonight. I've advised you not to go because, in my judgment, it could be dangerous. It's just an unnecessary risk."

"Bill, he's right," Chief says. "No question about it."

Reilly smiles briefly, shakes his head. "I told you that I intend to be there. I told you and I told Jim. How many times do I have to say it? I'm a stubborn Irishman, okay? Whoever did this, a kid, a practical joker, a psycho, a Satanist, or just some asshole with a grudge, he's just not gonna intimidate me. I just flat-out refuse to be intimidated."

Mairs glances at his watch. "In that case, we'll have to start the security precautions immediately. We've got—it's now almost two-forty-five. So we've got about four hours of good daylight left and a total of more than nine hours to get set, which should be adequate."

"Spell it out for us," Chief says.

"Number one," Mairs says, "we block off Thirty-third from Ninth to Tenth avenues. Two, the Bomb Squad will search the entire school, room by room, floor by floor, plus the school grounds. Three, they'll search adjacent buildings, garages, vehicles in the street, the works, from manholes to streetlights. Four, I'll assign a total of fifteen Emergency Service Division sharpshooters to assume positions on roofs and in windows of the school and adjacent buildings. Bill, I want you out of the immediate vicinity until eleven-fifty-five. At that time, my advice to you—my strongest advice as a professional—is to allow ESD to do its job, to provide maximum protection. If you insist on going ahead with this, I want you to arrive in front of that school in a bulletproof limo, accompanied by me. That's step five, a critical step, and it's the safest environment I can recommend under the circumstances. At that point, given a worst-situation scenario, our most serious vulnerability would be exposure to airborne incendiary devices lofted into the target area. Obviously, this is always extremely difficult to anticipate and defend against. We've seen projectiles fired with a relatively high degree of accuracy from weapons as basic as bazookas. Fired from as far away as five city blocks, although the range is generally much shorter. Projectiles ranging from armor-piercing rockets to homemade tear-gas grenades. Naturally, the limo will be equipped with gas masks. Finally, in the event we were forced to vacate the limo, we would need helmets and vests, and I will insist that you wear both, as I intend to do. That's it, Bill. Except to say that I think you're crazy to go through with it."

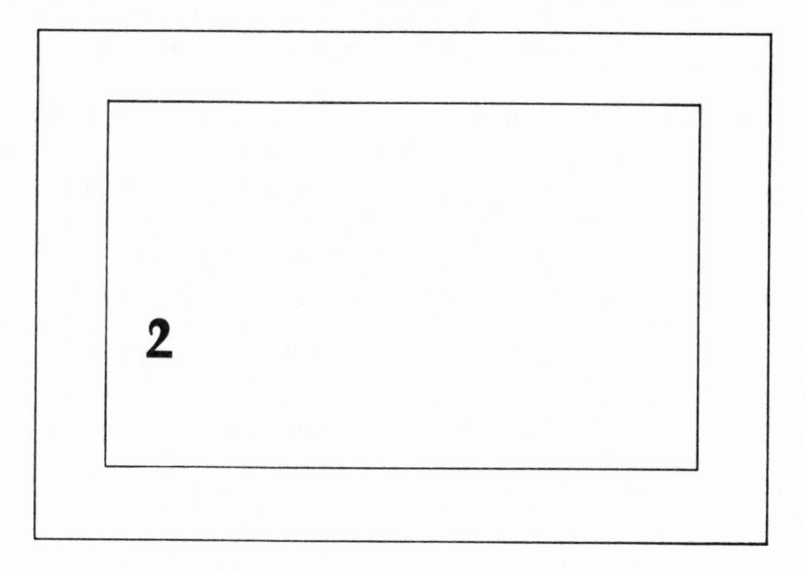

THE BOMB SQUAD operates out of the Sixth Precinct, 233 West Tenth, nice little tree-lined Greenwich Village street, shady, quiet on Sunday. I go in, show my gold, ask for Lieutenant McCartney, the commanding officer, he's expecting me. Desk sergeant tells me second floor, points out the stairs, says, "Look for the bomb." Look for the bomb? Climb the stairs, turn left, walk down the hall, here's this big World War II bomb suspended from the ceiling, says BOMB SQUAD on it, points toward the squad-room door. Can't possibly miss it, these guys don't fool around. I go in, large rectangular room, fluorescent lights, linoleum floor, desks all over, quite a few detectives on duty. Show my gold, ask for Lieutenant McCartney. I'm told he's in the conference room off to the right, be right out. Thing that catches your attention in this room almost immediately, there's this gigantic display board on the wall to my left, takes up the whole wall, this thing's got head-and-shoulder photos of every member of the NYPD Bomb Squad going all the way back to 1903 when it started, looks like maybe 120 or more officers. Very impressive display. There's a framed history in the middle of the photos, three printed pages under glass. Although I've been a cop for thirty-one years and observed the Bomb Squad in action all over the city, probably hundreds of times, I don't know that much about its history, so I step over and glance at this thing, I'm curious.

Interesting stuff, tell you a few highlights. This is the oldest and largest non-military bomb squad in the United States. Also one of the most specialized professional police units in the country. Roots were formed in April 1903, under the leadership of Lieutenant Guisseppi Petrosino, and it was first known as the Italian Squad, had just five officers. Reason it was formed, seems there was a wave of bombings directed against a bunch of Italian merchants on the Lower East Side because they wouldn't give in to extortion demands made by a secret society called the Black Hand. Merchants turned to Petrosino's Italian Squad as their prime protection. Progress was slow but sure. Then, on March 12, 1909, when Petrosino was in Sicily exchanging information with Italian authorities, he was shot dead. After that, two major things happened: One, information exchange programs with overseas police were broadened; two, as a result of the success of the Italian Squad, a big push was made to recruit other ethnic minorities into NYPD to work within their respective communities. It paid off.

Then we've got a real Bomb Squad working, there's a significant decrease in extortion activities, but that didn't stop the bombings, of course; they just changed direction. For the next decade or so, bombing incidents took on a distinctly political nature, all kinds of extremists began using explosives as a means of advancing their causes. One example, in the so-called Black Tom Explosion of 1916, almost two million pounds of munitions were exploded on a strip of land off the Hudson River. Two million pounds. Quite a bang.

Skip to the end of World War I, you got an epidemic of anarchist bombings that culminate in the famous Wall Street Bombing of September 16, 1920. That day, known as Bloody Thursday, a horse-drawn wagon loaded with explosives was detonated between the J. P. Morgan Building and the U.S. Assay Office at Broad and Wall, killing thirty-nine and injuring three hundred. Bolshevik fringe group was responsible, called themselves the American Anarchist Fighters.

Okay, this period of political unrest gradually subsided, next you're into Prohibition, 1920–1933, and the Bomb Squad has to focus attention on various rival syndicates that used bombing as their common instrument of terror. Sometime during the mid-1930s (the exact year isn't known), the Bomb Squad merged with the Forgery Squad, and the union lasted until 1940—a year that would mark a critical turning point for the Bomb Squad, entirely as the result of a single incident.

On July 4, 1940, an employee at the British Pavilion of the New York World's Fair discovered a package that was subsequently determined to be a bomb. Detectives assigned to that pavilion removed the device from the building and carried it to the perimeter of the fairgrounds, near the Polish Pavilion. Two detectives from the Bomb Squad, Joseph Lynch and Ferdinand Socha, arrived on the scene and began to examine the package. Within seconds, it exploded, killing Lynch and Socha instantly, and injuring four others.

As a direct result of this tragedy, the Bomb Squad was detached from the Forgery Squad, completely reorganized, and the art of bomb disposal was approached in a far more scientific manner. Emphasis was placed on research, additional public funds were allocated for safety equipment, and new recruits were required to undergo a ninety-day training period. Exercises included constructing and dismantling a variety of explosive devices, learning the uses of a wide range of safety equipment, and studying the techniques of bomb investigation.

Now, this next thing, I can relate to this, I remember it as a kid. From 1941 to 1957, the Bomb Squad was plagued by a lone bomber who hid or exploded an estimated forty-seven devices throughout the city. George Metesky, the Mad Bomber, remember him? He'd worked for Consolidated Edison, he claimed he'd been cheated out of his pension, that's why he targeted all the bombs for Con Ed installations. Took NYPD sixteen years to collar this guy.

Historical sketch goes on to say that the most significant increase in major bombing incidents began in the late 1960s with a host of well-organized, militant, revolutionary outfits, ranging from the Black September Group to the notorious FALN, and the potential for death, injury, and personal property damage increased dramatically. Today, it's still going on, of course, only the characters have changed; terrorism continues at an accelerating rate, with no plateau in sight.

Fortunately, the Bomb Squad's kept pace with change. In addition to being the biggest and most experienced police unit of its kind in the country—by a wide margin—it's also the most technologically sophisticated. Today, you see the Bomb Squad in action around the city, it's really something special, makes you proud to be in NYPD. Response vehicles are equipped with portable X-ray systems, fiber optics, listening devices, specially trained dogs from the Canine Corps, all kinds of high-tech safety equipment like Water-Gel fire blankets, SAFECO bomb suits, bomb blankets, phosphorus incendiary suits, and state-of-the-art custom robots called Remote Mobile Investigators, or RMIs. These robot vehicles, they're like unmanned moon buggies, low and sleek with rows of little tires; they roll up to a suspected explosive device, they X-ray it from various angles, see what's inside, they listen to it with very sensitive mikes. If the technicians decide it's potentially dangerous, the robot picks it up gently, takes it over to one of the bomb-containment vehicles, loads it aboard, then it's transported to the squad's large and isolated Demolition Range out at Rodman's Neck in the Bronx, where much of the research and development activities are also conducted. The squad's thirty-seven bomb technicians are all graduates of the Redstone Arsenal training course in Huntsville, Alabama, but their training continues on a year-round basis.

Lieutenant McCartney comes out of the conference room now, walks over, introduces himself, shakes hands. Big, good-looking guy, early forties, bald pate, strong chin, sparkle of humor in his eyes. He escorts me into his office, to the left of the display board, just off the squad room, leaves the door open. Relatively large office, desk in the far right corner near the windows, walls have big maps, cutaway diagrams of demolition enclosures, and NYPD organizational charts. Glass cabinet contains dozens of odd-looking bombs and incendiary devices. Desk itself holds a clean red bundle of maybe a dozen sticks of TNT, looks ornamental, but what do I know? We sit, he leans back, arms braced behind his head, says Vadney briefed him on the basics.

"I'll supervise the search myself," he tells me. "But let me explain a few things before we leave, John. The most competent person to search a particular area is the person who occupies that area. Now, a perfect example," he points to his briefcase on the floor near the desk. "Is that suspicious? In other words, you don't know if that belongs there or not. I do, okay? I know it *can* hold twenty-seven pounds of plastic explosives, but I also know that it doesn't, because I brought it here this morning."

"I understand."

"Okay? So, as far as the Bomb Squad, if there's a threat at St. Michael's, who's the most competent person to search the school with us?"

"The principal," I tell him. "Sister Mary Garcia. She'll be there to open up for us."

"Excellent. Now, in terms of priorities, we'll search public access areas first. In other words, if I'm going to deliver something to the school, exactly where would I be allowed to deliver it? Next, we cover the private areas. But let me tell you this up front, John, let me just get this off my chest. And I went on record with Chief Vadney about this. If the decision was left to me, there's just no way in the world that I'd allow Commissioner Reilly to *be* there, okay?"

"Understood."

"Okay? I mean, I know he's stubborn about this, he's absolutely determined not to be intimidated and all, but if it was up to me, as a professional, I simply wouldn't allow him to *be* there, period."

I nod, shrug, take out a cigar.

"And I feel very strongly about that, John. So, anyhow, let's get down to it. Now, if there's a device inside the building and the commissioner is outside the building. Okay. Public access areas first, but then we'll do the area of the building that would be in the closest proximity to where the commissioner will be located. So, when we get there, we'll have to determine exactly where the commissioner's limo should be parked. Now, St. Michael's School, as I recall, we're talking about a very substantial stone structure. So, if we're able to work back through one or two substantial walls, to search the rooms in that particular area, what's the level of threat to a person on the street? Okay? You'd have to have a mega—you'd have to have an incredible device. St. Michael's is a well-fortified structure with block walls, maybe reinforced concrete and plaster. We're not talking about plyboard and plasterboard. Okay, back to the level of threat. We can go in there and search, but we could also go in there and tear the walls down, destroy the place. The level of threat in this particular instance doesn't justify the destruction of property."

"No way, Bill. There's no specific threat, nothing. Vadney and Mairs just want to touch all the bases on this thing, to take all necessary precautions."

"Yeah, well, you can't blame them, since the commissioner's involved. It's the same basic principle as dignitary protection. We do probably eight hundred searches a year for dignitaries. For example, the president's wife is in town. We've done three searches for her already today. Since last night at six-thirty, we've done a total of five for her. That's the reason I'm working today, Sunday, it's nothing unusual. I mean, there are one hundred and fifty-nine heads of state associated with the U.N., and we provide dignitary protection for all of them. Any request made by the Secret Service or the State Department, we do the bomb search service, it's routine."

"On average, how many actual bomb threats do you have a year?"

"Nine thousand."

"Nine thousand a year?"

He smiles now, sits forward. "Yeah. Nine thousand bomb threats and I'd say about nine hundred jobs. About ten percent. Where we have, quote, suspicious packages, where we have to go through our disposal process."

"That's in all five boroughs?"

"Yeah. Doesn't matter if the FBI has a bomb or the Secret Service has a bomb or the State Department or the Port Authority or the airports, anywhere in the city, it's our bomb, it's our responsibility."

"Nine hundred actual responses?"

"On a yearly average, yeah, last three years."

"I've always been curious, are your people paid significantly more than—?"

"No. Absolutely not. That surprises a lot of people, John, but it's true. As you know, the people here are detectives, we're in the Detective Bureau. The organizational structure is complicated these days, but I work for Chief Vadney. I'm a commander of a unit within the Arson Explosion Division, and the division is under the Detective Bureau. A police officer who arrives here is eligible to be promoted to detective about two years later. But he's paid no more than any other detective in the bureau, okay? And he doesn't arrive at that designation with any greater speed than he would in the normal process. Every officer who comes in here is a graduate of the Hazardous Devices School in Alabama, the only bomb technicians' school in the country. That training is only the introduction to what he needs to learn. A person here doesn't reach maturity for approximately two years. And that process includes what we call in-service training."

"What's that actually entail?"

"Okay, for one thing, we make twelve bombs a month. I have the diagrams of every recovered explosive device in the free world. We've made every fusing system of every recovered device. Now, I have six teams here. Each month, each team creates two devices, and another team must confront these two unidentified devices. They must be able to X-ray it, read the X-ray, interpret it, explain the fusing system, develop a rationale as to how they'd disrupt it, and then do it. And I monitor their success rate in accomplishing that. This goes on continuously. Matter of fact, I'm in the process of doing something that's going to become a—within the business, it's restricted material—but I have a series of tests that I've just done on a total of seventy different devices. And our success rate in defeating these devices is ninety-seven percent. Which I'm very proud of. I mean, I'm in contact with bomb technicians in Spain, England, France, West Germany, and I'm very pleased with what occurs here. I don't know how to be humble about it—we're absolutely the best in the world. People in here are very competent."

Goes like so, I shoot some other questions at him, can't help it, I'm very curious, but now we're both glancing at our watches. It's about 3:15, we're supposed to meet Sister Mary Garcia at the front door of the school at 3:30; that's a short drive from here, but we've got to get moving.

We go out in the squad room, McCartney selects an officer to accompany him in the response vehicle, Detective Mark

McIntyre, he introduces us, we shake hands. Kid looks to be in his mid-twenties, about six-one, 165, thick dark-brown hair, unparted, thick mustache, very white teeth, muscular build. Looks you right in the eye, I like that in a kid, no bullshit about him. Young Tom Selleck–type guy.

Now the three of us go downstairs, out the side entrance into a small courtyard, and McIntyre opens the gate of a little kennel in the building. He goes in, snaps a leash on a sleek-looking Labrador retriever, one of two explosive-detection dogs that are "on duty" today; the other is a German shepherd. As we walk toward the garage, he explains that the squad maintains two canine facilities, one here, one at the Demolition Range out in Rodman's Neck, which is the main training and exercise area. All these specially trained dogs are rotated between the two locations on a regularly scheduled basis to ensure they receive exposure to actual field work as well as constant reinforcement and updating. Basically, they're conditioned to associate the odors of various explosives with food; when they smell an explosive odor, they salivate. According to McIntyre, in the fifteen years they've been used by the Bomb Squad, no dog has ever been injured in the line of duty and—get this one—no dog has ever failed to locate an explosive device when one has been present. Quite a record. This one's named Fred, he's nineteen months old, short gray-white coat and intelligent eyes, a real beauty. He's sniffing my trousers as we walk, he can smell Daisy, that's our dog at home, a six-year-old little Pekingese, she's a real pisser, tell you about her later.

Bomb Squad shares the Sixth Precinct garage on Charles Street, the rear of the station house. Two response vehicles are parked side by side, both are vans, a Ford and a Dodge, sparkling clean, painted identically, top half white, bottom half blue with a vertical white stripe holding the big NYPD logo plus bold letters: BOMB SQUAD. McIntyre opens the rear doors of the one on the end, the dog jumps in, I get my first close-up view of a robot vehicle. Long and almost as wide as the van, six little tires, looks like a TV dolly with an X-ray camera. All the other equipment is stowed neatly like on a boat. McCartney and McIntyre get in a conversation with one of the cops in the garage, I tell them I'll see them at the school.

St. Michael's is at 425 West Thirty-third Street between Ninth and Tenth avenues, one block west of the General Post Office. It's on the north side of the street and, together with its connecting Catholic church, occupies most of the long block. Across the street is an office building and a big Edison parking lot, about half full today. Years ago, the entire area between Thirtieth and Fifty-eighth streets, west of Eighth Avenue, was named Hell's Kitchen, one of the worst crime areas in the city, old tenements that housed famous gangs like the Gorillas, the Gophers, and the Kitchen Mob; some of them had more than five hundred members. Today, most of the tenements are gone, at least in this immediate vicinity, replaced by office buildings and parking lots, but St. Michael's High School somehow survived it all.

I arrive before the Bomb Squad van, I double-park near the entrance, stick the NYPD card on my dash, arm the burglar alarm before I get out and lock up. Front facade of the school is this classic nineteenth-century architecture with stately pillars and all, dark with soot, but no graffiti in sight. Across the length of the building is a high black wrought-iron fence, enclosing a narrow space between the sidewalk and the school. Off to the left of the entrance, a black iron grillwork deal extends out from the stone wall, about eight feet above the walkway, and holds the circular pedestal where the statue was bolted. So, whoever stole the statue had to get inside the iron fence, which looks to be maybe six feet high, unbolt the statue, and then—? Somehow lift the four-foot-tall solid-bronze statue over the fence? Extremely difficult. I don't know how much it weighed, but it must've been very heavy. Could it have been lifted over the fence by one man? No way. At least, not in my opinion. There must be a gate in this fence.

There is. The long fence is interrupted by the stone archway of the entrance to the school and there's a narrow gate in the fence with a big old-fashioned padlock. I make a mental note to ask Sister Mary Garcia who has keys to that padlock and to ask Jim Mairs how hard it would be to pick that old lock.

It's early, it's only 3:25, nobody out front, so I walk over to the entrance, lean against a pillar, light up a cigar, and glance at the empty pedestal again. Couple of seconds later, I hear the sharp sounds of two deadbolt locks clicking and I turn to see one of the two heavy wooden doors open. A female figure stands there in dark silhouette, lighted from behind, and as I turn around I experience this split-second flashback, or hallucination, still don't know what to call it, haven't had one of these in years. Scenes from my childhood. It's over in seconds, but a sick, dizzy sensation lingers. I blink, use the pillar for support, clear my throat, try to smile at the dark figure in the doorway. "Sister Mary Garcia?"

No answer. The silhouette is motionless. Now I squint, I see it's not a female figure at all, it's a man, relatively tall and lean, wearing a dark garment that looks like a priest's tunic. Before I have a chance to walk toward him, the heavy wooden door closes. It doesn't slam or anything dramatic; it just closes quickly and clicks, with the dark figure behind it. Strange thing is, the figure remained absolutely motionless. So how did the heavy door close?

I'm standing there leaning against the pillar now, still experiencing the sick, dizzy sensation. I drop the cigar, step on it, squint at the door again. Question comes to mind almost instantly: Is this another hallucination? No. No way. This is real, this happened. What the hell's going on here?

I don't know, but I'm going to find out. Okay, I pull myself together, straighten my tie, button my blazer, walk to the door, look around for a bell. No bell. I knock. No answer.

Knock harder. Nothing. Now I turn the knob. Door's unlocked. I open it slightly, look inside. Big marble foyer is brightly lighted. Directly ahead are glass display cabinets holding dozens of sports trophies. Now I clear my throat, call out: "Hello, anybody here?" Voice sounds hollow with all the marble. Nobody answers. I raise my voice: "Sister Mary Garcia?" Voice seems to echo. Then silence. Now I step inside, glance around, look behind the door. To the left and right of the foyer are dimly lighted hallways lined with steel lockers and the marble floors are highly polished. Can't be certain, but I think I hear sounds coming from the end of the right hallway. I go back, close the door quietly, listen again.

Click-click. Clack-click-clack. Soft, almost rhythmic sounds, somehow familiar. Definitely coming from the end of the hallway to the right. *Click-clack-clack-click.* Pause. *Clack-clack-click.* Where the hell have I heard those sounds? Where? When? Know that feeling? A quick, vague spark somewhere back in your mind, your memory. Can't get the spark to ignite.

Okay, ordinarily I wouldn't do this, and I don't know how to explain it, but I have this almost irresistible compulsion to walk down that hallway. I'm standing there, I'm starting to breathe quickly now, I can't believe this. I've just got to walk down that hallway. It's long and dim; the overhead lights from the foyer illuminate only about a third of its distance. Then, way toward the end, I can see a slim white rectangle of light from an open doorway and the light glistens across the marble floor.

I walk slowly, leather heels sounding hollow on the polished marble, punctuating the soft, familiar sounds that now seem less rhythmic, with longer pauses: *Clack-click-clack . . . clack-clack . . . click . . . click.* My shadow starts off short and dark, gets longer with every step, begins to fade as I enter the darkness. I continue along at a slow, steady pace, aware that

I'm breathing quickly, aware that it's warm and stuffy in here, that I'm starting to sweat. Then I feel something that makes me angry for some reason, despite the fact that I have no control over it: I feel the beat of my heart. Adrenaline's starting to pump through my body. Makes me angry because it doesn't happen all that often on the job, at least not anymore. It's usually only triggered during very rare moments when I realize I'm in serious danger. I'm angry at myself, but then I think: You're not listening. Your body is telling you something and you're not listening. Now, as I'm nearing the lighted doorway, I unbutton my blazer, reach back, unsnap the safety strap on my holster.

"Sister Mary Garcia," I call out. "Are you in there?"

Silence for a moment, then: *Clack-click-click. Click-click-click-clack.* Tempo's increased, sounds are louder. I flatten myself against the wall to the right of the doorway. My face is dripping sweat now, I'm still breathing hard, and I feel the beat of my heart. What the hell's wrong with me? I take several deep breaths, try to resist the urge to draw my weapon before going in. I clear my throat, but when I call out, there's a definite shake in my voice:

"Police! Come out of the room with your hands in sight!"

Silence. Five seconds. Ten. Now I draw my revolver, hold it high, drop to my knees as I enter the room. Bright fluorescent light. A classroom. Rows of empty desks. No sound. I stand, press my back against the wall, glance around. Nobody's in the room. Nobody. No other doors, windows are closed, blinds drawn. Nowhere anybody could hide. But those sounds were definitely coming from in here. I'm absolutely positive. When I'm sure I'm alone, I holster the gun, walk up the center aisle to the teacher's desk. The entire blackboard is covered with carefully printed words. Bright white chalk against glossy black. Suddenly dawns on me, *that's* what I was hearing: Chalk on a blackboard. Somebody printing words.

Soft, rhythmic, familiar sounds from my youth. Sounds that came from this room.

There's got to be an explanation. I look around carefully again, walk across the front of the room, examine the five rectangular slabs of the blackboard, walk slowly to the back, observing every desk, every square foot, floor to ceiling, wall to wall. Next, I go to the windowed wall, pull up all six venetian blinds, try to open the windows, but all six are locked. Now I stand against the back wall near the door again. Spooky, have to admit it, but I'm calmed down by now, I'm trying to think logically, I know there's got to be a rational answer. Then I glance up at the blackboard again, read a few lines for the first time. Everything's printed in meticulous upper- and lowercase letters:

> Ol sonuf vaoresaji, gohu IAD Balata, elanusaha caelazod: sabrazod-ol Roray i ta nazodapesad, Giraa ta maelpereji, das hoel-qo qaa notahoa zodimezod, od comemahe ta nobeloha zodien; soba tahil ginonupe pereje aladi, das vaurebes obolehe giresam. . . .

Goes on like that, fills all five slabs of the blackboard. I don't know what language it is, of course, I don't have a clue. Complete gibberish to me. But for some reason, just reading that one carefully printed sentence makes me feel suddenly cold.

Me, I've had enough of this weird shit, I get out of that classroom in a hurry. Walk double-time down the long dark hallway, into the bright foyer, then out the door.

Nice to be in the fresh air again. As I walk into the sunlight, squinting, I'm relieved to see the Bomb Squad van double-parked behind my Nissan; its rear doors are open and McCartney and McIntyre are back there playing with the dog. When I go over to join them, I see Vadney's late-model, dark-blue Ford Fairmont coming slowly up the street, Mairs in the passenger side. Chief double-parks in front of my car, comes back to talk with us, but Mairs stops to admire my car. He's always been a car nut, he's even got scale-model classics all over the bookshelves in his office, Ferraris dominating. Now he walks around, checks out the turbo cowl, the T-top windows with their Windex shine. Must say, it looks like it was just washed, which it was, yesterday. I sashay over there feeling like the veteran sports car jockey that I'm not.

"Yours?" he asks.

"Yeah."

"Eighty-four?"

"Yeah."

"Eighty-four and still no dents."

"Not a scratch."

"You should have at least one dent in this thing, John."

"Why's that?"

"So you can stop worrying about your first dent."

"Maybe I like to worry."

"Keep it in a garage?"

"Yeah."

"In a custom car cover?"

"No. Don't have a cover."

He frowns. "You don't have a custom car cover?"

"Naw."

"John, do you realize what could happen to this car?" He runs his fingertip along the door, inspects it carefully. "Look at that. Go ahead, just look at it. Know what that is? Soot. You're picking up soot on this thing, John. Out in the open air like this? You kidding? You realize what this shit can do to your car?"

Chief comes over with McCartney and McIntyre. "So where's the principal? Sister Mary What's-her-face?"

"Not here yet," I tell him.

Glances at his watch. "Can't depend on anybody these days."

"Front door's open," I say.

"Yeah?" He turns to McCartney. "Okay then, Bill, let's get started."

"Wait a minute," McCartney says. "Hold everything. The door's unlocked? How come? Who's in there?"

I take a deep breath. "Don't know exactly. I might just as well level with you guys; something strange is going on here. I got here early, I went up—"

"Knew it," Chief says. "Knew it. Knew we'd run into trouble here, I could feel it in my gut."

"What's going on?" Mairs asks me.

"I got here early, I was standing by the entrance, waiting for Sister Mary Garcia. Now I hear somebody snap open two deadbolt locks on the door, I thought it must be her. Door opens and this—looked like a man—this figure stands there in silhouette, couldn't see his face. Wearing what looked like a priest's tunic. Before I can get over there, the door starts to close. This dark figure's just standing there, he doesn't move a muscle, but the door closes. Heavy door, too, you'll see. Okay, I go over to the door, I knock, nobody answers. I try the door, it's unlocked, so I open it and call out the sister's name. Nobody answers. I go in, foyer's brightly lighted in there, I look around, nobody's in the foyer. Now I hear this sound coming from one of the halls off the foyer. Familiar sound, a series of soft clicks, but I just can't place it. Seems to be coming from a lighted classroom down this long dark hall. I'm curious, naturally, so I walk down the hall. I stop outside the open door, stand off to one side of it, because I don't know what I'm getting into here. I call out the sister's name again. Nothing. Sound continues, it's definitely coming from that room, no question about it. Okay, now I know something's real strange here. I draw my weapon, I call out 'Police,' I order the person to come out. No answer. Clicking sound stops. I wait, then I duck inside. Classroom's empty. Totally empty, nobody in there. I mean, I give it a good long look, it's empty. No other doors, all the windows are locked, nowhere to hide. I look at the blackboard, front of the room, it's covered with writing. Suddenly dawns on me, those were the sounds I was hearing, somebody was writing with—printing, rather—printing with chalk on that blackboard. Now, this next thing, you'll have to see for yourself. The writing on that blackboard is a foreign language of some kind. Don't think I ever saw a language like that before. It's not French, Spanish, German, anything like that. Very strange-looking words."

"I want to see this," Mairs says. "Walt, maybe you guys better wait for the principal, huh?"

"Yeah, good idea."

Mairs and I walk to the front door. As usual, I'm trying to keep a certain sense of perspective about all this, a sense of humor; I've developed that ability over the years, and it's been psychologically helpful. But this time, to be honest, it's very difficult to do that. The more I think about what happened, the more strange it seems. I know what I saw, I know what I heard, but then, when I tried to follow up, it's like my senses were deceived. I'm a realist, I tend to believe there are logical explanations for most phenomena, if you dig deep enough.

Anyhow, we go in, we walk down the long dark hall toward the lighted classroom, we pause just outside for a few seconds and listen. Silence. We walk in, Mairs first, he gives the room a once-over, then he goes up to the blackboard and studies the words.

"Son of a bitch," he says. "It's Enochian."

"What?"

"The ancient language used in Satanic ritual. E-*no*-key-an. It's believed to be older than Sanskrit."

"Any idea what it says?"

He smiles briefly. "John, come on, I'm not a linguist, for Christ's sake. The only reason I recognize it at all, it's quoted at some length in *The Satanic Bible.* Very interesting part of the book for me. LaVey quoted from the famous nineteen Enochian Keys, then translated them into English, into what he called his 'unexpurgated' version."

"What're the Keys for? What do they mean?"

He narrows his eyes at the words. "Apparently, until very recently, they've been shrouded in secrecy, incorrectly translated by design, euphemisms used to camouflage meanings, this sort of thing. The original manuscripts, or scrolls, are thought to be proclamations from Satan himself, revealed in the fifth or sixth millennium B.C., the virtual dawn of recorded history."

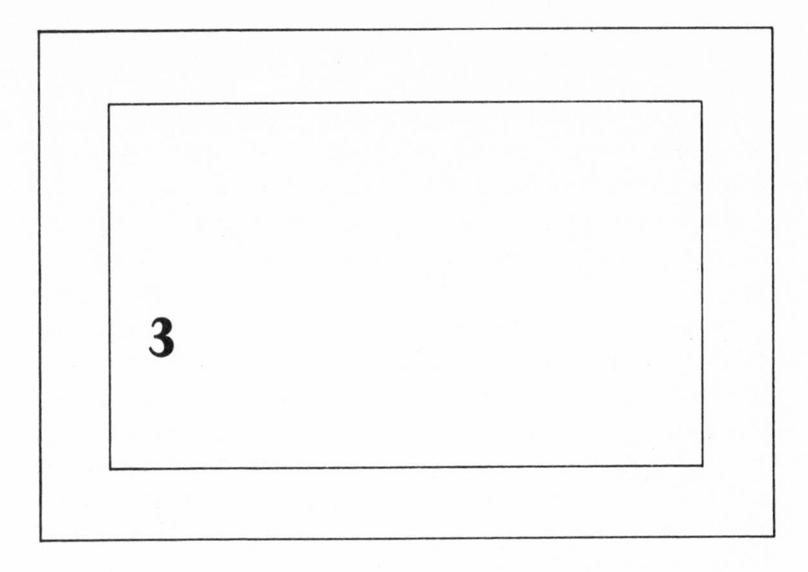

3

SISTER MARY GARCIA arrives at 3:40, small and slim in a modern and well-tailored summer habit. She's not what I expected at all and it's a pleasant surprise. I suppose the words "sister" and "principal" conjured up stereotypes in my head, childhood memories of stern old ladies in stiff white cowls, long black veils and robes, and heavy rosaries dangling at their sides, I don't know. Modern dress helps, of course, but that's only half the story here. First off, she's young, no more than thirty-five, if that, and, despite the absence of makeup and jewelry, she's—how can I put this? She's naturally feminine. That's it, that's the only way to describe her. Lovely complexion, dark arched brows, long lashes framing dark-brown eyes. Thing that catches your attention right off—ready for this?—she's got dimples. Yeah. Just little ones when she smiles, not what you'd call "cute," that's just not the word. These dimples are just plain—attractive. Know what I mean? Okay, I know, I'm choosing my words carefully here, it's a throwback to my Catholic upbringing, what can I tell you? When I was a kid, nuns were nuns, kind of a holy neuter-gender-type deal, you just didn't describe them as feminine or attractive, right? At least *I* didn't. I mean, it was all different back then.

Anyhow, if you can picture this, we're all standing out there on the sidewalk in the late afternoon sun, we're talking with her, five cops towering over this lovely young lady. We ask her some routine questions about the door and the classroom, try not to upset her. No, she didn't unlock the front door; in fact, she hasn't been to the school all day. No, the janitor doesn't work here in the summer. Yes, about five other people have keys to that door; she gives us the names, she'll get us the addresses and phone numbers. Tell you something that comes across as we talk: She's relaxed and we're not. How come? Number of factors at work here, not the least of which is the fast realization that Sister Mary Garcia, in addition to being surprisingly attractive, is also very bright. Comes across easily, she's not looking to impress anybody. Also, she's got a good quick sense of humor. Like, the reason she was late, she says she was reading, she simply lost track of the time. Reading. Nobody asks her what she was reading, of course; we assume it was something on the order of St. Paul's Epistle to the Thessalonians, stuff like that. She volunteers the information with a big smile, says she was reading John D. MacDonald's latest Travis McGee novel, *The Lonely Silver Rain,* twenty-first thriller in the series, she just couldn't put it down. Must say, that loosens us up a lot, we all glance at each other and laugh. Me, I happen to be a fan of John D. MacDonald, I think he's terrific. All I can say, thank God he doesn't use many four-letter words.

Bill McCartney explains how he intends to conduct the search; he wants her to accompany them through the public access areas first, but before that he thinks it might be a good idea for her to take a quick look at the open classroom (we haven't told her any details about what I experienced in there), see if she can spot anything that seems out of place or doesn't belong there at all.

McIntyre goes back to the van to get the dog, Fred, then all of us go into the school. Soon as we enter the lighted foyer, I can see Sister Mary's concerned. She checks the condition of the two deadbolt locks (both Medeco and perfectly okay), glances around the foyer, walks over to the trophy display cases, inspects them carefully, then heads for the lighted classroom down the long hall. McCartney walks beside her, followed by Vadney and Mairs, then McIntyre, Fred, and me. Our shadows are vivid on the polished marble floor, lengthen and become lighter, finally fade as we enter the dark area. Our footsteps make hollow sounds, punctuated by Fred's sharp clicks.

When we reach the pale yellow rectangle of light across the floor in front of the open classroom door, Fred makes a low sound in his throat. Not a bark, not a growl, not a cry. More like the soft, low, throaty sound that our own dog makes when she senses someone approaching our front door, long before the doorbell rings, long before my wife and I can hear footsteps or anything else, and seconds before she jumps up and scampers to the door. Fred's deep-throated sound is almost identical, but he doesn't scamper to this door. He stops dead.

McIntyre calls to the others: "Wait a minute, don't go in there!" When they stop and turn, he gets down on one knee, strokes the dog under the chin, speaks quietly. "What, Fred? What is it?"

Fred's bright eyes are riveted on the doorway, his ears are back now, and he starts to growl softly. McIntyre removes his leash quickly, motions for us to stand back. We do. Fast. Fred crouches, walks slowly into the band of light, hesitates for just an instant, sniffing, then enters the room cautiously, head down, ears back, continuing to growl, teeth slightly bared now, tail held high.

We all jockey for position outside the door, watch silently as Fred moves slowly up the center aisle, growling softly, claws clicking. His head darts left and right as he glances between the rows of desks. When he reaches the teacher's desk, he pauses, sniffs around, head low, circles the desk clockwise, walks to the far left corner, sniffs the end of the blackboard, turns left, continues down that aisle all the way to the back, where he's out of our sight. Now he passes the door on his way to the right rear corner, glances at us from the corner of his eye, growling, and he's out of sight again. He appears gradually, walking up the aisle next to the windows, turns, goes to the teacher's desk, pauses, sniffing, then turns and heads down the center aisle toward us, jogging rather than walking now, ears still back, tail high. We stand aside as he comes out, passes through the band of yellow light, stops at the far side of the hall, faces us.

McIntyre goes over to him, frowning, gets down on one knee, strokes him under the chin, pats his side, then moves his hands over the dog's back, legs, and chest. "Good boy, Fred, it's all right, good boy." He turns, still frowning, looks up at McCartney. "Lieutenant, he's shivering. His whole body is shivering."

As I say, it's difficult to keep a reasonable sense of perspective about all this (much less a sense of humor), because we can't seem to get a handle on any of it. What happens, while McIntyre tries to calm the dog down outside, we go in the classroom, at least we know there's no explosive device in there. The room's empty. Sister Mary Garcia studies the language on the blackboard, says she's never seen anything like it before, so we decide not to volunteer any information for the time being. Also, she doesn't recognize the printing style, it's not like that of any of her teachers. She takes her time wandering around the room, doesn't see anything unusual, anything out of place. Finally, she goes to the teacher's desk, opens each drawer, finds only the usual stuff—pens, pencils, several boxes of chalk, a couple of rulers, a box of paper clips, this kind of thing. So what the hell did the dog sense? Before we leave, I go around the room and sniff things—desks, blackboard, chalk, walls, venetian blinds, windowsills, windows—trying my damnedest to pick up any strange odor. Nothing. So what'd the dog sense? It had to be something. I mean, whatever it was obviously spooked him. Now I think, okay, if it wasn't an odor, could it have been a sound, an ultrahigh-frequency sound that couldn't be heard by us, but could be picked up easily by a dog?

Definite possibility. It's a well-known fact that dogs and certain other animals have a hearing range that includes VHF, UHF, SHF (superhigh frequency), and in some cases even EHF (extremely high frequency)—the highest known frequency. That might help to explain why Fred's ears were back; he could've been feeling some degree of pain. Mail carriers in some areas of the country routinely use high-frequency sound devices to protect themselves against the attack of dogs; certain sound frequencies, far above the range of human hearing, can actually stop dogs in their tracks, scare them off, without damaging their eardrums. But where would such a sound come from in this classroom? I look around the walls and ceiling for public-address speakers. There's only one, a small speaker high on the wall above the center of the blackboard, undoubtedly connected to the office. They had the same sound system in my grammar school and high school; announcements could be made to all classrooms simultaneously or to any one individual classroom. So that's a possibility, sure, but you'd need a key to get in the office and you'd have to have technical knowledge about how to operate the system's console. Seems too obvious to me, but I intend to check it out anyway. Next question: Could the sound have come from outside? Outside the building? I don't know that much about the capabilities of high-frequency sound, but I'll certainly find out.

Of course, the same basic principle of sensory perception applies to odors. Dogs have an almost incredible sense of smell, a supersensitivity to odors that's far beyond the range of man. Could it have been a combination of the two? Painful, frightening sound combined with some kind of foul odor? I mean, he wouldn't growl like that at sound alone, would he?

I'm a trained observer, that's really what I get paid for, so my first approach to anything like this is to carefully examine the physical possibilities for logical assumptions. Many cases I work have at least some aura of mystery at the beginning because, let's face it, in major crime cases these days we're dealing with people the courts call "career criminals," whose techniques are relatively sophisticated, and whose tools tend to be increasingly high tech. True of major crime cases, but what're we talking about here? The theft of an old statue of St. Michael the Archangel from outside a school. A note to the commissioner, quoting scripture, and telling him to be at the school tonight at 11:59 if he wants to find out who did it. That's the kind of crime we're talking about. So far. So what's all this weird stuff all about? I don't know, I don't even have a solid clue at this point. My radar's starting to pick up confusing signals, some sort of unknown factor is present, and that always serves as an intuitive warning to me. Warns me there's probably much more going on here than I realize. So I'm taking nothing for granted, I'm not going to assume anything until I have more information.

Also, I'm not going to be hooked into the easy emotional reaction. Don't get me wrong, I'm intensely aware of this emotional element, and I'd be a liar if I said it didn't disturb me. It does. Very much so. I mean, after seeing that figure at the front door, hearing the chalk sounds, finding the writing, learning it's Enochian, then watching the dog walk around that room, I'm well aware we're dealing with phenomena that, on the face of it, are frightening. But the sum total of all my training, thirty-one years of police work, has been directed at finding, or attempting to find, logical, realistic, believable explanations that will stand up in a court of law. In other words, evidence that can be believed beyond a reasonable doubt. That's all I'm saying here. Satan? The presence of a dark, unknown force in nature? Scares me, sure, absolutely, I admit it. Scares almost everybody. But I'm a detective, not a priest. My first reaction to this thing is emotional, I can't control that, but my first responsibility is to think logically. That's what I intend to do. That's my job. If all this stuff turns out to defy the rules of logic, I'm open to the ramifications of that. But I'll give it my best shot first.

So now, what happens next, Sister Mary begins to lead McCartney, McIntyre, and the dog into the school's public access areas, and Vadney, Mairs, and I tag along, we don't want to miss anything at this point. We go back to the foyer, take the hallway to the left of it (she snaps on the lights), walk about halfway down, turn right, into another hall that leads directly to the office. Office is the main public access point in the school, she tells us, it's where all routine deliveries are made (except for the cafeteria), and all visitors have to get a pass here to go anywhere else in the school.

She unlocks the two Medeco deadbolts, turns on the lights, we follow her inside. Long counter to the left, two desks behind it, big rectangular waiting area to the right with six wooden chairs and a coffee table, a private office straight ahead in back, separated by frosted-glass walls and a closed door with the finely printed word: PRINCIPAL. She goes to that door, enters alone, we see her dim silhouette move across the frosted glass to the right, then back to the left, where she snaps on a lamp. Now she comes out.

"All right, Lieutenant," she says. "Let's start with the waiting area, then behind the counter, then the two desks here, then move on to my office."

Off they go into the large waiting area, it's lined with built-in bookshelves, three walls of them, floor to ceiling, all kinds of plaques and certificates and academic knickknacks separating groups of books. She wanders around now, giving the shelves a close look first, Fred's sniffing everything in sight. Me, I go my own way, stroll behind the counter, hands in my pockets, glancing around, casual as you please. But I'm looking for something very specific. I'm looking for the sound-system console. Can't find it out here, so it must be in the principal's office. No reason to ask permission, we're all working together, so in I go. Good-sized rectangular room, old mahogany desk to the left holds a lighted lamp, three chairs face the desk, wooden conference table in the center of the room, eight chairs, then off to the right at the far end of the room, there it is. Big black vertical deal built into the wall, looks old-fashioned by today's Silicon Valley stereo standards, lots of dials and switches, little black levers for every classroom, all neatly labeled; microphone stands in the corner. Wait a minute, here's an update built into the side here, looks like a modern stereo system: AM/FM stereo receiver, graphic equalizer, dual cassette decks, semiautomatic turntable. I peek into the little windows of the tape decks, see if there might be cassettes in there. Sure are. Now I look around for the eject button, left deck, find it, press it. *Click.*

"Detective Rawlings!"

Startles me, I turn fast. Sister Mary Garcia stands in the doorway, frowning, hands on hips. I give her an innocent glance. "Yes, Sister?"

"May I ask what you're doing?"

"Just admiring your stereo system."

She walks toward me, keeps her voice low but cold. "Is that a fact?"

"Yeah. I'm—kind of a stereo freak."

"I see. Do you often tamper with other people's equipment?"

"Tamper?"

"Tamper."

"Of course not, I was just—"

"You ejected one of the cassettes. I heard it."

"Yes, I did. I'm sorry, I didn't mean—"

"Do you think being a detective gives you license to tamper with privately owned equipment like this?"

"No, I don't. Absolutely not."

She glances at the left tape deck. "The cassette you ejected happens to be one of my favorites, the Grieg Piano Concerto in A Minor. Is that what you wanted to know?"

"Yes. I'm really very sorry. Please accept my apology."

When she sees that I'm sincere about it, her eyes change and her voice softens. "This stereo is one of my few luxuries, Rawlings. I listen to it during the school year mostly, when I'm working late, which is quite often. I'd hate to have anything happen to it, y'know?"

"I understand. May I ask a question?"

"Sure."

"Do you normally keep this private office locked?"

"No, I don't. Maybe I should, but it just seems superfluous to me, because we've got those two deadbolts on the office door itself."

"And how many people have keys to that door?"

"Only three. The janitor, the AP, and me."

"What's an AP?"

"Assistant principal, that's Sister Frances Barbella. You already have her name, she has a key to the front door, too, she's one of the five. And you have the janitor's name, Anthony Salinger, he's on vacation now, but he doesn't live far from here; I'll get you his address and phone number."

"Excellent. Just one last question, Sister Mary, I'm curious.

These stereo tapes in here, can you program the system so the tapes can be heard in any given classroom?"

"Oh, certainly. We don't normally pipe music to the classrooms, but we play it from noon to one-thirty in the cafeteria every day during the school year."

"I see. And who's authorized to operate the system on a daily basis?"

"Just Sister Frances and me. Why do you ask?"

I shrug. "Beautiful piece of equipment. I don't blame you."

"And delicate and sensitive—and temperamental, as I'm sure you know. That's why we won't—if you want the truth, Rawlings, nobody else is allowed to even touch it." She smiles then, briefly, dimples showing slightly, and starts for the door. "I really have to get back and help."

I stay where I am.

She hesitates at the door. "Coming?"

In that split second before I move, the thought flashes through my mind: She doesn't want me to see the other cassette, the one in the right-hand tape deck. Don't know why, can't explain, I just think it, feel it, know it. Something in her eyes, her voice, her mouth, her posture, standing there waiting, blinking, hand on the door frame.

I nod, smile, follow her out of the room.

By six-thirty that evening, everything seems to be under control, the Bomb Squad guys have covered all public access areas with Sister Mary, including the kitchen and cafeteria, the gym and its grandstands, the locker rooms and shower rooms (visiting basketball and volleyball teams use those facilities), and all lavatories on all six floors throughout the school. Lieutenant McCartney, in consultation with Vadney and Mairs, has decided that Commissioner Reilly's limo should be parked directly across the street from the empty pedestal where the statue had been, a distance of approximately forty-five feet. The pedestal, eight feet above the sidewalk, is welded to a wrought-iron fixture that extends out from the stone wall; it's twenty feet to the left of the entrance. What's behind that wall? Turns out to be a lavatory, a fairly big one, it's already been searched, of course, but now McCartney, McIntyre, and Fred go to work on that room again with extreme care—toilets, urinals, sinks, soap dispensers, paper-towel holders, they even use a ladder to examine the sprinkler system and the two smoke detectors.

Now they want to inspect the outside of the building, the stone blocks and distinctive old windows that make up the front facade of the ground floor, particularly around the area of the pedestal. That means they have to get inside the high black wrought-iron fence that encloses the narrow walkway between the school and the sidewalk. Sister Mary needs the key to the old-fashioned padlock on the gate of the fence, but she doesn't have it on her regular key ring, so she has to go down to the janitor's office in the basement to get it. Vadney volunteers to accompany her down there, a gesture she seems to appreciate.

Key they bring back is an elaborate old-timer and it's tied with a strip of ancient rawhide to a six-inch-long wooden cylinder with the word GATE carefully lettered on it in longhand, but almost illegible now. When I ask her who might have a duplicate key, she says she's never seen a duplicate in the four years she's been principal and, in fact, the only time that gate's ever opened, to her knowledge, is when the window washer comes, once a month during the academic year.

"Is it always the same man?" I ask.

"Yes, always. His name is Jack Trowbridge, he's not with a service, he's an independent. He's been washing these windows for—well, at least four years now, I know that."

I jot down the name. "Is it possible that he might have a duplicate key?"

"I suppose it's possible, but I doubt it. I think Mr. Salinger always opens the gate for him."

"Always?"

"Rawlings, look. I know Mr. Trowbridge, okay? I mean, I've known the man for four years, I write out his check every month. He's an honest, hard-working, thoroughly dependable man."

"I'm sure he is. But I'd like to talk to him."

She nods, leans against the gate, watches McCartney, McIntyre, Vadney, Mairs, and the dog moving around inside the fence. In the warm, diminishing sunlight, they're inspecting the stone facade, the windows, even the standpipe.

"I'll give you the man's number," Sister tells me coldly now. "And his address. I suppose you'll want to go and see him. Assumed guilty until proven innocent, right?"

"Sister Mary," I say quietly, "you have to understand something. This is the way we work. We talk with anybody who we think might be helpful. We ask routine questions, that's all. We ask for their help. We try to be polite, most of us."

She meets my eyes for a second, then continues to watch the men work. "Rawlings, come on, get serious. Who do you think you're talking to? Some sheltered virgin straight out of a convent? I grew up in this city, down on West Fourth Street. So spare me this hype about 'we try to be polite,' okay? I don't buy it, I've seen you guys in action all my life. What you really try to do, most of you, is to be tough and oblivious. Oblivious to the filth you have to wade through every day. Try to be polite? Most New York cops don't know the meaning of the word. How can you be polite when you're dealing with arrogant, obnoxious animals and airheads most of the time? It'd sour anybody. You assume they're guilty because most of them are. You don't trust anybody because it's excellent insulation, you never get disappointed that way."

I wait a beat, then keep my voice calm. "You're making a generalization that's just not true. You know it's not."

"Do I? Do you trust *me?*"

"Of course. But it depends on what you mean by trust. You can't place trust in somebody who's a complete stranger."

"That was obvious in my office."

"I'm not—sure what you mean."

She turns now, fast, eyes glaring. "Rawlings, come on, let's cut the hype. You were snooping around my office on your own because you were looking for something. Frankly, I resent that, I resent the implication, the suspicion that I'm trying to hide something. Instead of snooping around, why didn't you just come out and ask me?"

"First of all, Sister Mary, we don't suspect you of anything. Second, before you arrived here this afternoon, several strange incidents occurred in that classroom, the one we searched. We decided not to tell you about those incidents because it wasn't necessary for you to know. At least, not right away."

"It wasn't necessary?"

"That's correct."

"Rawlings, I'm the principal of this school. Everything that happens here is important to me. Everything. I think I have a right to know what's going on, don't you? For example, that writing on the blackboard, what's it mean?"

"We don't know what it means yet, but we know what language it is. It's called Enochian."

She blinks, frowns. "Enochian? Oh, my God."

"Do you know—?"

"Yes, of course. It's the ancient—it's the language of Satanic ritual."

"That's right. Commander Mairs identified it. He's going to have it photographed and translated."

"Good. I want to know what it says as soon as you know. I have a right to know that. Now, come on, what else? What were the strange incidents? And what were you looking for in my office?"

"I was looking for a tape cassette, that's all. It was just a hunch I was playing, I wasn't at all—"

"What cassette?"

"—sure it was there. Sister, it was strictly a hunch. I was looking for a tape recording that might have certain sound effects that could've been piped into that classroom on the public-address system."

"Sound effects? Of what?"

"Maybe the sounds of chalk on a blackboard. Maybe some kind of ultrahigh-frequency sound that would be picked up by a dog. Maybe both sounds, one following the other on the same tape, I don't know. The whole idea was a long shot, but sometimes I play long shots."

"Okay, obviously I'm not going to understand all this until you tell me what happened before I got here. What about the strange incidents, what were those all about?"

I hesitate, glance away. "I'm not trying to evade the question, Sister, but those things were—well, more of a personal nature than anything else. I'd rather wait until I have more information, if you don't mind."

"Okay, let's back up a little. You ejected one of the tape cassettes on the stereo, the Grieg concerto. You saw that, but not the other one. Why didn't you ask to see it?"

"Actually, I didn't see the first one. You told me what it was. I didn't get a chance to look at it."

"So why didn't you ask? Why didn't you simply ask to see both of them?"

"You were plainly upset. I didn't want to—"

"That wasn't it, Rawlings. Tell the truth. You didn't ask to see them because, for some reason, you actually suspected I had something to hide. So you decided to wait, right? You decided to check out those cassettes later when I wasn't around. Right?"

Again, I hesitate, glance away.

"Right? Tell the truth."

"That's—yes, all right, that's true."

She takes out her big key ring, holds it out to me. "Go

ahead. Right now. Check it out. The two office keys are"—she finds them and shows me—"right here, these two Medecos. Go ahead. Check it out."

I thank her kindly, take the key ring, go back in the school. I know she didn't touch the stereo when the Bomb Squad guys were in her office because I watched her carefully. She didn't even go near it. Now I go in, I see the cassette in the left-hand tape deck is still in the ejected position. I slide it out. Label on the top side confirms what she said: Grieg's Piano Concerto in A Minor. Stuttgart Philharmonic Orchestra. Matthias Kuntzsch, conductor; Eugene List, pianist. Flip side is Rachmaninoff's Piano Concerto No. 2, same orchestra, conductor, and pianist. I slide it back in. Find the eject button for the cassette in the right-hand tape deck, press it. *Click,* out it comes. Top side, Brahms's *Double Concerto.* New Philharmonia Orchestra. Kurt Masur, conductor; Ruggiero Ricci, violinist. Flip side, Schumann's Fantasy in C Major. Same conductor, same violinist, but the Leipzig Gewandhaus Orchestra. Slide it back in, start looking around for other cassettes. No cassette storage shelves on the console.

I glance around the office, go over and check the two bookcases. No cassettes, but I'm sure she must have many others stored somewhere. I go behind her desk, snap on the lamp, try the wide middle drawer. Locked. Same with the side drawers. I check her key ring. Nothing small enough to be a desk key. Now I sit in her chair and think: What am I doing? If a sound-effects tape was in fact in one of the two tape decks, playing a high-frequency sound while we were in that classroom, Sister Mary wouldn't have had time to eject it and replace it when she went briefly into this office to turn on the desk lamp. Would she? Her image flashes through my mind: *She goes to that door, enters alone, we see her dim silhouette move across the frosted glass to the right, then back to the left, where she snaps on a lamp.* Fact of the matter is, with fluorescent lights throughout the office, including her private office, she didn't need to snap on the desk lamp anyway. But if she went in for the sole purpose of turning on the desk lamp, why did she walk way over to the right first, then walk back to the left, where the desk is? Could she have reached the stereo in those few seconds? Yes, she could have. But if she ejected a cassette, I would've heard it, the machine makes a sharp click when you eject a cassette. There was no click, I'm sure of it. Then why did she walk to the stereo? To turn it off? Yes, that's possible. And if that's what she did, then I'm left with only two logical assumptions: Sister Mary or her assistant principal left the stereo on by mistake after one of the cassettes finished playing, a common mistake, I've done it myself, and she simply saw the red light on and went over to turn it off; or, following my theory, one of the two cassettes in that machine right now could be a sound-effects tape, despite what the label reads. You want to put sound effects on a professionally produced musical tape, you just cover the little hole in the cassette, then record over it. No sweat.

Only one way to find out. I get up, walk back to the console, eject the cassette in the left-hand tape deck. *Click,* out it comes. Labels are authentic, no doubt about that. Top side is labeled the Grieg concerto. Now I look to see where the tape is on the spools. This one, the tape is all the way over to the left, at the beginning, ready to be played. So it couldn't be that one. I slide it back, press the eject button for the cassette in the right-hand tape deck. *Click.* Top side, Brahms's *Double Concerto.* Where's the tape on the spools? All the way over to the right. Finished. Okay, I slide it back in, turn on the stereo, press the rewind button for the right-hand cassette. As I watch it rewind, I think: Just suppose you're right? Suppose it really *is* a sound-effects tape? Suppose it starts out with those rhythmic chalk sounds on a blackboard, maybe fifteen minutes or so, then seems to play silently for the rest of the tape, at a frequency you can't hear? What the hell does that prove, other than the satisfying fact that your theory is correct? Does it prove that Sister Mary Garcia had anything to do with it? No way. And I've got to keep that in mind. Because, look at it logically: It's entirely possible that she actually *did* see the red light on the stereo as soon as she entered her office and quickly went over to turn it off. Absolutely. What's more, if it's a sound-effects tape, and if she knows damn well it is, then why would she hand me the office keys and tell me to go check it out? Why the hell would she do that? Would she think I'd just look at the labels and that would be that? Would she think most cops would do just that? Would she?

Tape stops, all rewound to the left, ready to play. I look around for the "play" button, find it, press it. Silence. Five seconds. Ten. I squint through the window of the tape deck to see if the spools are turning. They are. Now I check the public-address console. All the little black levers for each room in the school are turned down, with one exception: Classroom 119 is turned up. I flick the lever down. Still nothing. Silence. I glance at the labels under each lever, find the one marked OFFICE, flick it up.

Double Concerto, Brahms.

I stand there listening to it for maybe a minute, hit the fast-forward button, listen, hit it again, keep hitting it to the very end. Beautiful violin concerto. Haunting.

Who made the chalk sounds?

What spooked the dog?

Gives me a strange, cold feeling.

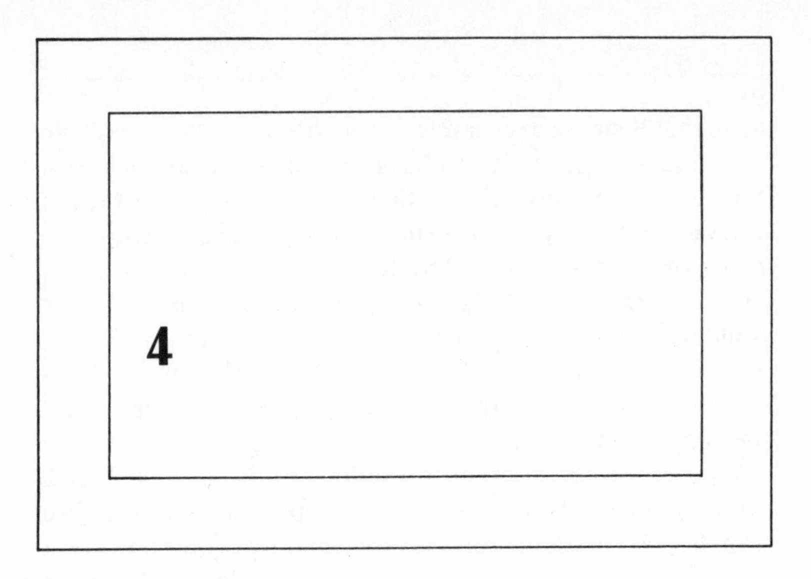

COMMISSIONER REILLY'S LIMO arrives right on schedule, 11:55 P.M., and parks directly across the street from the empty pedestal. It's a long black Caddy, bulletproof, equipped with a telephone and police radio, plus walkie-talkies. Jim Mairs is in back with Reilly; the driver is from the Emergency Service Division. All three men are wearing bulletproof vests. Nothing's been left to chance, the Bomb Squad guys have covered a wide area, including the office building across the street. West Thirty-third Street has been blocked off from Ninth to Tenth avenues for about an hour now. Seven private cars that were parked in front of the school all day (illegally, there's a block-long yellow curb out front) have been towed away, so now the whole area is about as open as possible. Mairs has stationed a total of fifteen ESD sharpshooters in strategic locations—three in opened windows of the school, two on the school's roof, four in windows of the office building, two on its roof, one at each end of the street, and two in the main entrance of the rectory, to the right of the school, where Sister Mary Garcia and quite a few other nuns are watching from various windows. Just around the corner of the office building, in the Edison parking lot, McCartney and McIntyre are waiting in the Bomb Squad van; parked right next to it, and manned by two Bomb Squad technicians, is one of the squad's state-of-the-art Bomb Disposal Vehicles with a spherical trailer called a total containment vessel, capable of containing all fragments and gases from a bomb, should it explode within the vessel en route to the Demolition Range at Rodman's Neck in the Bronx.

So we're ready for just about any contingency, with the possible exception of airborne incendiary devices lofted into the area, but Vadney has unmarked cars cruising the six nearest side streets running parallel to Thirty-third between Ninth and Tenth avenues. We're all in contact with the limo via walkie-talkies, of course, and Reilly, Mairs, and the driver are equipped with gas masks and riot helmets, in addition to the vests, should they have to vacate the vehicle.

Vadney and I stand just outside the entrance to the office building, because it's the closest to the limo, about thirty yards away. Across the street, the school is completely dark. Streetlights provide the only illumination now, throwing reflections across the glossy top of the limo. We can hear traffic noises from Ninth and Tenth avenues.

Chief glances at his watch. "Christ, this is ridiculous, Little John. Y'know that? This is totally fuckin' ridiculous. All this manpower and money? I mean, we don't even know what the fuck we're *lookin'* for here. We shouldn't even *be* here."

"You gave him your advice," I say. "You and Mairs both. What else can you do? He's the commissioner."

"He's a stubborn Irishman. That's what he is, that's what it boils down to. A plug-stubborn ignorant Irishman. And a civilian to boot, that's what sticks in my craw. A civilian who doesn't know shit about standard protection procedures, but flat-out refuses to take the advice of professionals. Right?

That's what it boils down to, that's what sticks in my fuckin' craw. Even Bill McCartney—God knows, Bill McCartney's one of the coolest pros in the whole department—he came right out and told me, he says he wouldn't *allow* it in dignitary protection. Wouldn't *allow* it. Okay? Wouldn't expose his men to such unnecessary risk. I mean, threat or no threat, we're dealing with some kinda slimebag sicko here, it's implicit in his behavior, Little John. I mean, it's *implicit.* It's implicit in his *behavior,* know what I mean?"

"No question about it."

"No question about it. Even Bill McCartney, he came right out and told me, he says he wouldn't allow it. That he'd go on record as—how'd he put it? Oh, yeah, 'disavowing,' that's it, that's what he said, 'disavowing responsibility.' Says he'd put it in writing to me if it involved dignitary protection. The irony is—know what the irony is?"

"What's that?"

"The irony is, he's never had to do that. I mean, he reports to me, he's been in that job four years now, and he's never had to do that. Disavow responsibility, I mean. For dignitary protection because they wouldn't follow his advice. Know why? I'll tell you why, this is the irony, Little John, listen up. He's never had to *do* that because they've never *done* that. Huh? And we're talkin' about *dig*nitaries here, presidents, prime ministers, kings, sheiks—very, very heavyweight foreign shitheads of state here. Right? He tells 'em not to *be* some place at some time, they just don't *go.* Period. Why? Because he's head of the oldest, biggest, most experienced and technologically sophisticated bomb squad unit in the whole fuckin' free world, that's why. I mean, he just doesn't screw around, he *knows,* and they *know* he knows. They know fuckin'-A-well *right* he knows. He says dump, they squat, no questions, no arguments. Presidents, popes, queens, first ladies, they *squat.* Right? That's the irony, buddy-boy, that's what sticks in my craw. That some ignorant Irishman tells us all to go take a flyin' fuck. What time is it?"

I hold my watch up to the streetlight. "Eleven-fifty-eight."

"Minute to go." He unbuttons his jacket, reaches back on his left hip, fast-draws his Motorola walkie-talkie. Takes a deep breath. Frowns as he places the mike to his lips. Changes his whole tone of voice: "Angel Two to Angel One, over."

Static, then Reilly's voice: "Angel One, over."

Static. "Less than sixty seconds and counting here, ready to mark." He holds his Omega Astronaut Moon Watch to the light, frees the index finger of his right hand from the walkie-talkie, holds it poised over the button to start his chronograph sweep second hand. "Eleven-fifty-eight and twenty-six seconds; twenty-seven, twenty-eight, twenty-nine, *mark thirty.* And counting."

Silence now except for distant traffic noises from Ninth and Tenth avenues. Streetlights glow yellow-gold, throw bright patterns of color across the long limo's polished top, hood, trunk, like water; windows reflect the light, but you can't see inside. Slight breeze coming east from the Hudson now, warm, humid, smells a little like sewage. I look at the dim silhouette of the long, dark, six-story school; all the windows reflect the streetlights except the three that are open, dark, where the sharpshooters wait. Look higher, I can see the heads and shoulders of the two sharpshooters on the roof, hatless, motionless, like statues, one at either end. Now I glance at the sky. Scatter of stars, no clouds in sight, not much smog because it's Sunday, can't see the moon from where I'm standing. Whole atmosphere is a bit eerie now, the stillness of it, reminds me of some artsy, moody black-and-white photograph.

Static, then Vadney's voice, softly: "Ten seconds and counting. . . . Six, five, four, three, two, one. Eleven-fifty-nine."

Nothing happens. Five seconds. Ten. Fifteen. Silence, stillness, slight breeze, smell of sewage. Me. I don't like this at all. My mouth is dry, my breath is coming faster, my heart's starting to pound. What're we doing here? Could this be some kind of weird, sick practical joke? *We shouldn't be here. This is a mistake. Something terrible is going to happen here, I can sense it, I feel cold. Who made the chalk sounds? What spooked the dog?*

Then, at exactly midnight, something happens that's almost impossible to believe. Suddenly, on the pedestal where the statue had been, eight feet above the fence-enclosed walkway, a lighted figure appears: A large and coiled king cobra, yellow-brown hood puffed out with black crossbands, thick neck bolt upright maybe three feet high, jaws wide, white fangs glistening. In the first few seconds, as all of us stare in shocked disbelief, the thing seems to be moving, fat hood quivering. Acting on pure instinct (no order was ever given), one of the young sharpshooters in a window of the office building takes a shot at it with his high-powered rifle—*BOOM!* Scares the crap out of us, Vadney and I drop down fast, we don't know what the hell's happening until we hear the slug hit the stone wall and ricochet with a sharp whine. Obviously missed, the big snake's still coiled, neck high, hood puffed, jaws wide. Seconds later (again, no order was given), another shot—*BOOM!*—this one from a window of the school, I see the flash; misses again, hits the pavement with a spark, kicks up a spray of cement.

Limo's headlights snap on, engine roars, tires burn and squeal, it lurches ahead, then catapults down the street.

That's it, like a nervous chain reaction, seems like maybe nine sharpshooters open up on the snake simultaneously, sounds like rapid-fire competition at a shooting range. I'm still crouched with Vadney, I'm watching, I'm shaking with the noise and vibrations, I can't believe this is happening: *BLAM!-BANG!-BOOM!-WHINE!-WHAM!-PING!-BAM!-POW!-BAM!-ZING!* Pedestal, fixture, wall, walkway pulsate with sparks and chips and smoke and splattering slugs, everybody's pulling triggers as fast as they can, all nervous energy, maybe ten seconds of deafening nonstop fire, but the lighted cobra doesn't move a muscle, like the slugs are passing straight through it.

Then the figure vanishes.

In the abrupt silence, the pedestal is dark again, barely visible in the glow of the streetlights. Smoke billows around it, then begins to rise. Stone wall behind it is crisscrossed with maybe fifty or sixty long black ricochet burns from the high-powered slugs. I glance at my watch; whole thing happened in less than thirty seconds. Vadney and I stand up now, frown at each other. Me, I'm dumbfounded, I've never seen anything even remotely like this in thirty-one years on the force. And, yes, it frightens me, I admit it, my legs are shaking.

Vadney gets on his walkie-talkie: "Hold your fire! Maintain your positions until further notice. Angel Two to Angel One, over."

Considerable static, then Reilly's voice: "Angel One, over."

"Immediate problem apparently resolved. Commencing investigation. Suggest you remain out of area until further notice, over."

"Roger."

Chief snaps off the walkie-talkie, shakes his head, speaks to himself: "*Now* he takes my advice." Snaps it on again. "Angel Two to Angel *Four,* over."

McCartney's voice: "Angel Four, over."

"Investigate the area from your vehicle, over."

"Roger."

We hear the van's engine start immediately, then watch its long headlight beams swing out of the parking lot to our right and head west, very slowly, toward the school. When the van approaches the area of the pedestal, McCartney turns on a spotlight from the passenger side. The bright white circle of light moves slowly along the charred and chipped stone wall behind the pedestal, over the wrought-iron fixture that's sustained obvious damage, then stops on the pedestal itself, its circular shape torn and twisted. Finally, when the spotlight moves down to the walkway behind the fence, the van stops there, blocking our view from across the street. All of us are curious now, we know they'll find the big snake somewhere down there on the walkway, probably with most of its head, hood, and upper neck blown away.

After inspecting the area from the van, moving the spotlight slowly back and forth across the whole length of the walkway, McCartney gets on the walkie-talkie: "Angel Four to Angel Two, over."

"Angel Two, over."

"Reporting negative progress so far. Not a trace of it. Request permission to leave vehicle and continue search with flashlights, over."

Chief hesitates. "Permission granted, but proceed with extreme caution. Draw your weapons, Bill, that thing's undoubtedly holed up somewhere in the area, probably wounded, over."

"Roger. Leaving vehicle now with weapons drawn."

We see Mark McIntyre get out of the driver's side, service revolver in his right hand, lighted flashlight in the other. Actually, the "flashlights" they're using are big lanterns with adjustable heads, six-volt batteries, and flashing red lights in back. He leaves the van door open, walks around the front, passes through the headlight shafts, joins McCartney on the sidewalk. They go to the left first, moving slowly, playing their lantern beams inside the fence, trying to cover every inch of the walkway area.

Chief squints, watching them. "Little John, I don't know what the fuck's going on here, but I'll tell you something. I'll level with you. I never saw anything like that in my life. I can't believe what I saw. That big snake, whatever it was—"

"King cobra."

"Yeah? Y'sure?"

"Positive. Saw 'em in the Bronx Zoo. Some of 'em grow to about twelve feet, something like that."

"They deadly poisonous?"

"Deadly."

He nods, frowns. "How many rounds were fired? Any idea?"

"Hard to say. Every sharpshooter seemed to be firing except for the two at the ends of the street, the two on the school roof, and the two at the rectory door. So that's—nine men were firing. I'd say they each fired four, five rounds. Maybe a total of forty rounds."

"In a period of what? Ten, twelve seconds?"

"I'd say about ten, yeah."

He shakes his head. "Unbelievable. Unbelievable that they could all *miss* the sucker in ten seconds with forty rounds. I mean, these guys are all experienced marksmen, best in the ESD. Plus they all got infrared night scopes, all of 'em, Mairs told me that himself. Ten seconds to drop a snake that big?"

"Okay, but the most important thing, they finally hit him; he's either wounded or dead somewhere in there."

"How could they possibly *miss* for that long?"

"First off, confusion. Nobody gave an order, at least I didn't hear one. Second, it's a big snake but a relatively narrow target, even with a night scope. Third, when everybody's firing all at once like that, high-powered rifles, you're contending with tremendous vibrations and noise."

He shrugs, glances at his watch. "Maybe you're right, maybe I'm just—and where'd the light come from, that's another thing. That weird light?"

"Looked like it came from—I don't know."

"Looked like it came from where?"

"I don't know, Chief. Whole thing happened so fast."

"No, come on, you were gonna say *where.* Say it."

"To my eye, in those first few seconds, it looked like it came from the snake itself. I mean, I know that sounds weird."

"No. No, it doesn't. Hate to admit it, Little John, to myself or anybody else, but that's how I saw it, too. Like the fucker was somehow—luminous, I don't know. Then"—he snaps his fingers—"he's gone."

I shrug, watch the lanterns. "I'm sure one of the shots hit him, Chief. Stands to reason. They'll find him in there someplace."

"If they don't, we could be in deep shit, Rawlings. I mean, think about it. What the fuck would we *tell* people? Huh? That this big snake suddenly appeared on a pedestal at exactly midnight and he—he seemed to be—well, *glowing?* That at least nine of our best sharpshooters fired a total of like forty rounds of high-powered ammo at him in a period of ten seconds, but they all *missed?* That we searched high and low for him, but couldn't *find* him? So, to the best of our knowledge, he's now loose in the *neighborhood?* Huh? This twelve-foot-long deadly poisonous king cobra's out there slithering around in the general vicinity of Hell's Kitchen? Think about it. Know what'd happen if the *media* got wind of this? All it'd take is just one eyewitness account. That's all. Just one cop, one nun, one civilian who's standing down the street there behind the police barricades, who saw the whole thing. We'd have media people comin' out our *ears!* What the fuck would we *tell* 'em? That it's not true, that it never happened? They'd have us by the nuts on a downhill drag! I mean, Jesus Christ, I can see the front-page headline in the *News:* 'Cops Lose Cobra That Glows in Dark!' Huh? He'd do that, Casandra would do that, you know he would, he'd eat us up and spit out the pieces for days! Reilly and me, we'd be the laughingstock of the city for days on end: 'Hey, Chief, ya catch that big *glowworm* yet?' Oh, shit, how do I get *into* these things? Why *me?*"

I wait, watching his pained expressions, visualizing all this stuff, then I say quietly, "They'll find him, Chief."

But I'm wrong. They don't find him. After McCartney and McIntyre search every inch of the walkway from outside the fence and come up empty, Vadney gets Reilly on the walkie-talkie, asks him to come back for a strategy meet. Turns out the limo just circled around and parked down at Thirty-second and Eighth near the post office, so they arrive back at the scene within a couple of minutes. Okay, Reilly and Mairs get out now, Vadney and McCartney bring them strictly to date. Idea of a twelve-foot deadly poisonous cobra slinking around the neighborhood doesn't sit too well with Reilly, he orders an exhaustive search of the whole street from Ninth to Tenth avenues, bringing in all available personnel. Mairs gets on his walkie-talkie, orders his fifteen sharpshooters to report to him in the street. Chief uses the limo's radio, puts out an emergency call for all units in the general area to proceed immediately to St. Michael's High School, no sirens.

Eight squad cars and six detective units respond within five minutes or so, park helter-skelter in front of the school and rectory. Chief's in his element now, leans back against the limo in the glare of crisscrossed headlights, pulsating red and blue emergency lights, and the monotone of police radios. His Duke Wayne sky-blues are narrowed, his arms are folded, coat off, collar open, tie yanked down, sleeves rolled up, badge and ID clipped to his shirt pocket, and he's surrounded in the street by sixteen uniformed cops, twelve detectives, fifteen ESD sharpshooters, and four Bomb Squad technicians, a captive audience of forty-seven armed but inexperienced snake hunters. Standing to his right, Commissioner Reilly and Commander Mairs; to his left, Commander McCartney and me. All these cops out there are looking at me, frowning, exchanging glances as if to say: Who the fuck's *this* clown? Me, I button my blazer, straighten my tie, adjust my badge, stand up to my full five-ten, look back at them as if to say: Special

Deputy Snake Hunter Rawlings, *that's* who. Friends in high places.

Chief raises his voice above the police radios and general din of conversation: "Okay, hold it down, men, listen up! Listen up, now, we don't have much time here. Bottom line, as most of you probably know by now, we've got a potentially dangerous situation on our hands here. There's a snake loose somewhere in this street, a big snake, a king cobra."

Lots of expressions and postures change. Rows of eyes dart streetward, glance left and right. Gum chewers stop chewing.

"Consensus opinion," Chief continues, "he's probably holed up somewhere in or around one of these buildings. Description: Approximately twelve feet long. Weight unknown, but presumed heavy. Yellow-brown skin, hooded upper neck with black horizontal stripes. This thing is known to be deadly poisonous and should be considered extremely dangerous. Therefore, your orders are to shoot on sight and shoot to kill. Last known whereabouts, the general vicinity of the empty pedestal on the wall over there, inside the fence, but by this time he could be inside the school, inside or outside the rectory over there to the right, and possibly inside or outside the connecting church to the right of the rectory. We'll concentrate on those three buildings first. Now, we're gonna break you up into two-man teams. All Emergency Service Division officers will report to Commander Mairs here, of course, for specific team assignments within the school itself. All uniformed officers and Bomb Squad technicians will report to Commander McCartney for team assignments within the rectory. All detectives will report to me for team assignments around the exteriors of all the buildings and the interior of the church. Now, before reporting to your commanding officers, listen up, hear this: I want all police vehicles in the street here to be lined up facing north, toward the school, headlights on high beams, spotlights on full. First line 'em up in one long, even row, then back 'em up against the south curb there and park 'em. Right? Now, that's so all of us can have a clear, unobstructed view of the street, curb, sidewalk, the little walkways behind the fence, plus the exteriors of the school, rectory, and church. We don't want any surprises around here. All right, questions? Any questions? Okay, let's go to work."

Search starts in earnest at 12:25 A.M. Only men not directly involved are Commissioner Reilly and his driver, who watch from the limo. Must say, Chief's idea of lighting the street, sidewalk, and buildings is an excellent one, he's got a total of nineteen vehicles lined up against the south curb, including both Bomb Squad trucks, the limo, his own car, and even mine. I took mine from the parking lot and positioned it at the very end of the row, east side, next to the big Bomb Disposal Vehicle. Both are parked directly in front of the entrance to St. Michael's Catholic Church. Not that I'm asking for any special consideration or protection, I'd never do that, but I just figure it's a real nice spot to be, it couldn't hurt. All the windows on all six floors of the school and rectory are lighted now, plus all the beautiful stained-glass windows of the church, so we've got an entirely different atmosphere going, a whole new perspective. Sister Mary Garcia has even turned on the spotlight at the base of the big white stone statue of Christ just outside the rectory.

Chief's left me on my own, at my request, so I have the flexibility of just wandering around outside, watching the two-man teams of detectives work the exteriors, cautiously, using flashlights for all shadowed areas behind the fences. I go over to the lighted statue of Christ, it's really quite imposing, bright white in the spotlight, to the right of the rectory's entrance. It's behind a black wrought-iron fence similar to the one around the school, except much lower. The statue is larger than life-size, standing maybe seven feet high from its pedestal. Christ's pose is a familiar one, depicted in many paintings: He's looking down at me, left hand pointing to his heart (visible on the outside of his garment), right hand extending down and outward, palm up. On the wall behind the statue, high above his head, an excerpt from the Bible is chiseled into the weathered stone, block capitals etched in gold:

COME TO ME
ALL YOU THAT LABOR
AND ARE BURDENED
I WILL GIVE YOU REST

I hear footsteps in the street, turn and see Commissioner Reilly walking directly toward me from his limo. Can't see his face or clothes because the headlights and spotlights make him a dark silhouette, but I know it's him by his walk. Not a doubt in my mind. When you observe the way people walk, as I often do, sometimes it can give you subtle insights. Now, Reilly, he's got what I'd call a modified New York street-fighter's walk: Head down, shoulders hunched, arms swinging, posture leaning forward. I say "modified" because his body language isn't all that tough or threatening, it's just intense, determined to get where he's going. Reinforces my first impression of him at his office this morning. I suppose if I had to use just one word to describe this guy it'd be "tenacious." Don't know why I identify with tenacious people, but I do, I usually like them. Must have something to do with my personality.

We nod to each other, now he stands there next to me, I can see him better in the light from the statue: Short, well built, dark-eyed, collar opened, tie pulled down. He looks up at the inscription in silence for a while, then speaks quietly. "Brings back memories."

"I'll bet it does."

"You a religious man, John?"

"In my own way."

"Nothing formal, huh?"

"Afraid not."

"Same with me. You recognize that inscription?"

"It's familiar."

"Matthew, eleventh chapter, twenty-eighth verse. Only thing is, it's not strictly accurate. It was shortened and anglicized so it'd fit symmetrically into the four lines there. In the original Greek and in the King James version it reads: 'Come unto me, all ye that labor and are heavy laden, and I will give you rest.' When I was a student here, that used to bother me. That they changed the words. Because at the very end of the Bible, in Revelation, twenty-second chapter, nineteenth verse, John says: 'And if any man shall take away from the words of the book of this prophecy, God shall take away his part out of the book of life, and out of the holy city, and from the things which are written in this book.' Things like that used to bother me. I used to think: Wow, they changed the word of God for economy, so it'd fit neatly on a wall." He smiles, shakes his head. "I was a sensitive kid."

"Nothing wrong with that."

"No, I guess not."

"Obviously, you studied the Bible closely, huh?"

He nods, looks toward the school. "Let's go take a look at the pedestal. I want to see how much damage was done."

As we walk, our tall shadows on the rectory wall are splintered by all the headlights and spotlights. Looks like we're walking with a small crowd. Breeze from the Hudson is stronger now, still warm, still has the smell of sewage.

"Walt told me what happened to you this afternoon," he says.

"In the school, yeah."

"At the front door and in that classroom."

"Right."

"What do you make of it, John?"

"I honestly don't know, sir. I only know—"

"Call me Bill."

"—what I saw and heard. At this point—and I'm sure of that, I'm sure about what I saw and heard. But at this point, to be honest, it beats the shit out of me. Doesn't make any sense at all."

"He said you saw a dark figure open the front door."

"Right. He looked like—he was dressed just like a priest, y'know? Long black tunic? Tall and lean. At first I thought it was Sister Mary Garcia. It happened fast, he just stood there for a couple of seconds, then the door closed. But he didn't seem to move, that's the thing, he didn't seem to close it himself. Then, when I go and open it, the foyer's empty."

He nods, slows his stride. "Okay, tell me this. About how much time elapsed? Between the time the door closed and the time you opened it and looked around. Can you remember that?"

"Yeah, let's see. I went up and knocked first, I remember that. No answer, so I knock harder, there's no bell, y'know? Still no answer, so I open it a little, just enough to see the lighted foyer, I could see the trophy cases. And I call out Sister Mary Garcia's name. That's the only name I had. No, wait a minute, first I called out—I said something like 'Anybody here?' That's right. Something like that. No answer, so then I called her name after that. Still nothing, so then I go in. I'd say—I don't know, maybe half a minute. I see what you're getting at, yeah."

"Half a minute, right? That's plenty of time for somebody to walk from the front door to the classroom down the hall."

"That's true," I say, and I think: *Or to go the other way. To go down the opposite hall, to the left, where, about halfway down that hall, there's another hall that leads directly to the office.*

"Now, Walt said you heard chalk sounds coming from that classroom, somebody writing on the blackboard, right?"

"Yeah. But nobody was in that room, Bill. Those writing sounds continued until I walked all the way to the classroom. And they were definitely coming from that room. Then, just as I got up to the door, they stopped. The room was lighted but empty. And the writing, the Enochian writing, filled the whole blackboard, all five slabs of it. That's another thing; it would've taken quite a while to fill that whole board. Jim Mairs had one of his men photograph the entire thing this afternoon. Says he'll get it translated as soon as possible."

"Yes, he told me. That should be interesting, to see what it means. Whoever's doing this, he's gone to a hell of a lot of trouble, I'll say that. But there have to be logical answers. If this guy's trying to scare me, he'll have a long wait."

The gate leading to the pedestal is open and two detectives are at the far end of the walkway with flashlights. We go in, take a close look at the damage to the pedestal, its wrought-iron fixture in the wall, and the badly scarred wall itself, which took most of the slugs. The cement walkway directly under the pedestal is chipped and cracked and debris is scattered all over the place—chunks of stone from the wall, bits and pieces of iron, fragments of the high-powered copper-jacketed slugs, and shattered glass that catches the light.

I take out a cigar now, bite off the end, spit it out, light up. I know it's bad for my health and all, but it's a luxury for me to do it once in a while, particularly when I'm tired and tense. Tense? Yeah, tense, although I've been doing my best to hide it. Tell you why. To me, the most unnerving thing that's gone on here, reflected in almost all the faces and voices I've observed closely, is the determined, conscious effort to do very physical things, to talk about all the very tangible factors, to avoid (or at least postpone as long as possible) that time when we're all going to have to think about what we've seen. That time when we're all going to be alone with our thoughts, and our fears. That's right. And I'm talking about our fear of the unknown. I'm no exception, I don't want to think about it. I know that sooner or later I'll have to drive home tonight, alone, and think about it, and I dread that. As I said before, and as I keep reminding myself, I'm a realist, I honestly believe that most physical phenomena can be explained in terms of logic, if you dig deep enough, and if you don't let emotion get in the way. Fear of the unknown is a powerful emotion, probably based on instinct more than intellect, I don't know, but I suspect most of us have it in spades, if we're honest with ourselves. We don't like to think about it or talk about it, because fear of the unknown goes deep, deeper than we want to go. Me, I hate it, I don't want to think about it. But I have to. In this case, I just have to.

Okay, cards on the table; exactly what am I afraid of here? Can I face that, can I spit it out honestly, without making a fool of myself? I'll give it a shot. I'll try. Within reason, of course. I mean, I'm not going the whole nine yards. But, briefly, here it is. Although I was raised as a Roman Catholic, I don't practice any formal religion any more. Don't get me wrong, I'm not an atheist. Far from it. I have a much stronger belief in God today than I've ever had. That's the honest truth. But then, having said that, I must also acknowledge a deep fear of the unknown, of another force in nature that's very much in evidence, all around me, every day of my life. Call it evil, call it a dark, cosmic force, call it Satan, I don't care what you call it. It's there. It just can't be denied. Maybe I'm more aware of it as a cop, I'll give you that, no argument. But it's there. I don't understand it, I don't think anybody understands it. But, obviously, we all acknowledge its presence. The evidence is just positively overwhelming, right?

So I'm standing there, I'm puffing my cigar, I'm looking at the torn and twisted pedestal where we all saw what we saw, and can't deny that we saw it, but don't really want to talk about it, or even think about it, because it's too hard, and now I look up at the stars. And I say to myself: Come on, John, face up to the possibility, at least. Just the remote possibility, that's all. The possibility that we were all in the presence of something that can't be explained by logic, that can't be understood, but that can't be *denied.* Admit to the possibility, that's all. Why not? Why should that be so painful, so frustrating, so totally unacceptable? Why can't you step over that line? Doctors do, scientists do, theologians do. They admit openly to the presence of weird phenomena that they don't understand, that they don't think anybody understands. Why can't you? Why can't you admit to the very real possibility that you may have been in the presence of Satan?

I shake my head, take a deep breath, glance down at the debris on the walkway—chips of cement, chunks of stone, bits of iron, flattened slugs, shattered glass that catches the light.

Shattered *glass?*

I toss my cigar away, take out my handkerchief, kneel down, pick up the fragments, examine them carefully before I drop them in the handkerchief. And, for the first time since this whole thing began, I can't help smiling. Then laughing silently, deep down inside, where the little boy is, the real me inside myself.

Are you listening, Satan?

Are you laughing, too?

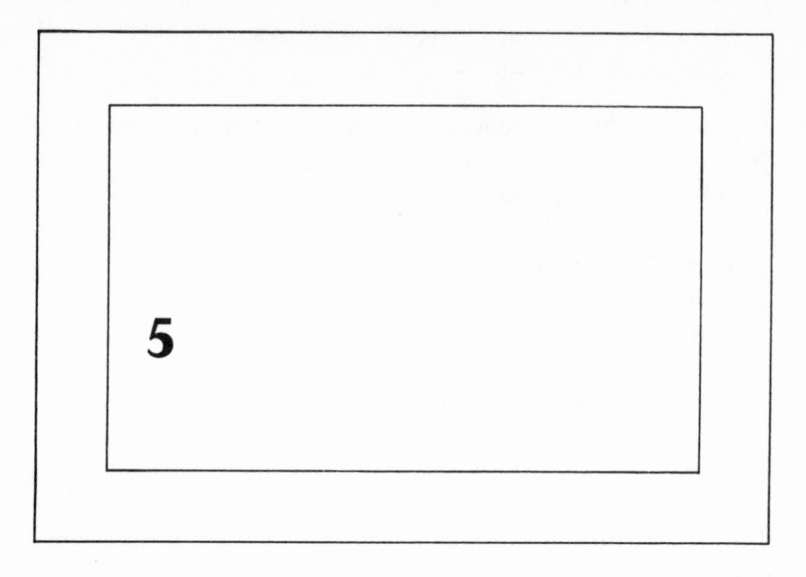

5

MONDAY MORNING, August 25, I grab a cab at Penn Station about 10:30 and head straight for the Police Academy, 235 East Twentieth, that's where our Forensic Lab is located. Relatively modern building, finished in 1964 when Abe Beame was mayor, eight floors of light-tan brick weathered soft soot gray. Me, I went to the old Academy, but I happen to love this one, it's a whole different world. Like, you should see the Ballistics Unit here, top floor, that's high tech all the way, probably the best in the country. Security's extremely tight around here. You show your shield and sign in at the lobby desk, then you get off the elevator and you're in a big steel cage. You show your gold again, you're buzzed in, you sign in again, then you're supposed to have an appointment with a specific officer in the lab, which I do, I called from home before I left. Happen to know the commanding officer, Lieutenant Diaz, Louie Diaz, we go back a long way. Desk sergeant calls him, he comes out to meet me himself. Haven't seen him in a couple of years now, but it doesn't matter.

Doesn't matter. First time I met this kid, I thought of him as somebody from the old neighborhood. Know what I mean? Still feel that way. Always will.

He comes out, he's smiling, he goes to his fighter's crouch, he bobs and weaves, he's looking to fake with the right, stick the left jab. Louie's about forty now, maybe he's gained a few pounds here and there, but he still looks like a welterweight, which he used to be. Real good amateur, Golden Gloves finalist, champion of his army division. Grew up as the only Spanish kid in a tough Sicilian neighborhood in the Red Hook section of Brooklyn, graduated from Queens College. Classic Spanish features, jet-black hair, dark complexion, thick lips, but his eyes are the thing. Always thought of his eyes as Brando eyes. Yeah, Brando, in *On the Waterfront,* remember that? Remember that famous scene in the taxi, Brando and Rod Steiger? He turns to Steiger in that dim light, reflections moving on his face? And he says, real soft, "It was you, Charley." Right? Remember those eyes? Okay, that's him, that's Louie, that's a wrap on this kid. Period. End. Boom. Windows of the soul. When he weighed 147 pounds, he was beautiful.

We walk through the lab, he's got at least twenty forensic technicians hard at work here, reading newspapers, sipping coffee, gassing on the phone. Leads me into his corner office, sunny southwest view, not bad for a kid from Red Hook. Sit down, have a cup of coffee, light up a cigar, shoot the shit for a while. He knows all about what happened last night, of course, hundreds of cops know by now; before the morning's over half the department will know. You kidding? Didn't make any of the papers, but NYPD's got a grapevine you wouldn't believe, particularly on juicy stuff involving top brass. So the word's out on the snake, the sharpshooters firing without orders (Mairs is considering official reprimands for all nine ESD men), and the emergency search, but that's it, that's all the rank-and-file know, thank God. When I went home at about one o'clock, they were still at it; Mairs was making arrangements for a fresh ESD team to take over at 2:30 and search until 7:30, when rush-hour traffic would make the emergency logistics too complicated. Bottom line, they never found the sucker.

"So what's happening?" Louie asks.

I reach in my blazer pocket, take out the folded handkerchief, put it on his desk. "Like you to take a look at some glass."

He frowns, takes a peek. "What y'got here, diamonds?"

"Picked 'em up under the pedestal."

"Yeah?" He pokes his finger around, frowning at the fragments, maybe two dozen in all. "Yeah, y'got a real treasure trove here, John. Here's—just off the top of my head, don't make book on this—now it looks to me like you got part of a light bulb here, plus something else, I don't know what this is." He glances up, tries to keep looking scholarly. "We're looking for snakeskin, right?"

Can't help laughing, this is vintage Louie.

He keeps frowning. "John, you were up real late, right? I mean, it happens to all of us. You had a couple of belts and all, I understand, believe me, I been there myself."

"Take a look at one of the thicker pieces."

He finds one, the longest, maybe half an inch square. Turns, holds it up to the window, studies it, finally gets serious. "Yeah, I see what you mean. Some kind of—looks like gray-green swirls or something." Now he picks up the phone, touches two buttons, continues to study it. "Dino, come in for a minute, huh?" Hangs up, turns back to the handkerchief, pokes around, selects a piece of very thin glass. Opens the top right-hand drawer of his desk, takes out a small clear plastic evidence envelope, drops the two fragments inside.

Tall kid with a mustache appears at the door, knocks on the frame. "Lieutenant?"

"Come in, Dino. Like you to meet John Rawlings of the Nineteenth. Dino Passarelli."

We shake hands, say hello.

Louie hands him the plastic bag. "Two samples of glass. Put 'em under the scope, huh? See what we got."

"Yes, sir."

"And, Dino, close the door, huh?"

He waits till the door's closed, sits back, puts his feet up on the desk. "So how's it going, John? Bring me up to date, it's been a while."

"Same routine, Louie, robbery detail mostly. Still got us up on Ninety-fourth, real shithole."

"Oh, yeah, that's right. How long you been up there now?"

"Over a year. Seems like five. Chief's got me on special assignment now, as of yesterday. Manna from heaven. Called Lieutenant Barnett this morning, commanding officer, told him the good news. Told him it was top-secret shit. He says good luck. He says he wishes somebody'd throw some top-secret shit in his cage once in a while."

"I know what he means, John. I know exactly where the man's coming from, believe me."

"Yeah? You? What're you, bored or what?"

"That's the word, John."

"No. I can't believe it. You?"

"Me. It happens. Tell you the truth, I envy you. I really do. I was much happier on the street. That's a fact, buddy, that's no shit. Of course, I didn't know it at the time, you never do. Remember when we were over in Brooklyn South, all those guys, Big John and them? Remember those times?"

"Like yesterday."

"Shit, I was just a kid back then. Chasin' crooks, kickin' butt. Drinkin' beer with you clowns over to O'Hanlon's. You and Big John and them." He takes his feet off the desk, swivels to the side, looks out the window. "We had fun. I mean, okay, we didn't know shit, right? But we had a lot of laughs back then. I remember that."

"You were ambitious, Louie."

"Yeah. Yeah, that's true, I was. What'd I know, right?"

In the pause, I puff my cigar, watch his profile, he's still looking out the window. Finally I clear my throat, do my imitation of Rod Steiger, he always liked that: "How much you weigh, son?"

Gets a smile out of him, but he won't look at me.

"When you weighed one hundred and forty-seven pounds, you were beautiful. Could've been—"

"Could've been a contender, yeah, right. So what happens? I start taking exams up the gazoo and now I'm a *pre*tender. Okay? Commanding officer of the fuckin' police lab. Stuck behind a desk, where I belong. Remember how I used to study for those exams? Remember that, John?" He swivels around, faces me. "Know what I am now? I'll tell you what I am now. I'm an administrator. That's right. Ad-*min*-istrator. That's what I am, that's what I do. I push papers around, I sign documents, I give orders, I write memos, I go to meetings, I write reports, I worry about my budget. That's what I do. I'm not a cop anymore. No way. I'm like a corporate executive. I don't *do* forensic science, I *manage* people who do forensic science. Specialists. Highly trained technicians who do the work: Chemistry, physics, biology, pathology, metallurgy, document examination. Except a lot of the daily routine involves blood-alcohol analysis in DWI cases, plus drug-related cases ad infinitum, so we're talking real glamorous stuff here. If they want somebody from forensic to appear in court as an expert witness, they don't want me, they want one of my people, they want a specialist. So where does that leave me? Sitting behind a desk. I don't even get to appear in court, for Christ's sake."

I shrug. "Take the captain's exam, maybe they'll move you out of here. How long you been in this job now?"

"Three and a half years already. Yeah, excellent suggestion, take the captain's exam. Matter of fact, I'm studying for it now. Know what'll happen when I pass it? Headquarters. Yeah, I'll lay you odds, headquarters. Another desk job, higher pay, more administrative responsibility. That's what happens to ambitious cops."

Goes like so. Ten minutes later, there's a knock at the door, Dino Passarelli comes in with his report. Sits down, hands Louie the plastic envelope, puts on his glasses, refers to some notes on his pad. Looks very serious and scientific with his glasses, speaks quietly but with authority.

"I studied both fragments under the Leitz," he says, turning to me. "That's one of the most powerful microscopes we have in the lab. The thin glass is definitely part of a high-intensity light bulb, possibly as powerful as three hundred watts. The thicker fragment with the swirls is part of a developed photographic plate of the silver halide group of light-sensitive emulsions, common to most films, but this one appears to be a holographic plate because of its extremely high resolution. Resolution is expressed in lines per millimeter. Most photographic plates or films don't have the capability to resolve more than fifty to one hundred lines per millimeter, but holograms require between fifteen hundred and three thousand lines per millimeter. Are you two familiar with holography, holographic projections?"

"Vaguely," Louie says. "Give us a quick rundown."

Dino removes his glasses, sits back, chews on one of the earpieces. "Well, holography's been around since the late nineteen-forties, but it's gained tremendous popularity over the past eight or ten years. What it is—let's see if I can describe it briefly. It's basically a three-dimensional image stored on a high-resolution photographic plate. The original photograph is shot with a laser beam, that's the key. But then the developed plate can be projected in space with ordinary white light or high-intensity light. It's supposed to be the most accurate three-dimensional illusion of reality ever discovered."

"Let me get this straight," I say. "You photograph something using a laser beam and a special photographic plate. Then you develop the plate. Then you can project the thing with ordinary light. And what you see, the image you see, is a three-dimensional image in space. It looks absolutely real and solid, but it's actually not there."

"That's essentially correct," Dino says. "Naturally, taking the photo is much more complicated, but the end result is a hologram, a three-dimensional illusion of reality. It's become a whole new art form. There's even—if you want to know more about it, there's a museum down on Mercer Street, the Museum of Holography."

"You been there?" Louie asks.

"Yes, sir, about a year ago. They've got all kinds of holograms on display, all sizes, shapes, techniques, lots of books on the subject. I thought it was fantastic."

"Where on Mercer Street?" I ask.

"Between—I think it's between Canal and Grand."

Louie looks at me, glances at his watch. "You going?"

"You bet."

He stands, goes to get his coat. "This is very technical stuff, John, you need help from Forensic. Definitely. Not only that, you need a partner down in that area, SoHo's a real jungle these days."

SoHo (means south of Houston Street) is anything but a jungle today, but it's a kick to have Louie with me. What's happened down here over the past fifteen or twenty years, the area's gradually evolved into a kind of art district, what they call avant-garde art, and a lot of artists live and work in the lofts around here, but they have to prove they're real artists of some kind before they can live here. That's a fact, that was done to prevent SoHo from becoming too expensive for artists, like what happened to Greenwich Village. It's bounded by West Houston, Canal, Sullivan, and Broadway, and it still looks like the industrial warehouse district it was back in the nineteenth century. Back then it was called Hell's Hundred Acres because of the frequent fires that swept through the warehouses. Interesting thing is, not many of them actually burned to the ground, because the majority of them were cast-iron buildings. Cast-iron architecture was very big down here between roughly 1860 and 1890. Most of the old warehouses and lofts have dates on the front, that's how I know it's true. In fact, cast-iron architecture is so important to the city, the area was designated as a historic district in 1973; means they can't change the exteriors. Today, you wander around here, you see tons of little art galleries, boutiques, restaurants, and bars, but light manufacturing still goes on, that's what makes it so congested. Streets are jammed with trucks backed up to the old loading docks of the warehouses, racks of new clothes are all over the sidewalks, it's a real mess in the daytime, crowded, dirty, noisy, garbage cans stink like hell, but the place has character, tradition, history you can see, if you like stuff like that. Me, I love it, I thrive on it, always have, always will, what can I tell you, I'm a New York freak.

Dino was right about the Museum of Holography, it's between Canal and Grand, 11 Mercer Street. Old cast-iron facade with big white pillars, makes it look stately, distinctive black lettering on the frieze above the pillars. Louie double-parks next door in front of the Empire Sporting Goods Building No. 3, sticks his NYPD card up on the dashboard. Off we go, up the stoop, through the double doors, I'm really looking forward to this.

First thing that grabs your attention inside, boom, there's a large holographic projection just off to our right, a country landscape of some kind with a road leading into it and—this is no shit—Louie and me, we're standing right in the middle of that road. Okay, this is hard to swallow, I know, you'd have to experience this thing, but the road extends straight out from the landscape and we're standing right on it. Hell of an optical illusion, we glance at each other, we can't help laughing, it's a very, very weird sensation. Now we look around, the place is fairly crowded, exhibits all over. Desk is to our left, three bearded guys and a girl selling books and stuff, we buy two tickets, three bucks each, we get a little program, two sheets. One's an exhibition guide, "From Innovation to Tradition," the other's titled "Questions Asked Most about Holography."

First floor is dimly lighted so you can get the full effect of the three-dimensional images. We walk around slowly, study each hologram, the title, author, and date. Many in the first gallery here are plates within frames, suspended from the ceiling by almost invisible wires, and lighted by rows of high-intensity track lights mounted in the ceiling, so the images seem to float in the air at average eye level, looking so real and solid it's difficult to believe they're illusions. Others are in glass cases on pedestals or in specially designed mountings or behind glass cases built into the walls. There are five general categories in this exhibition: Manipulation of Image, Manipulation of the Hologram, Manipulation of Space, Holograms as Sculpture, and Manipulation of Light. One I like best looks like a permanent display, a 120-degree wall-mounted glass deal with a girl's head and shoulders inside; as you walk past her, she puts her right hand up to her lips, blows you a kiss, then gives you a wink. Louie, he can't believe this shit, he walks back and forth in front of this thing maybe a dozen times, kid must be starved for affection. Most of the people wandering around in here are relatively young and the majority are typical tourists—Japanese, French, German, British—and almost all have cameras slung over their shoulders, although taking pictures is strictly forbidden. Last thing you want in this joint are flashbulbs popping.

When we go downstairs, we come to a gallery with a display called "In Perspective: The Development of Holography,

1948–1978." First thing is the head of a man in a glass case, scholarly looking old gent with white hair, glasses, and a thin mustache. Inscription says it's Dr. Dennis Gabor, the inventor of holography, who received the 1971 Nobel Prize in physics for his discovery. We walk around his head, we study the face, eyes, glasses, mustache, ruddy complexion, he looks totally alive, like he's standing up in a vertical box with only his head visible, a mime trying to mimic a mannequin. Talk about Madame Tussaud's? This guy won't even melt. This guy's not even there.

We see the three main galleries, the theater/gallery, plus a traveling exhibition called "Through the Looking Glass" that's already been to forty cities and six countries, spend about an hour studying the various effects. I got what I came for, I understand the basic idea, the fundamentals, the possibilities. Of course, I have a lot of questions. Explaining this to Vadney, who'll then try to explain it to Commissioner Reilly, might be a bit tricky, so before we leave I browse the bookshelves up front and select two books, *How to Make Holograms* and *Holography Handbook: Making Holograms the Easy Way,* the only one in the place that comes complete with its own little hologram. Okay, with tax, they come to around thirty-eight bucks, but I can put it on the expense account. And it's necessary research. I don't know who or what I'm dealing with here, but at least I'm starting to learn part of the person's methodology. In this case, an attempt to intimidate and/or frighten Reilly. Why? I don't have the slightest idea.

Louie's having a ball, of course, he's a street detective again, wants to make it last as long as possible, so he suggests that we should both meet with Vadney this afternoon and bring him up to speed. Says he can back me up and lend some forensic authority with his technological and scientific background and vocabulary. We both laugh when he says that, but I agree, I want him with me all the way. Truth is, he doesn't really have a technological or scientific background (he majored in psychology at Queens College), but he's got an absolutely fantastic vocabulary—when he feels like using it. You'd have to know Louie, he's a complicated guy, totally brilliant, but he holds back, he doesn't want to come across as an egghead. When I worked with him in Brooklyn South, back when he was still into his amateur boxing, it was obvious to the whole squad that the kid had a multiple personality: Thoughtful, polite, and relaxed in almost any social situation; meticulous, demanding, and ambitious at the precinct; arrogant, tough, and thoroughly street-smart in undercover work. Hell of an actor when he worked undercover. One case we worked together, organized crime case, Louie went into deep cover, he assumed the physical, emotional, and mental role of an Italian hood so convincingly that sometimes he had to remind himself of his own identity. Yeah. He'd lose himself in the role, he was that good. But he nailed the guy we were after in that case. Nailed him good.

Anyhow, so now he drives me down to headquarters, we park in the underground garage, take the elevator to the lobby, go through the whole ID routine, desk sergeant calls Vadney's secretary, Doris Banks, she gives thumbs up, we sign in, clip on our floor-coded red badges, up we go, top floor, top-secret shit, I'm shining my shoes on the backs of my trousers, you never know who you might run into up here in the celestial hierarchy.

Louie straightens his tie. "Nineteen years on the force, I only met Vadney four times. Believe that? Four fuckin' times. Personally, I mean, him and me."

"Stick with me, Louie, I move in fast company. Heavyweights."

"Yeah, right. Imagine that? Three years CO of the police lab, I get to talk private with the Duke four times."

"But he calls you up all the time, right?"

He smiles, pushes back his hair. "Oh, yeah, well, it stands to reason, John. You kiddin'? CO of Forensic? Man's on the phone to me five, six times a day, minimum. Beggin' for my technical expertise. Beggin'. I mean, it's embarrassing, know what I mean? Half the time, I gotta put him on hold, I'm too busy solvin' the biggies, I got a line waitin' outside my office."

"You met his new secretary?"

"John, what's the matter with you? Doris Banks, yeah, I met her, sure, but you gotta get updated here. She's not his secretary any more, she got promoted, she's his administrative assistant now."

"Oh, yeah, I forgot."

"What's the matter with you, I thought you moved with the heavyweights here."

"Yeah, well, only the commissioner and them."

"The commissioner? The commissioner's a civilian, for Christ's sake, I'm talking about the brass, the top brass. When was the last time you worked with Vadney?"

"Vadney?" I give it careful thought. "Yesterday."

"Yeah, yeah—before that?"

"Before that? Last December."

"Last—? I don't believe this. This is unbelievable. That was the last time you worked with the brass, last December, eight months ago? I mean, John, what's the matter with you?"

"Just lucky, I guess."

"I mean, you gotta get some ambition here, John, you could get lost in this department, y'know that? Don't you think it's about time you got a little ambition?"

Elevator doors open, we step out laughing softly, feels like the old days. Louie ushers me to the right, tells me to stick with him, he knows the way to Vadney's office. Says he'll introduce me around headquarters after the meeting, get me some contacts. Says he's got clout up the gazoo. Kid's a pisser. Not only that, he's shorter than me, he's only about five-nine,

I got a full inch on him, I'm walking tall down the hall, what can I tell you? Instant marriage. Doesn't get any better than this.

Doris Banks's office is just outside Vadney's; it used to be a tacky waiting room, every time I walk in here now I have to blink, I can't believe what she did to this place. When Doris moved in here, October 1983, she brought her living room with her. Changed the decor from Bronx cheer to Bloomie's chic. White marble tables in three corners graced by black marble lamps throwing soft golden cones. White designer couches and chairs surrounding a glass-and-chrome coffee table that holds strictly current magazines, plus neatly folded final editions of today's *Times* and *Journal,* plus cut-glass ashtrays that no self-respecting cop would leave a cigar butt in. I mean, you wouldn't even think about it, it'd blow the whole nine yards here, the interior decorator would mess his Sassoons. Oil paintings of old Manhattan street scenes in fancy frames, individually lighted. Spotless light-gray fitted carpet; white sheepskin rug under the coffee table. Me, I always check my shoes for dogshit before I walk in here. Who picked up the tab for all this elegance? Not Vadney. No way, and he's always quick to point out that not one red cent of taxpayers' money was involved. No, it was Doris's husband, J. W. "Will" Banks, retired self-made multimillionaire. Gives her anything she wants. "Within reason," he says. Met him last December, looks like a mean son of a bitch, but Doris says he's a pussycat. "When he's asleep," she adds. I always said this about Doris, this kid don't take no shit from nobody. No place, no time, no where. Like her style.

She greets us at her glass-and-chrome table/desk, looks classy as ever in a fashionable off-white pantsuit. Blond hair has a nice sheen in this light, hazel eyes sparkle with the usual hint of mischief. Stands up, shakes our hands.

"Little John, Louie, nice to see you."

"Hey, Doris."

"Hey, Doris."

"I told the chief you're here, he'll see you in a minute."

"So, what's new, Doris?" Louie asks. "How's the new job?"

"Nice title," she says. "Nice new calling cards. No money, no power, no perks. I still handle all his paperwork, write his memos, take his calls, make his appointments, cover his derriere. Still, I don't have to go around chasing snakes on Sunday nights."

"You would've loved this one," I tell her. "Big king cobra, beautiful specimen. Nice warm smile, pearly white fangs."

"Yuck. Sounds like something my husband would bring home as a house pet. Tell the truth, Little John, weren't you scared? I mean, when you were out searching for it?"

"Me, scared? Searching for a twelve-foot-long deadly poisonous king cobra at midnight? Come on, Doris, you know me better than that. No way. I was too terrified to be scared."

"You're an honest man." She picks up the phone, presses two buttons on her console. "Detectives Rawlings and Diaz to see you." Listens, turns her back on us now, whispers into the receiver: "No, I told you. *Diaz,* Lieutenant Diaz, CO of the Forensic Unit. Right." Hangs up, turns around. "He's in a wonderful mood today. Wonderful. He didn't get much sleep, he had horrible nightmares. He kept dreaming that a big, fat, slimy snake was wrapped around him. Turned out to be his wife. Go right in. Hope you have good news."

"Doris," Louie says, "we're gonna make his day."

In we go with our books and papers, ready to explain the logical facts behind the strange saga of the snake that wasn't there to a man who, logically speaking, may not be there himself. Office hasn't changed much in eight months, it was newly decorated about the time Doris moved in. Not that she influenced him all that much, he'd been trying to get new furniture approval from Reilly for years. Chief finally got so pissed off he went out and bought it himself, two-year installment plan. Yeah. Of course, Doris's urging didn't hurt, she even helped pick it out. His desk is actually a highly polished teakwood conference table, twelve feet by six feet, chrome-plated legs, with twelve modern executive armchairs. He presides at the far end next to his matching teakwood commode with his telephone console, squawk box, and assorted high-tech toys. Same twenty-six NYPD-blue filing cabinets along the three walls. Wait a minute, here's something new since my last visit: Cozy little sitting area in the corner by the windows, one long white sofa, two matching chairs, glass-and-chrome coffee table in the middle. Expensive status symbols. Wonder how many installments?

Chief stands when we approach, motions to the conference-table chairs nearest him. Doesn't look too bad; sky blues are bloodshot, he's frowning at Louie like he can't quite place the face.

"Rawlings, Diaz, sit down there, what y'got?"

"Good news, Chief," I say.

"Yeah? I could use some."

"Think we found your snake," Louie says.

"Yeah? Y'*found* him? Holy jumpin' Christ! *Where? When?* How'd ya *do* it?"

Louie clears his throat, takes out the little plastic evidence envelope, places it proudly in front of him.

Chief frowns. "What's this?"

"Two pieces of very special glass," Louie says. "John found them under the pedestal at the school last night."

"Two pieces of—? Where the fuck's the *snake?*"

"Chief, ever hear of holography?" I ask.

"Holography? Yeah. What's it mean?"

Louie clears his throat again, pulls out his sheet titled "Questions Asked Most about Holography," reads the first question and answer in a soft but scholarly tone: " 'What is holography? Holography is a completely new way to make three-dimensional images, using laser light. It is one of the most interesting parts of modern technology. It was invented by Dennis Gabor, who received the nineteen-seventy-one Nobel Prize for his invention. Images made with holography are called holograms.' "

"Holograms?" Chief asks. "What's all this shit got to do—?"

Louie holds up a finger for silence, calmly reads the second question and answer: " 'What is a hologram? A hologram is a piece of film or *glass* coated with a photographic emulsion that has been exposed to *laser light* reflected by an object. Instead of making a flat image on the surface of the emulsion like a photograph, a hologram has no image at all. But when you shine a *light* on the hologram, a *three-dimensional* image appears to *float* behind the hologram, or in front of it. Holograms can be so *realistic,* you want to *touch* the image. But when you try, you find out that there is *nothing there.*' "

Chief narrows his eyes, picks up the plastic envelope, opens it, slides out the two fragments of glass, inspects them carefully. He swivels around, opens a drawer in his teakwood commode, takes out a small magnifying loupe, swivels back, places it over the fragments, hunches over with his right eye almost touching the loupe. "Are they both part of the same hologram or what?"

"Thicker one's the hologram," I tell him. "Thin one's part of a high-intensity light bulb. I found quite a few fragments of both under the pedestal and around it."

Chief rearranges the pieces, takes another squint through the loupe, whispers, "Son of a bitch."

"Forensic identified them this morning," Louie says. "Then John and I went down to the Museum of Holography to observe exactly how it's done. Fascinating technology, Chief, you should check it out."

"Yeah, I will. Rawlings, tell me something."

"Yes, sir."

"Where was the hologram hidden? In the pedestal itself?"

"That's my assumption. In that circular wrought-iron base

where the inscription was, the donors' names. And I believe the light bulb was directly under it. I'll have to check it out."

He looks up at me, blinking, pushes back a cowlick from his forehead. "How was the light turned on?"

"Chief, I'll have to—"

"By remote control or what?"

"I don't know," I tell him. "I'll have to go back to the school today and examine the inside of the pedestal in daylight. You remember that big statue of Christ just outside the rectory?"

"Yeah. Yeah, I do, the big lighted one, sure."

"That's right, it was brightly lighted," I say. "Okay, here's my assumption. The statue that was stolen, the one of St. Michael, I'm assuming that was routinely lighted, at least during the school year. Because, after all, St. Michael's the parton saint of the school, right? I'm assuming it was probably lighted by a simple automatic timing device, the same kind of twenty-four-hour automatic timer that's used commonly today in homes, offices, whatever. Keep in mind I'll have to go over there and check this all out. But I'm guessing that whoever placed that hologram inside the pedestal simply programmed an automatic timer inside the school to light the bulb at exactly midnight and turn it off—I don't know—maybe a minute or two later. Except the hologram and light were shattered by bullets within ten seconds. Reason it took that long is obvious. All nine ESD sharpshooters were aiming at the three-foot-high image of the snake, rather than the pedestal. What undoubtedly broke the plate and bulb were the ricochets."

Chief sits back now, hands clasped behind his head, gazes at me with his bloodshot eyes. "Little John, I gotta hand it to ya, buddy-boy. How'd you—? Everybody else searched that little walkway in there, all that debris in there. How'd you know what to look for?"

"I didn't."

"You didn't?"

"No, sir. I just saw some fragments of glass shining in the lights, in the glare of all those headlights, y'know? And I thought: Where'd the *glass* come from? I hadn't seen any glass around, up to that time, and there aren't any windows in that particular area."

He nods. "So you just took a long shot, huh?"

"Well, not exactly."

"No?"

"When I got down and examined the glass, especially the thicker pieces with the swirls, it struck a spark back in my mind. I knew I'd seen glass like that before, I just couldn't remember where. Then it hit me. In nineteen-seventy-nine, my wife and I saw a holographic image projected through a window at Cartier on Fifth Avenue. Anybody who saw it couldn't possibly forget it. What it was, it was the hand of a woman holding a beautiful diamond bracelet with her fingertips. The image was projected out over the sidewalk there on Fifth, close to the window, so it appeared to float in the air."

"I remember that!" Louie says. "I saw that! It drew crowds for weeks, it got a lot of press. Cartier's window, sure."

"That's right," I say. "There was a story in the *News* about one woman, she thought it was the work of the Devil, she tried to attack the image with her umbrella. They ran a picture of her and all. Anyhow, my wife and I, when we saw it, I think it was a Saturday night, we were in town for a show, we went over and read the sign inside the window, telling what it was and all, and we studied the holographic plate, and how it was lighted from behind. So that's how I remembered. That's how I remembered that particular kind of glass."

Chief sits forward now, shakes his head. "Gotta hand it to ya, Little John, wish I had more like ya. What's that word you always use to describe intuitive shit like that?"

I shrug. "Intuition."

"Yeah, that's right, intuition. Okay, tell me one more thing before we all go in to see Reilly, to explain all this. Does your intuition tell you anything about *who* we might be looking for? About what kind of weirdo would pull a stunt like this?"

"Yeah," I say. "Whoever it is, he's extremely intelligent. He's playing sadistic head games with the commissioner right now, trying psychological torture, working on his fear of the unknown. I think it'd be a mistake to underestimate a guy like this. In my judgment, we're dealing with a dangerous psychopath."

"What the hell you think he *wants?*" Chief asks.

"I think it's too early to tell."

"What's your *intuition* tell you?"

"That his motive is revenge. That he's following a meticulous plan. That it's entirely possible he intends to kill the man."

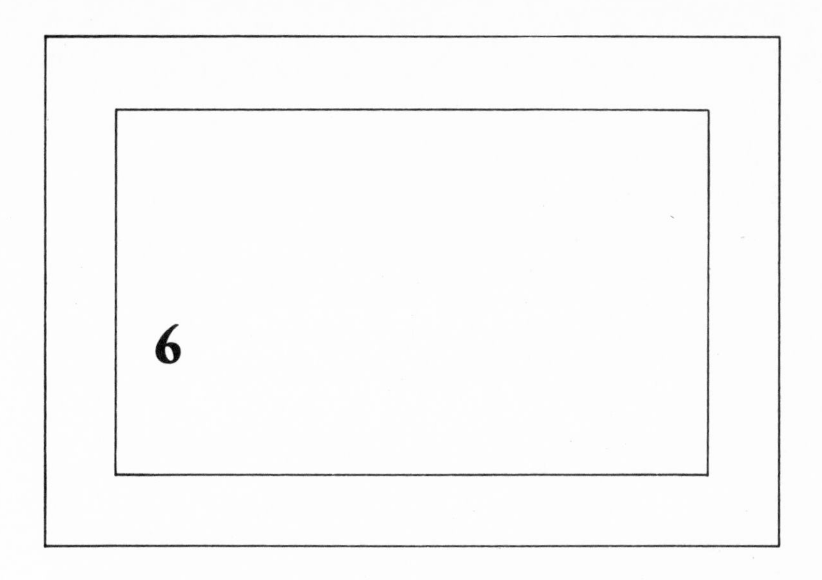

6

AFTER THE CONFAB with Commissioner Reilly, during which we alert him to take extra security precautions, Louie and I grab lunch at Wendy's (he's a junk food freak like me), then go over to St. Michael's, meet with Sister Mary Garcia in the rectory, and explain the whole thing for the third time. She confirms my assumptions on the technical aspects. Turns out the statue of St. Michael was routinely lighted at night during the school year, turned on and off by a twenty-four-hour automatic timer located in the basement near the janitor's office. She takes us down to the basement, opens an unlocked electrical box, shows us the timer. It's a simple little device called Intermatic Time-All, has a plastic dial like the face of a clock, a knob for automatic operation, and two sliding tabs, "on" and "off," to set at the desired times. Right now it's set to switch on at exactly midnight and shut off at 12:05. According to Sister Mary, the device hadn't been used since the school year ended. Who shut it off? Janitor. Since the electrical box wasn't locked, anybody with a key to the basement could've set the timer. Who has keys to the basement? Only the janitor, Anthony Salinger, the assistant principal, Sister Frances Barbella, and her, to the best of her knowledge. She's already given me Salinger's address and phone number, now I ask if she'd be kind enough to call him, ask him to come over to the school and speak with us, just routine questions.

We go back to the rectory, wait in the living room while she makes the call. Salinger agrees to come over, says he'll meet us out front at two o'clock.

That gives Louie and me roughly half an hour, I'd like to show him around, let him see everything firsthand, so Sister Mary gives me the keys to the front door of the school, tells us to go ahead, but be sure to return the keys before we leave. She walks us to the rectory door.

"Detective Rawlings," she says, "I want you to take a good look at that wall out there."

"The wall?"

"The wall behind the pedestal. In case you hadn't noticed last night, it's badly damaged and so is the pedestal. Who's going to repair it? Who's going to pay for it?"

"I'll find out," I tell her. "I'll see to it personally. We'll get two or three estimates for you and we'll see that it's repaired as soon as possible."

She smiles, shows her dimples. "Who's this 'we' we're talking about, Rawlings?"

I glance at Louie. "Community Relations?"

"That's my guess, yeah. Give it a shot."

"I'll make a call," I tell her. "I'll check it out personally. I'll get somebody over here."

"Today?" she asks.

"I'll call this afternoon. I'll try my best."

Seems to satisfy her. Louie and I go out, down the stoop in the bright sun, walk over to the school. He takes one look at the wall and pedestal, he gives a soft whistle. In sunlight, the damage looks extensive. It's a relatively small area, but it looks like it was hit by shrapnel from a bomb. Wall's cracked, chipped, crisscrossed by dark ricochets, it'll need custom stonemasonry. Circular part of the pedestal will have to be replaced; custom ironwork. Whole thing looks like an expensive job. Shooting snakes ain't cheap.

Now we go up to the front door, I unlock the two Medeco deadbolts, Louie holds the door wide open as I look for the light switch. Find it, turn on the foyer lights. Louie comes in, closes the door, snaps the locks. I light the hall to the right, we walk toward the classroom, heels clicking on the marble, and I explain what happened in there. My voice echoes a little, sounds spooky, but I can't help it. Louie, he's listening to all this stuff, he's nodding, he's going "Uh-huh," he's shifting his shoulders like a fighter, but I can tell he's not overjoyed by what he's hearing. I know by his voice, I know by his eyes. I'm not saying he's scared, at least not yet, I'm just saying he's not exactly relaxed.

We get to the classroom, I reach inside, snap on the lights. Nothing's changed. Rows of empty desks, window blinds drawn, entire blackboard is covered with those carefully printed words. Bright white chalk against glossy black. Louie takes it all in, gives with his soft whistle again, walks down the aisle for a closer look. I make a mental note to call Jim Mairs this afternoon, see if he's found somebody to translate it yet. Probably not. Question flashes through my mind: Where in hell do you find somebody who can translate Enochian? No pun intended. Probably some egghead at one of the universities in town could do it, no sweat.

"Let me get this straight," Louie says. "Let me run this down, stop me if I'm wrong. Front door of the school opens, you see a dark figure standing there. Now the door closes. You go up, you open it, the guy's gone. Now you hear the chalk sounds from down the hall, somebody's writing on the blackboard. You walk down the hall, the classroom's lighted, you stand outside, the chalk sounds stop. You go in the room, there's nobody in here. No other doors, windows are locked, nowhere anybody could hide. But there's all this weird shit written on the blackboard here. What's it called again?"

"Enochian."

"Enochian, yeah. Which, that's the ancient language of Satanism, right?"

"Of Satanic ritual, Louie. At least that's what Jim Mairs thinks it is. He had somebody from ESD photograph it all and now he's trying to get it translated."

"Okay." He sits on the edge of the teacher's desk, folds his arms, glances around the room. "So now, next thing, the Bomb Squad guys come on the scene here, they send in their dog to sniff for explosives, but he gets real spooked. He starts growling and all, his ears are back, he senses something in this room. He doesn't find anything, but he comes out and he's—his whole body is shivering?"

"Yeah. I mean, he was scared, Louie. Obviously, something scared him real bad."

"So your idea, you think it might've been some kind of odor or high-frequency sound, right?"

"That's all I—those were the only logical alternatives. To me, at least."

"What'd the Bomb Squad guys think?"

"Louie, it just beat the shit out of them. They'd never seen one of their dogs react that way before."

He frowns, loosens his tie now, unbuttons his collar, turns to look at the little loudspeaker built into the wall above the center of the blackboard. "So next you check out the public-address system up in the office?"

"That's right. Two tape cassettes in the console up there. Classical music. I checked them out personally. But here's something I didn't tell you. The number of this classroom is one-nineteen. On the public-address console there's a little lever for every classroom, every room in the school, the gym, the cafeteria, all that. So they can pipe messages to all rooms or to any individual room. Now, on that console, only one lever was in the 'up' position, the 'on' position: Classroom one-nineteen."

Louie blinks, glances away, smiles. "I'm glad you told me that, John. I mean, that gets us back to earth, know what I mean?"

"Only too well."

"It was done by sound, it had to be. Sound effects of chalk on a blackboard, then high-frequency sound. Somebody was up in that office, they played a couple of tapes. That lever explains the whole fuckin' thing."

"It's a slim clue, Louie, one little lever. But it's all we got."

"Who has keys to the office?"

"This guy Salinger, the janitor, plus the assistant principal, who's a nun, and Sister Mary Garcia, of course."

"After we meet Salinger, let's take a good look at the guy's background. Run him through the NCIC computer, the works. And we want his fingerprints, we'll tell him it's routine, we'll take him down to the Tenth Precinct."

"Oh, sure. I agree. Absolutely."

"John, I know that look in your eye, I know that tone in your voice. You'll check him out, you'll go through the whole routine, but you think it's too pat, right? You think he's too obvious?"

"Yeah, I do. I mean, I haven't even met the guy yet, but everything I know so far seems to point to him. All circumstantial. How the hell would a high school janitor pull off all this technical shit? Holography, high-frequency sound, the Enochian language. It doesn't add up. Something strange is going on here, Louie. And it—I don't mind telling you, it unnerves me."

"What kind of stuff you talking about?"

"I don't know. It's just my radar's been picking up very strange readings right from the beginning."

"John, look at me. Come on, look me in the eyes, man, talk to me."

I look him in the eyes, but I have difficulty finding the words.

"Talk to me, John. Come on. What is it?"

"I just have a feeling that we're into something much, much more complicated than we think. That we're into intelligence that—it gives me a strange sensation. It's hard to explain. Like we're in the presence of something genuinely—evil. I don't know what."

"Keep talking. Come on. Tell me this: Who do you think was that figure you saw at the front door? That dark figure. Talk to me, John, say it out."

I take a deep breath. "I don't know. But it unnerves me."

He waits. Then, softly: "You believe in Satan, John? The truth. You and me."

"Do *you* believe in him?"

"Yeah, I do. I'm not ashamed to admit that, why should I be? I was brought up as a Catholic, same as you. We had it drummed into our skulls all through grammar school and high school. You kiddin'? Yeah, it's hard to talk about it, but I believe something's there, the presence of evil, the force we call Satan. Now, come on, I've answered the question honestly, now you answer it. You believe Satan exists, in one form or another?"

"In one form or another, yeah, I suppose I do. I believe in the strong presence of evil, which I've felt since yesterday afternoon. Call it what you like."

"Who was that figure at the front door, John? Is there even a remote possibility in your mind that it—that you could've been in the presence of something supernatural? In the presence of Satan?"

"A remote possibility? Yes."

At two o'clock, we're standing outside the front door waiting for the janitor, Anthony Salinger. Traffic's relatively heavy, cars and cabs and trucks heading west toward the tunnel in the warm sun. Steady flow of people in and out of the office building across the street, parking lot off to the left is jammed, but the sidewalk in front of the rectory and school is virtually empty. Now here comes this old guy riding a bicycle on the sidewalk. Slow. So slow, it looks like he might lose his balance. Irony is, the bike's a sleek racing-style job, handlebars hung low. Now he comes closer, you should see this, he's a white-haired old black man, he's got a white goatee, he's hunched over the handlebars, long thin legs riding high on the pedals, intense expression on his face, like his mind's on the 1988 Olympics, but the message never reached his body. He passes Louie and me, pulls up in front of the pedestal, gets off his bike carefully, leans it against the wrought-iron fence. Stands there now, hands on his hips, studying the damaged wall and pedestal. Somehow I know this guy's Anthony Salinger, don't ask me how, so I take a long hard look at him. Tall, maybe six-foot-three, lean but not exactly skinny, I'd guess maybe 165 pounds. Short, curly white hair and trim white goatee combine to make his face seem unusually black. Age? Difficult from a distance, but I'd guess sixty-five to seventy. Wears a long-sleeved, snug-fitting blue workshirt tucked into tight black jeans, and blue Adidas sneakers with the three white stripes on the sides. He's frowning, he looks angry, his lips are moving like he's cussing to himself.

"It's him," I tell Louie.

"Got to be."

We walk over to him slowly. Closer we get, the more he seems to resemble someone I've seen before. Then it hits me: Redd Foxx. I mean, taller, thinner, older, but the sharp facial features of Redd Foxx.

He keeps studying the wall and pedestal, dark eyes moving

up and down, side to side, doesn't even glance at us when he speaks—suddenly, sharply, spitting out the words like he's known us for years: "Diaz, Rawlings, this is unconscionable, this is deliberate, reckless destruction of private property owned by the Archdiocese of New York."

"Mr. Salinger?" I ask.

"This will take thousands of dollars to repair, do you men realize that?"

"Yes, sir," Louie says calmly. "Are you Anthony Salinger?"

His eyes dart down to Louie. "The New York Police Department is legally obligated to pay for this. This afternoon, I intend to get written estimates from the best—not the cheapest, but the best—stonemason and custom ironworker in this city. I know who they are. I know their work, I admire their work. They're honest workers. They'll give honest estimates. They'll be here. I'll have written estimates in my hands by five o'clock this afternoon. Which I will then deliver to Sister Mary Garcia with my informed advice on exactly how to proceed in this matter. To wit: Copies of those estimates, together with a covering letter, will then be hand-delivered to the appropriate official at police headquarters at nine o'clock sharp tomorrow morning. If we do not receive written approval for the repairs within forty-eight hours, Sister Mary Garcia will contact the bishop's office, who will in turn contact—subject to the bishop's approval, of course—who will in turn contact the legal representatives of the Archdiocese and instruct them to initiate litigation proceedings. Litigation, gentlemen. Do you understand what I'm telling you?"

"Yes, sir," I say. "In my opinion, you'll receive cooperation from headquarters all the way. Litigation won't be necessary. In fact, I'll be glad to deliver the estimates and the letter to the right officer at headquarters myself. And I'll do my best to expedite the approval."

He looks in my eyes. "You're Rawlings, is that correct?"

"Yes, sir." I stick out my hand. "John Rawlings."

He shakes it firmly. "Anthony Salinger."

Out goes Louie's mitt. "Louis Diaz. Nice to meet you."

"Are you gentlemen from the Tenth Precinct?"

"No, sir," Louie says. "Detective Rawlings is from the Nineteenth Precinct and I'm the commanding officer of the Forensic Lab."

"Then you're not from the precinct of jurisdiction. Who are you reporting to?"

"Chief of Detectives Vadney," I tell him. "We're on special assignment."

He takes his hands off his hips now, folds them across his chest, seems to relax just a tad, glances at the damaged wall. "Will you gentlemen be kind enough to tell me exactly what happened here last night? And why it happened?"

I hesitate. "Personally, I'd be glad to tell you. I really would. But we're under orders not to discuss it. At this point, it's still classified information. It's under investigation."

"Rawlings, I know for a fact that police sharpshooters opened fire on somebody here last night, because Sister Mary Garcia told me so herself on the telephone. She saw it happen. Okay? She doesn't know who they were firing at, she couldn't see from her window, but she saw them firing and heard them and it scared the hell out of her. I mean, it scared hell out of every nun in the rectory, okay? And after it was over, she gave her permission for the police to conduct a search of the school, the rectory, and even the church. A massive search, involving dozens of police officers, she doesn't know how many. A search that continued until seven-thirty this morning, at which time they returned the keys to the buildings. Now, I know this, I know all this already, it's no secret. Do you deny that's part of what happened?"

"Mr. Salinger," Louie says, "we're not at liberty to confirm or deny anything. We're under orders not to discuss the subject. Try to understand our side of it."

"You ask me to come all the way down here, you expect my cooperation, but you won't even tell me what you're investigating. Try to understand *your* side of it? How about *my* side of it? You have any idea how that makes me feel? It's a clear indication to me that you consider me a *suspect.*"

"No, sir," Louie says. "All we want to do is ask you a few routine questions, see if you can help us out."

"Routine questions? Don't make me laugh, Diaz, don't insult my intelligence. Routine questions? You know I have keys to everything in this school. So, in your 'routine,' lazy, indifferent habits of investigation, you automatically *assume* that I'm a candidate to be involved in whatever's been going on around here. Even including—probably even including the theft of the statue, right? Okay, if that's the case, then the burden of proof is on *you,* not me. Arrest me on a specific charge, read me my rights, take me down and book me, let's get it over with. I'll be out in a matter of hours, I'll go straight to the ACLU, we'll start immediate litigation for harassment, false arrest, false imprisonment, discrimination, you name it. Please go ahead. Frankly, I could use the money."

"We have no intention of doing that," I tell him. "If you don't want to answer any questions, that's your legal right, and we respect it. My offer still stands to deliver those estimates and covering letter to headquarters and to try and expedite approval of the repairs."

"I appreciate it, Rawlings, but I think I'd rather handle it myself. Now, if you gentlemen will excuse me, I have some telephone calls to make from the rectory."

I hold out the keys to the school. "Will you return these to Sister Mary Garcia and give her our thanks?"

He nods, takes them. "Is there any damage to the classroom?"

"Classroom?" I ask.
"One-nineteen."
"No. No damage at all."

When we get down to headquarters about two-thirty, Vadney's in Commissioner Reilly's office, meeting's just started, Doris says he'll probably be a while, so we ask her to ring Jim Mairs, see if we could stop in for a few minutes. Turns out he's free, come on over. He's just down the hospital hall from Vadney. On the way, Louie tells me that although Forensic gets its share of requests from ESD, he's never actually been in Jim's office, it's all been done by phone, memos, and reports, which doesn't surprise me, that's the way things get done at headquarters. In any event, I feel almost obligated to brief him about this particular office, because if you walked in cold, you might get the wrong idea about Mairs. Chief tagged him with a secret nickname, "Commander Cuckoo," but it's not true, Jim just happens to collect weird shit, that's all.

We walk into his assistant's office, well-endowed youngster by the name of Amy Silin, kid's got Tiffany class, Cartier sparkle, knows how to package the gifts. Chief calls her "Moneypenny," gets his rocks off on that, she puts him down gentle as a Waterford goblet on a barnyard turd. Now she turns from her IBM PC, smiles, waves us inside. Jim's on the phone, he motions for us to sit, but there's no place to sit, as usual. Louie and I go over and lean against the windowsill, try not to gawk. First off, it's a paper chase in here, a blizzard of case files and reports and letters and memos and computer readouts stacked high on his desk, on his filing cabinets, on his chairs, even on the floor. But it's okay, it's completely organized (in his head), he knows precisely where everything is, right down to the last Christmas card. Floor-to-ceiling bookshelves are relatively neat, tons of research books in hard and soft covers behind a virtual menagerie of scale-model locomotives and classic cars and three-masted ships and unopened

Olympia beer cans. Valuable old Leica camera here, miniature Underwood typewriter there, antique British bric-a-brac everywhere. Which is fine and dandy. But then you start picking up on more imaginative stuff. Preserved frog that was squashed by a truck. Preserved bat hanging by a claw from the limb of a dead geranium plant. Preserved venus flytrap near the window, from which hangs a tiny birdcage that you can't see because it's draped in a black velvet cloth with the white letters R.I.P. You don't want to know what's in there, believe me, you don't.

Louie does. He nudges me, jerks a thumb toward the black cloth, keeps his voice very low. "What the fuck's in *there?*"

"Don't ask."

He thinks about it a while, glances around innocently, waits until Jim's not looking. Lifts the cloth, takes a quick peek. Drops it fast. Frowns. Shakes his head. Can't quite believe it.

"Told you," I tell him.

"Ho-lee shit."

What, exactly, is in there? Knew you'd ask. Deceased pet cockroach named Quint II. Big sucker, once the sole surviving heir apparent to the illustrious Quint I, stricken in his grime about five years ago, and buried decently somewhere in Jim's apartment, story goes, can't verify it. Quint II bought the cage just one year later, malady unknown. Jim just can't bring himself to part with it yet. Story goes, several of his friends have suggested, delicately, that it's time now, that a four-year mourning period is adequate, that it's appropriate to give the poor little chap a dignified resting place. But he can't do it yet, they were just too close. You know how you get attached to pets. So Quint II, he's still in there, on his once-slimy back, once-hairy legs straight up in that slow dance of death called "Rigor Mortis Cucaracha."

Thought occurs to me now, he could ask somebody to shoot a hologram of Quint II, then he could put the glass plate in the cage, add a small light bulb—presto, there he is in three-dimensional grandeur, maybe even standing up. Now a visitor comes in, you don't want him to see, just snap off the light. Gone, boom, empty cage hanging there. What a shame he didn't get it done before the roach croaked, right? While it was still big and healthy, bright-eyed, slime-backed, hairy-legged. What a happy hologram that would've made. What a happy man he'd be today.

Now I think: Hey, wait a minute, hold on here, that's an idea that could make me a millionaire. Wouldn't have to keep entering the Publishers Clearing House Sweepstakes anymore. I mean, many millions of people out there are deeply attached to their pets, love 'em like children, absolutely hate to see 'em go, right? Me, I could study my books on holography, buy the necessary equipment, the laser and all, and go into business for myself. Advertise in all the pet magazines, the whole shot: "Your Beloved Pet Can Live Forever!" Huh? What an idea! Wait a minute, what's the matter with me? "Your Beloved *Pet"?* How about: "Your *Beloved* Can Live Forever!"? Human *beings* I'm talking, husbands, wives, grandmas, grandpas, sisters, brothers, what have you? How about *that?* Hologram 'em in their prime, before their teeth go bad and their hair falls out. Shoot a life-sized hologram of your spouse sitting there in the living room watching TV. Then, when he or she passes away, project the hologram so your spouse is in the same familiar spot, sitting there in glorious three dimensions, smiling at some dumb sitcom like always. Lonely? Who's lonely? But then, if you get sick of 'em, if you remember all the shit you had to take from 'em, if you want instant revenge on the son of a bitch, just snap off the light. Boom, gone, empty chair. Talk about having the last laugh? And just think of the variations. Like, say your husband passes on, you're still an attractive lady, you want to start dating again, maybe you're looking to get married. So you have dinner with some distinguished dude, he takes you home, you invite him in for a nightcap, tra-la. One thing leads to another, now he starts in, he's looking to score, but you just don't feel like getting it on tonight. What's a mother to do? Simple. Snap on the hologram. Yeah! Distinguished dude turns around suddenly, here's your husband sitting right across from you, big as life, smiling! Distinguished dude levitates, screams bloody murder, messes his pants, he's out the door in a flash. Boom, problem solved. Of course, it's potentially dangerous, you could trigger an instant heart attack that way, but still. Does the job, right? I mean, just try to be selective, don't pull shit like this on any silver-haired gents with the shakes. Ramifications seem endless, here's a real growth industry in the making, maybe I could patent the idea, franchise it, have outlets all over the place.

Back to reality as we know it. Mairs finally gets off the phone, we bring him up to date on everything that's been happening, Louie explains the snake hologram deal for the fourth time today, he's on a roll, he doesn't even need his Q&A sheet anymore. Jim finds this stuff fascinating, sits back, listens carefully, asks sharp questions, takes notes, looks like a college professor with his high forehead that begins at the base of his neck. He agrees with us that Anthony Salinger seems much too easy a target, but we're going to check him out anyway, cover our asses.

"Anything on the translation?" I ask.

Jim frowns, nods a scholarly nod, stands without a word, steps gracefully as a Persian cat over two or three neat stacks of paper on the floor in front of the bookcase against the wall to his left. Slim fingers maneuver between a scale-model red Ferrari and a steam locomotive, extract a thick paperback book with a black cover. We can't see the title, all we see is the back, a big reddish photo of a mean-looking author, totally bald with piercing black eyes and a dark goatee. Weird red symbol behind his head, a five-pointed star enclosed in a double circle. Jim high-steps back, sits, opens the middle drawer of his desk, takes out five 8×10 black-and-white glossy photos. Holds them up for us: Enochian writing from the five slabs of the blackboard. Now he picks up the book, we see the title, white letters against black: *The Satanic Bible,* Anton Szandor LaVey.

He opens it, flips through to a section just past the middle. "My memory is better than I thought. As soon as I saw the writing, I associated it with the famous nineteen Enochian Keys. So, as soon as I got a look at the developed prints this morning, I turned to the Keys in LaVey's *Bible* and started comparing. Bingo. It turned out to be the First Enochian Key in its entirety. LaVey's English 'translation' was based on the English translation that was done by a Satanic cult called the Order of the Golden Dawn in the late nineteenth century. And, to his credit, LaVey acknowledges the English source translation. He calls his translation the 'unexpurgated' version, as revealed to him by 'an unknown hand.' The First Enochian Key is supposed to represent the initial proclamation from Satan." He looks up. "You—want to hear it?"

"Sure do."

"You bet."

"His format is simple, he presents the original Enochian on one page, then the English translation on the back of that page. Okay, here goes, the First Key: 'I reign over thee, saith the Lord of the Earth, in power exalted above and below, in whose hands the sun is a glittering sword and the moon a through-thrusting fire, who measureth your garments in the midst of my vestures, and trusseth you up as the palms of my hands, and brightened your vestments with Infernal light. I made ye a law to govern the holy ones, and delivered a rod with wisdom supreme. You lifted your voices and swore your allegiance to Him that liveth triumphant, whose beginning is not, nor end cannot be, which shineth as a flame in the midst of your palaces, and reigneth amongst you as the balance of life! Move therefore, and appear! Open the mysteries of your creation! Be friendly unto me, for I am the same!—the true worshipper of the highest and ineffable King of Hell!' "

In the silence that follows, Louie and I frown at each other with the unspoken question: *What?*

"Jim," Louie says. "That's supposed to be a proclamation from Satan himself?"

"Yes."

"You understand what he's talking about? I mean, in the last few sentences there? Well, the whole thing, but especially the end."

Jim smiles, glances at the page again. "He's saying that he's the Lord of the Earth . . . that he made us a law to govern the holy ones . . . that we swore an allegiance to him . . . that he has no beginning and no end. Okay, then it seems to get confusing, I agree. He says, 'Move therefore, and appear! Open the mysteries of your creation! Be friendly unto me, for I am the same!—the true worshipper of the highest and ineffable King of Hell!' Those last three sentences seem more like a prayer to Satan than a proclamation from him, but there's a good reason, a practical reason. The Enochian Keys were intended to be used in Satanic *ritual,* in the worship of Satan by Satanic cults such as the one founded by LaVey in San Francisco, called the Church of Satan."

"Yeah," Louie says. "That's what it sounds like to me."

"Jim," I ask, "have you read all nineteen Keys?"

"Yes. In fact, I read the whole book out of curiosity, but it's been a while, at least a year."

"What do you make of it?" I ask.

He glances out the window, gives it some thought. "Difficult question. It'd be easy to dismiss it all as a crock of shit, but that's just not the case. I remember an emotion I experienced when I finished the book. Late one night. About a year ago. I remember it vividly. I thought: You can't dismiss LaVey with a shrug or a laugh, you have to give the man credit. Because he's deadly serious and it's a deadly serious subject; it has been since the dawn of recorded history. Just think of what this guy is trying to do. Anton LaVey is seriously trying to explain an infinite idea with the tools of finite intelligence. Which is all we have. Which may be like trying to solve infinitesimal calculus with just a knowledge of basic arithmetic. But, the point is, he's *tried.* He's tried to formalize a religion that's in fact older than Christianity or Judaism, a religion that's never actually been formalized by any individual or any group in recorded history. It's the antithesis of the Judeo-Christian ethic, but it doesn't satirize that ethic, as so many other cults have done. It's a religion that's almost automatically hated because of its name, hated by people who know absolutely nothing about it—and don't want to know anything about it. If you want to know what it represents, I suggest you read the Nine Satanic Statements on page twenty-five. They're short and succinct. They'll surprise you."

He tosses the book to me.

I turn to page twenty-five and read:

THE NINE SATANIC STATEMENTS

1 Satan represents indulgence, instead of abstinence!

2 Satan represents vital existence, instead of spiritual pipe dreams!

3. Satan represents undefiled wisdom, instead of hypocritical self-deceit!

4. Satan represents kindness to those who deserve it, instead of love wasted on ingrates!

5. Satan represents vengeance, instead of turning the other cheek!

6. Satan represents responsibility to the responsible, instead of concern for psychic vampires!

7. Satan represents man as just another animal, sometimes better, more often worse than those that walk on all-fours, who, because of his "divine spiritual and intellectual development," has become the most vicious animal of all!

8. Satan represents all of the so-called sins, as they all lead to physical, mental, or emotional gratification!

9. Satan has been the best friend the church has ever had, as he has kept it in business all these years!

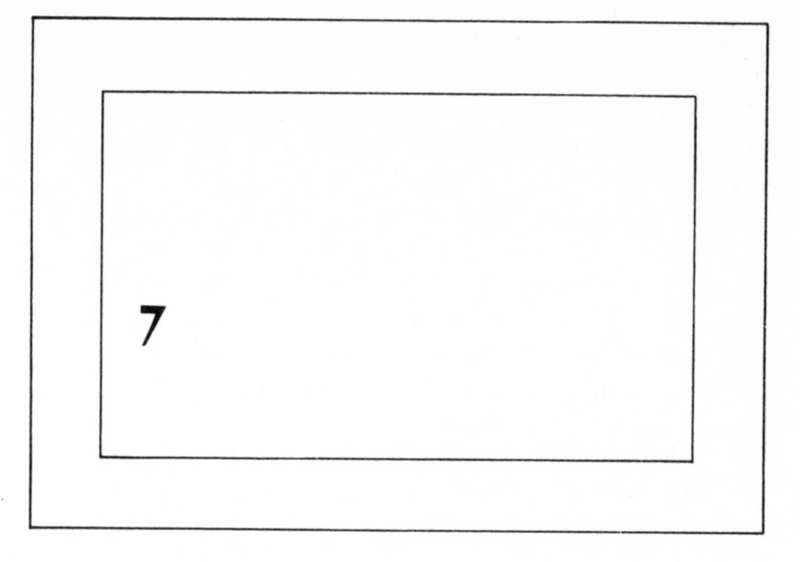

NEXT AFTERNOON, Tuesday, August 26, Chief calls me in for a meeting at 2:30, hits me with the news that I'm going to Harvard. With Reilly and him. We'll be there from Tuesday night, September 2, till Sunday afternoon, September 7. Reason? Seems Harvard University's celebrating its 350th anniversary (1636–1986), a big birthday bash that's been in the works for over a year now, with thousands of alumni attending from all over the country and the world. Reilly's an alumnus and he's been invited to speak at one of the 106 symposiums to be held Thursday through Saturday. He's in pretty good company. Other speakers include Secretary of Defense Caspar Weinberger, U.S. Surgeon General C. Everett Koop, Supreme Court Justice William Brennan, Secretary of State George Shultz, House Speaker "Tip" O'Neill, and many other high government officials. Foreign dignitaries include Prince Charles, who will deliver the keynote address, Sheik Yamani of Saudi Arabia, the Aga Khan, and the king of Nepal. Lecturing at the Kennedy School of Government will be Senator

Daniel Patrick Moynihan, who was once a full professor at Harvard, and Commissioner Reilly, an alumnus of the school, among other city and government bigwigs.

Talk about dignitary protection? This thing's got to be a nightmare. Chief says security clearances will be handled jointly by the Secret Service and Scotland Yard, they've had sophisticated strategies in place for months now, they've got teams of technicians up in Cambridge right this minute, they're looking to cover that campus like a tent. Still, it's not enough, Chief says. Because of the bizarre incidents at St. Michael's School, he cautions Reilly to play it safe all the way and take along his own personal plainclothes bodyguards. In a gesture of superb magnanimity, Chief offers the full-time six-day services of "the finest and most experienced detectives in the entire department"—him and me. Reilly accepts. What's he got to lose?

Chief's really pumped up about the trip, he's got our plane reservations, our accommodations, our detailed itinerary, the whole shot. I mean, to give you just one example, we'll be met at Logan Airport by Boston Police Commissioner Terrance Malloy (love that name) and whisked off to Cambridge in his bulletproof limo with a motorcycle escort.

"Sounds good to me," I tell him.

"*Good?!*" Chief sits back, hands behind his head, smiles at the ceiling. "Little John, you don't know the half of it. I mean, do you realize what an opportunity this is for the both of us? This is an *unprecedented* opportunity, buddy-boy. Just think of it. We're gonna get to *socialize* with Reilly for a change, lift a few grogs, let our hair down a little, get to know him and his wife on a *personal* basis."

"His wife's coming?"

"Oh, sure. Sure. From what I hear, she goes with him on all these political boondoggles. You kiddin'? Comes with the territory. Bill Reilly's a *politician,* his wife's part of the *team,* the all-important *social* aspect of the job. She's a knockout, too, she'd charm the tits off a pit bull, that lady. Funny thing, her name's Samantha, same as my wife's. He calls her Sam, same as me. Unfortunately, that's where the similarity ends. I mean, we're talking the difference between an Airedale and a fuckin' bloodhound."

"Your wife's coming, too?"

"Oh, sure. Absolutely. You kiddin'? That's a necessity at this level, buddy, you gotta go along with that all-important social aspect. Yeah, Sam's coming. Shit, when I told her last night, she let out this bowel-freezin' Comanche war cry that could be heard all over the block. This morning, she went off on a shopping spree I'll be paying off for years, a whole new wardrobe for the occasion, right? I mean, we're talking—at least five days and nights of formal festivities, cocktail parties, hobnobbin' with the blue bloods. Reminds me, I'll have to rent a tuxedo, for Christ's sake. So will you, buddy-boy, Reilly says it's mandatory at these blowouts. We'll be rubbing elbows with the likes of Moynihan, Shultz, Weinberger, Koop, Brennan, O'Neill, maybe even a few Kennedys and Roosevelts."

"May I ask a question?"

"Sure. Shoot."

"Am I allowed to bring my wife, too?"

Chief sits forward slowly, frowns, studies his clasped hands on the desk. Clears his throat. Glances at the door to make sure it's closed. "Little John, I knew you were gonna ask that question. That's one of the reasons I wanted us to have this little meeting in private. Just you and me, man to man. Now, I won't bullshit you, we've known each other too long. And, incidentally, this is strictly confidential information, John, your ears only. Now, the reason—the *ostensible* reason, okay?—for us to tag along on this blast, why I suggested it in the first place, is security. Okay? Dignitary protection, that's how we can justify it on the expense report. But there's another reason, Little John. And I'm taking you into my confidence now, this is strictly off the record. The other reason—I'll be candid about it—is political. Politically motivated. On my part. Okay? Now, sure, I know what you're thinking, it's only natural. You're thinking to yourself, Vadney? Politically motivated? Garbage! The man's a *cop,* thirty-four years on the job, came up the hard way, same as me, he's never played politics in his life! Now, okay, I know that's what you're thinking to yourself, buddy, I understand that. But I want you to try and understand something else. This is difficult for me, John, so bear with me here. Fact is, I'm fifty-five years old. Chief for fourteen years now, doesn't seem that long, but it is. Bill Reilly's forty-five years old. Commissioner for eight years now. And I have reason to believe he's getting antsy. *Antsy.* Know what that means? Know the political ramifications of that fact, what it could mean to me? And to certain other individuals, in the department and out? People with ambition? Political ambition? Huh?"

"Holy shit."

"That's right, Little John. Holy shit. That's exactly what certain other people would say if they got wind of this. Which they haven't. At least, not yet. That's why it's so important for me to take advantage of this opportunity. To get tight with this guy, to let him know how I feel about certain things. You have any idea how most decisions are made—*really* made, okay, in the real world—regarding political appointments?"

"From what I hear, it's who you know."

"You heard right, buddy. Who you know. Know how you get to know 'em?"

"Social aspect?"

"Social aspect. Bingo." He sits back now, hands behind his head again, smiles at the ceiling. "Ed Koch is one hell of a good mayor, maybe the best in our lifetimes, because he's a political animal. Plain and simple. He knows how things get done in the world of politics. He appointed Reilly commissioner eight years ago for a number of reasons, some of them Machiavellian, I'm sure, if the truth were known, because

Reilly's obviously going places in government. He's young, he's bright, he's tough, he's got all the credentials. I mean, he didn't earn his master's degree at the Kennedy School of Government so he could spend his career as a police commissioner. But the point I'm making, he was recommended for that job, recommended to Ed Koch, by some political heavyweights, including—get this—including the *previous* commissioner, Al Medwick. Remember him? Albert T. Medwick? Who's now *what* and *where?*"

"Democratic Congressman Medwick, Washington."

"Democratic Congressman Medwick, Washington. Bingo. What it comes down to, Little John, the bottom line, it's deceptively simple, but they all *know* each other. Huh? They all move in the same social circles—the *inner* circles—that's where the real power is vested, in political networking. The kind of political networking that usually leaves guys like me out in the cold. So, what I'm saying, this is an unprecedented opportunity for me. To come in out of the cold. Right time, right place, right circumstances. Know what I mean?"

"Yes, sir. Chief, one question: I'm not exactly sure what all this has to do with my wife."

"Your *wife?*"

"Yeah. Remember, I asked if I could—?"

"Oh, your *wife!* Sorry, Little John, I lost track of what I was getting at. You asked if you could bring her along. Perfectly legitimate question. Okay, here's the thing about that. Here's the problem. Security, buddy. Dignitary protection. As I said, that's the reason—the ostensible reason—we're going up there in the first place. To protect Commissioner Reilly. I mean, that's how we can justify the whole thing on the expense report. Somebody's got to look after him and his wife. I can't. I can't possibly concentrate on stuff like that while I'm networking. I'm sure you can understand that, Little John, it's a question of priorities. This political networking is a full-time job, and a tough one at that, on call night and day, a real ballbuster-type operation. So that leaves you. That leaves you in the driver's seat, John, I'm delegating full responsibility to you. Protecting Bill Reilly and his wife is a full-time job. Which means you can't waste time socializing. Which means, of course, you can't bring your wife."

"I understand."

"I know you do, buddy, and I'll tell you this, I'll promise you this: I'll make it up to you. In spades. Huh? I'm talking down the road, know what I mean? Because that's the way it works in the game of politics, y'know, it's called the spoils system. 'To the victor belong the spoils,' right? Down the road, if I should be lucky enough to actually land this job, some of that chocolate's gonna rub off on you, buddy, you're gonna get a taste. Ever wonder what it'd feel like to be a deputy police commissioner?"

"No, sir. Never did."

"How's it sound to you?"

"Chief, I'll tell you the truth, I'm happy where I am. Doing what I'm doing. That's a fact. I love my job. But, I must say, it'd be a kick to know the new commissioner's a friend of mine."

His forehead flattens just a split second before his ears move back, then he's into his all-out left-sided Duke Wayne molar-shower. "That'd be something, wouldn't it? God damn, after thirty-four years in the department? Think of the effect it'd have on the morale of the rank-and-file, huh? The cop on the street. To know that it's possible. To make it all the way to the top on your own. Huh? Step by grueling step, year after grueling year, no help from anybody."

Going home on the Long Island Rail Road that afternoon, I finish reading the *Post,* I'm smoking a cigar, taking in the green summer landscape of southern Nassau County, but I can't really enjoy it. Those familiar little suburban towns move past slowly in the soft sunlight—Valley Stream, Lynbrook,

Rockville Centre, Baldwin, Freeport—and for some reason my mind keeps returning to St. Michael's School and what happened to me there on Sunday. Two days have passed and I still can't shake it. I suppose Louie Diaz did me a favor when he put it to me the way he did. I can see his eyes when he said it, looking at me sideways, lids half drawn. *Who was that figure at the front door, John? Is there even a remote possibility in your mind that it—that you could've been in the presence of something supernatural? In the presence of Satan?* Remote possibility? Yes. I admit that, I have no serious problem with that. Because, as he said, it was drummed into us when we were kids and adolescents, all through grammar school and high school. I mean, we didn't even question it back then. It was a fact you lived with every day. It was in the Bible and everything in there was true. That's where the fact was established, that was the source. Were there any other "reliable" sources, pro or con? Never even bothered to ask. Never even looked up the word Satan in the card catalog at the library. So why should I do it now, at my age?

Because the subject happens to intrigue me now. So much so, last night I asked my wife if she could try to find some time today to stop in our branch library in Bellmore and see if she could dig up some books on the subject of Satan. I'm curious to find out what the eggheads think in this enlightened day and age. We have a first-class library system in Nassau County, modern as they come, so I'm hoping she found some up-to-date volumes on the subject. If so, no television for me tonight, I'll be into some spooky reading.

Well, I suppose now's the best time to tell you about our new house. I've been saving this. We moved on May 5, moved into a house in the same neighborhood, easy walking distance from our old place. In fact, Cindy and I moved all the small stuff ourselves, in our cars, over a period of a couple of weeks. Then I got an estimate for the heavy furniture from the most reasonable outfit in the county, Gomez. You'll never believe this, nobody does, but all it cost us was $200. Plus a $50 tip to the moving men, which they deserved. That's it, total moving expense. The house is about four years old, nothing conspicuous, two stories of Spanish-style architecture, red barrel-tiled roof, white stucco walls. Nice corner property at the end of a cul-de-sac. Actually, I saw this place being built, I used to walk the dog around this particular cul-de-sac in the early evenings, and I remember thinking how solidly it was being constructed. As I say, it's nothing spectacular, three bedrooms, three baths, living room, family room, dining room, good-sized open kitchen, and a large screened-in back patio where we do most of our living in the warm weather. Guy who lived here first sunk a great deal of money into it, inside and out, particularly on security, that's the most interesting part of the story. Elaborate black wrought-iron grillwork on the front entranceway and garage, with a big gate leading to the front door, then the same fancy grillwork on every window and every outside door. You should see this stuff, all custom work, must've cost him a small fortune. Now, behind all this grillwork—ready for this?—a continuous-circuit burglar alarm on every window and every door, one of the most comprehensive (and expensive) residential security systems I've seen. So, if a burglar wants to get in here, what's he do? Options are limited. First practical thing that comes to mind, he could wrap a heavy-duty chain around the grillwork of, say, a ground-floor window, attach that chain to a truck with plenty of horsepower, put 'er in gear, burn rubber, and yank the grillwork right out of the stone wall, where it's bolted. With all the neighbors watching, right? Now what? Now he has to face a continuous-circuit burglar alarm with an auxiliary-powered outside bell that would wake the dead and that's also monitored by a private security agency. Talk about paranoid? But that's not all. In the master bedroom upstairs, there's a big red "panic button" that can be pressed to ignite the alarm system instantly. Conclusion is obvious: This guy wasn't just protecting his property, this guy was out to protect his life.

Who was he and what was he so afraid of? Good question. I know his name, of course, but not much more. After living here for about six months with his wife and one child, he left in a big hurry. According to my neighbors, a moving van pulled up here late one night and the next morning the place was empty. Didn't say good-bye to anybody, but then, he didn't have any friends. House was vacant for just over a year when the bank finally foreclosed. That's why we got such a good deal on it. Nobody knows where this guy is, or why he took off, but he left one clue that I can develop into a whole scenario. He took every piece of furniture except one, a custom-made "dry bar" cabinet of laminated wood, thirty inches high, thirty-six inches wide, sixteen inches deep, built into a recessed area of a wall in the downstairs bedroom that was used as a study. On the left side of the cabinet was a mirror; on the right side was a glass door that opened to various-sized mirrored shelves, probably intended for glasses and bottles. First time I opened the glass door and looked in, I thought: Wait a minute, what's in the *other* side of this cabinet?

I examined it carefully. No door of any kind, no knob, no hinges, just solid laminated wood with a mirror built into the center. I opened the glass door to the right again, reached in, tested the mirrored shelves, pulled on them. No good. Mirrored wall to the left separated the two sides of the cabinet. I knocked on it, pushed it, tried to slide it. No way. Solid. What's the point in building a three-foot-wide cabinet when you only use a foot and a half of it? Something's got to be in the other side, right?

Well, you know how it is when you're moving, you're doing so many things simultaneously, you just don't have the time to spend on little mysteries like that. So I just put it on hold for a while, I figured I'd solve the riddle when I had the luxury of some free time.

About a month later, when most of our hundreds of boxes were finally unpacked and the house was beginning to look like a home, I was working in that room again, shaping it up to be my study, and I started to fool around with that cabinet again. What's in the other side? It's hollow, I knew that, I'd knocked on it enough times from every possible angle. Only one way to solve the mystery. Pry the top of the cabinet off. Ever try to pry laminated wood? Don't. Stuff splinters in small chunks. To be honest, I didn't really like the freakin' cabinet in the first place, it didn't fit in with my plans for the study, I didn't want a "dry bar" in there. So, when the top started splintering off in these little chunks, I thought, screw it, rip the sucker off, let's see what's in there. I got a crowbar and began tearing the top off, inch by painful inch, until I had an opening just large enough to get a flashlight into and shine it around.

Surprise. There was a second wooden top several inches below the first. By now I was sweating, I was tired, I was frustrated, and—hate to admit it—I was angry. Made an instant decision to rip off the entire left front side. Boom, I went to work with the crowbar, a wedge, a chisel, a hammer, and whatever brute strength I had left. Tell you something I learned. If you ever want to build a cabinet that'll withstand a bomb blast, use about a half-dozen layers of laminated wood. I slammed, I pried, I ripped, I chiseled, I pulled (with heavy gloves) with all my strength for a total of two and a half hours. Cindy heard the racket and came in a couple of times to try and calm me down, but by then it was an irrational battle to the death—me against *it.* Sometimes I'm like that with inanimate objects, it's embarrassing, what can I tell you? Even cussed at it. Yeah. Called it every name in the book. I know, I know, sometimes I'm a jerk.

Anyhow, when I finally got that front side half ripped away (had to break the mirror, of course) and played my flashlight in there, it was empty except for two strange objects: Two slender steel flange rails on the bottom, extending horizontally across the entire width, maybe six inches apart. I reached in and touched them. Each was a three-sided rail with the bottom side secured to the wood by screws. Now I played the light around, picked up some glints of steel up on the slab of wood that was the top beneath the cabinet top. Another set of identical steel flange rails extending across the width, about six inches apart. What the hell were they? Or what had they been part of? It beat the shit out of me. Of course, I was tired, I knew I wasn't thinking clearly, so I just sat down, lit a cigar, and kept glancing up and down at those steel rails. It didn't really hit me until I noticed that my fingertips had picked up thin streaks of black. I rubbed them together. Black grease. Where I'd touched the rails.

I jumped to my knees, swung open the glass door on the right side, pushed hard against the mirrored left wall. Whole mirrored side of the cabinet shuddered a bit. Then—*eureka!*—that side slid smoothly on the steel rails into the empty left side.

A dummy cabinet.

What was behind the now-empty *right* side?

A safe, of course. Not in the conventional sense, just an open box-like container of the same laminated wood. What was in the box? At first, I thought it was empty. Then, as I moved the flashlight beam around, I saw something sparkle in the far left corner. Looked like a piece of thick glass laying flat. I reached way in, picked it up, took it out in the light.

I remember my reaction the first time I looked at it: I thought it was some sort of Jewish religious symbol because it had a star in the middle, which I took for the Star of David, and it had Hebrew writing on it. I'll describe this thing to you. It's a circle of laminated glass, six and a half inches in diameter, with a small hole at the top for hanging it up. There are two layers of glass. Bottom layer is jet black; top layer is clear glass with a large red symbol in it. Symbol is relatively simple: A five-pointed star with each point touching a circle that surrounds it. That circle is enclosed in an outer circle. In the space between the circles, directly opposite each point of the star, are Hebrew language symbols. Within the star itself, which stands on just one point, is the long face of an animal; looked to me like a bull or a cow, possibly even a horse.

Showed it to Cindy, then showed her where I found it. She was intrigued by the dummy cabinet and the safe and all, but she didn't know what to make of the glass thing. In fact, her first reaction was about the same as mine, she thought it might be a Jewish religious symbol. Make a long story short, I didn't know what to do with it, I left it in the study. What interested me in this whole thing was the dummy cabinet. I mean, it was ingenious, it was beautifully built, and I felt terrible that I'd wrecked the top and side. Still, the best part of it was intact, the sliding mirrored shelves, so I decided to build a whole new cabinet around that, have my own hidden safe. Never built a cabinet before, took me about a month, nights and weekends, but it was worth the work. Modesty aside, it's a beaut. Two doors this time, makes it look more authentic. But only the right one opens, okay? Painted the whole thing white, so it blends in with the decor. Looks really professional. I'm proud of it.

But to get back to this glass thing. On July 4, we had a combination house-opening and Independence Day party, invited twenty friends, including Doris Banks and her husband, Will. Actually, they were the first to arrive, very punctual people, and they came all the way from Manhattan. So, naturally, we showed them around the house, upstairs and down. When the girls were in the kitchen, I showed Will my hidden safe, I couldn't help myself, I was so proud of it. And just after that, he spotted the glass thing, I'd left it on one of the marble end tables by the couch, and he was very interested in the thing. I asked him what it was.

Will, he looks at me with this puzzled expression, he always reminds me of a distinguished-looking Ty Cobb with his big beak and all, and he says, real quiet and confidential: "John, you really don't know what this is?"

"No."

"John," he says, "this is the Symbol of Baphomet."

"Yeah? What's that?"

He smiles, pushes back his white hair. "I can see history wasn't one of your favorite subjects. The Symbol of Baphomet goes all the way back to the early twelfth century, the First Crusade, it was used by the Knights Templar—I'm sure you've heard of them—when they lived in the Temple of Solomon in Jerusalem."

"Yeah? That explains the Hebrew writing, huh?"

"That's right. I don't read Hebrew, but I know what these figures mean because I'm familiar with the symbol and the stories about it. The Hebraic figures here are from the teachings of Cabala, a form of Jewish mysticism that dates from the first century. The word they spell is 'Leviathan,' a sea monster that symbolized evil in the Old Testament."

"Yeah? So that head in the center is the sea monster?"

He smiles again, gives me a look, points to the head. "Shit, John, does that look like a sea monster to you?"

"No, huh?"

"It's the head of a goat. See the horns up there? And the beard at the end of the chin? The Symbol of Baphomet was worshipped by the Knights Templar because it represented the Powers of Darkness. It's endured through the centuries as the classic symbol of Satan."

Almost two months have passed since he told me that. I can honestly say that it didn't mean all that much to me back then, except for the added insight it gave me about the guy who lived in this house. Based on the man's obsession with security, my gut feeling about him was—and still is—that he was in the drug trade, that the hidden safe was probably his stash place, and that he had to split fast when one of his deals went sour. Maybe he was on the stuff himself, a lot of them are, particularly on coke, because they crave the confidence it gives. So, what I thought back then, two months ago, if the guy belonged to a Satanic cult of some kind, so what else is new? Drug traffickers aren't exactly your normal taxpaying, churchgoing, homeowning model citizens. Also, I thought it's entirely possible that the Symbol of Baphomet belonged to his teenaged kid. I know he had a teenager because the smaller of the two bathrooms upstairs is professionally wallpapered in "graffiti" statements. Stuff like, "Is there intelligent life on earth?" Followed by, "Yes, but I am only visiting." Same bathroom our son John uses now. He's going on ten and he loves that wallpaper, but some of the real precocious lines are a bit over his head, he has to ask what they mean. So, I figure this kid was probably a teenager and, as I understand it, a lot of teenagers today are turned on by the occult.

What I'm trying to say is that up until last Sunday the whole ancient and ugly mystique of Satan and Satanism didn't really *matter* to me, one way or the other. That's a fact, that's really the way it was. I'm not saying I believed it was total bullshit, I've never believed that, not with my Catholic upbringing and all, but up until now all this stuff was always in the realm of the abstract and I've never been the kind of guy who kills himself with abstractions. That's changed now. In the space of three days. I don't like it, I don't want to deal with it, but in a strange way that I can't explain, it fascinates me too, the idea of a supernatural force out there revealing its presence. Revealing its presence to me. That frightens me, sure, but the idea has a kind of almost irresistible attraction. That's why I want to learn something new about the subject, to read what serious scholars think about it today.

Turns out I'm in luck. Cindy stopped in our branch library this afternoon, checked the card catalog, and came up with four relatively recent volumes: *Satan: The Early Christian Tradition,* by Jeffrey Burton Russell; *Satan's Power: A Deviant*

Psychotherapy Cult, by William Sims Bainbridge; *The Satan Trap: Dangers of the Occult,* edited by Martin Ebon; and *The Satanists,* edited by Peter Haining. Cindy's browsed through them, she suggests that I start with the one by Jeffrey Burton Russell, titled *Satan,* because it's the most recent, and because Russell is a well-known scholar, a professor of history at the University of California, Santa Barbara.

After dinner, I take her advice and settle down with *Satan* in my study while she watches television with John in the living room. *Satan* grabs my attention immediately, absolutely fascinating reading. To give you an idea of what Russell's doing, here's a quote from the preface:

> This book is the second volume in my history of the concept of the Devil. . . . The first volume, *The Devil: Perceptions of Evil from Antiquity to Primitive Christianity,* published in 1977, presented a cross-cultural survey of the idea of evil and then traced the development of the concept of the Devil in Hebrew and primitive Christian thought to the first century of the Christian era, by which time the main lines of the tradition had been established. . . .

Toward the end of the preface, Russell makes this statement:

> I am still inclined to believe that the Devil exists and that his works are painfully manifest among us. . . .

I like the way he starts Chapter 1, titled "The Devil":

> The problem of evil is the theme of this book. Why is evil done to us, and why do we do evil ourselves? No easy answers work; in human affairs the truth is often inversely proportional to the certitude with which it is stated. . . .

In Chapter 8, titled "Conclusion: Satan Today," he gets into the kinds of questions that really interest me, starting on page 222:

> To revert to the question of experience: a concept that does not respond to human experience will die. But the concept of the Devil

is very much alive today, in spite of opposition from many theologians as well as those hostile to all metaphysics. Indeed, the idea is more alive now than it has been for many decades, because we are again aware of the ineradicable nature of perversity in our own behavior, a perversity that has been more evident in the twentieth century than ever before. Well-intentioned efforts to reform human nature by education or legislation have so far failed, and rather spectacularly, as they break like waves against the rock of radical evil. We have direct perception of evil, of deliberate malice and desire to hurt, constantly manifesting itself in governments, in mobs, in criminals, and in our own petty vices. Many people seem to have the additional experience that behind all this evil, and directing it, is a powerful transhuman, or at least transconscious, personality. This is the Devil. . . .

And, finally, I like the last paragraph on page 230:

The corollary for the Devil is as follows: the Devil is not a principle; the Devil does not limit God's power; the Devil is a creature; the Devil is permitted by God to function; the Devil has some purpose in the cosmos that we cannot grasp; the Devil is God's enemy and our enemy and must be resisted with all our strength. This is true whether the Devil is an ontological entity or the personification of the "demonic" in humanity.

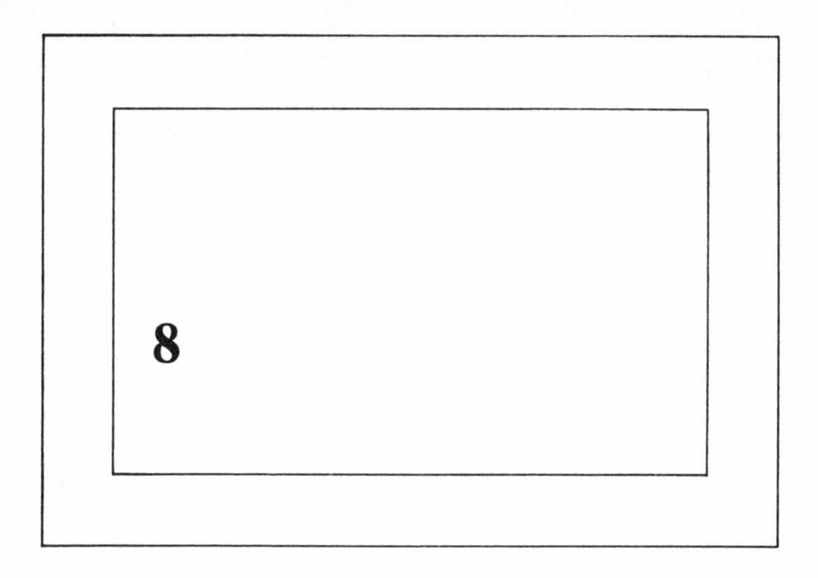

TUESDAY, SEPTEMBER 2, 1986, we take off for Boston on Pan Am's Flight 582, departing Kennedy at six in the evening, arriving Logan at seven. Would've been a lot easier to grab a shuttle flight from LaGuardia, but Vadney insists on the "regular" flight, a Boeing 727, because it's less crowded and therefore offers a higher degree of security. That's what he says. My opinion, the real reason is that this flight offers first-class service and the shuttle doesn't. Me, I'm not complaining, I get to fly first class for one of the few times in my life. Bill and Samantha Reilly are in the bulkhead seats, 1A and 1B; Walt and Samantha Vadney are directly behind, 2A and 2B; and I bring up the rear, aisle seat 3B, nobody next to me. Dignitary protection on a boondoggle ain't cheap. First-class round-trip fare happens to be $416, tax included. Multiply that by five, you get a nifty $2,080 on the expense report. What's the shuttle fare? Knew you'd ask. Just $138 round trip, no reservations, no seat assignments, no frills. That times five equals $690. Difference of $1,390. But, come on, we're talking the all-important social aspect here, huh? Champagne before takeoff, unlimited name-brand booze in flight, dinner with wine, dessert with coffee and liqueurs, nice folksy atmosphere all around. Service? All the attention that can be crammed into an hour. Especially since we're the only passengers in the whole first-class section. Like having our own private jet. Ah, politics, it grows on you.

Time magazine's out today, dated next week as usual, cover story caught my eye at the newsstand in the terminal, headline reads:

HARVARD
350 AND GOING STRONG

Nice painting of Harvard's president on the cover, Derek Bok, salt-and-pepper hair, bushy brows, warm smile, looks more like a board chairman than an egghead. Since I don't know much about Harvard or exactly what's going on over the next four days, I start reading right after takeoff, armed with a very dry Beefeater martini on the rocks with a twist, while Bill & Walt & Sam & Sam jump into their social stuff. Cover story takes a total of nine full pages, touches all the bases past and present, including a one-page sidebar on Bok himself. Apparently, they're pulling all stops for this birthday bash, lots of glitz, which raises the eyebrows and dander of quite a few scholarly gents. I can understand why. I mean, you'd have to read this stuff; the sheer bulk of famous heavyweights who went here is so staggering it's laughable. Name a scholarly field, Harvard's got a glut of Nobel and Pulitzer prizewinners in it. Government? Six presidents, count 'em, from John Adams to John Kennedy. Today, the Kennedy School of Government is the only one of its kind at any U.S. university, there are 700 full-time students, the best and the brightest, and it welcomes more than 600 government officials every year.

Surprisingly lively eight pages of history and stats (Harvard has a $3.5 billion endowment and an annual budget of $650 million), now I sip a second martini, turn to the one-page sidebar about Bok himself. Don't know what I expected, but here's a refreshingly offbeat-type guy. Basketball star at Stanford, also Phi Beta Kappa. Joined the Harvard law faculty in 1958, became dean of the law school in 1968. In 1971—at the age of forty-one—he became president of the university. Been in the job fifteen years now and he's only fifty-six. Enough to give some guys a bigger hat size, but not Bok. Listen to this one: He still tools around Cambridge in his old beat-to-shit VW Bug, just had a red paint job. Always flies tourist class, gets a laugh when he sees some of his grant-rich professors up in first; his salary is less than he pays some of his deans. This guy is the first prexy since 1911 who won't live in the presidential mansion on campus. For many years he played basketball as head of a campus team named "Bok's Jocks." Yeah, basketball, *my* game. Now, get a load of this: Six years ago, at age fifty, he's in a tight game, he's dribbling down the court like crazy on a fast break, he lets loose with a running lefty hook shot—*boom!*—sinks it! Bok's Jocks are fallin' down, suckin' air, they can't believe this shit. What's he do? Decides to retire on the spot, then and there, top of his game, hangs 'em up forever, calls it a career. I mean, this is my kind of guy. What's he do now? Tennis, two or three times a week. There's a picture of him on this page, looks like he's still in excellent shape, relatively short and lean like me. Of course, he gets his share of criticism. Sidebar tells how a lot of his time is taken up lately by the problem of divestiture of Harvard's stock in firms doing business with South Africa—$416 million worth. Takes constant flack from alumni and students. Story goes, last spring students are demonstrating outside his office, they're chanting: "Hey, hey, Derek Bok, throw away your racist stock!" Know what he does? Goes outside and tries to reason with 'em. Yeah. Tells 'em he's always been strongly against apartheid, but he opposes total withdrawal. Tells 'em exactly what his position is and why. Like his style. Like to meet this guy, shoot a few hoops with him, know what I mean?

Pleasant flight all the way, we touch down about 6:55, gold September twilight in Boston, taxi to the gate, lots of chatter from the first two rows, New York's Finest are feeling no pain. Door opens, here's this distinguished-looking gentleman standing on the boarding bridge with his lovely wife, I know in my gut it's Commissioner Terrance Malloy, it's just written all over him. Introductions all around, I take a close look at this guy. Remember John Houseman in those terrific TV commercials for Smith, Barney, how they make money the old-fashioned way? That's him, that's Terrance Malloy, he's even got the dark three-piece suit. I mean, this is real Boston stuff, conservative four-in-hand tie, white pocket hankie, handshake like a vise: "It's a pleasure to meet you, Mr. *Rah*-lins."

Off we go to the baggage claim area, ten-minute wait for our luggage, then Vadney and I have to wait a few minutes longer for the Pan Am captain to retrieve the steel "personal effects" container from the carousel and discreetly return the revolvers we surrendered to him before boarding. Sam and Sam have a total of four giant suitcases between them, plus two fat garment bags, in addition to one case each for Reilly, Vadney, and me, so we get a Skycap to load it all on his dolly. Malloy leads us out to a long gray Caddy limo with antennae for shortwave radio, phone, and TV. Gray-uniformed chauffeur opens the doors, helps the ladies in, then goes back to give the Skycap a hand. I climb in, sit on one of the upholstered jumpseats next to Vadney. Malloy sits forward, reaches between us, presses a button just below the TV screen. "Dry bar" rolls out silently, complete with cut-glass decanters, crystal tumblers, silver ice bucket, silver tongs, and lemon twists. He slides back, smiles thinly. "Ladies and gentlemen, the bah is now open, let the festivities begin."

"Terry," Sam Reilly says. "Wait a minute, what's going on here, what happened to the motorcycle escort?"

Malloy's eyelids go half-mast. "My deah young—"

"You forgot!"

"My deah young lady," he scolds gently, "this is haadly a presidential motta-kayd."

Peals of laughter. Peals. Wish you could see Malloy's wife laugh, her name's Margaret, he calls her "Mags." She hears the peals, her Irish eyes twinkle, fill instantly with tears, her thin lips part to pearly pony's teeth, then her throat goes: "Haah! Haaah! *Haaaah!*" On and on. Alarming at first, could be she's choking on something. Sam Vadney's watching with her bloodhound eyes, she's got a more controlled laugh herself, her jaws snap open to a glittering gold mine: "*Ya!* Ya-ha! *Ya!*-ha-ha! *Ya!*-ha-ha-ha!" Phonetics to that effect.

Chauffeur jumps in now, removes his cap, fastens his seat belt, starts the engine almost soundlessly, we glide away in air-conditioned comfort, oblivious to the Back Bay riffraff, off to Hah-vid in the gathering dusk.

You could get used to this shit. Me, I pour myself three fingers of brandy, enjoy the view, I've only been to Boston a few times in my life, always on a case. Chauffeur takes the Sumner Tunnel under Boston Inner Harbor, then Atlantic Avenue northwest, winds southwest on Storrow Drive past huge Massachusetts General Hospital, hangs a right, crosses Longfellow Bridge over the Charles River Basin. Now Bill Reilly decides to be our tour guide, he's in familiar territory. Says we're on Memorial Drive heading southwest, that's M.I.T. coming up on our right. We go around a big horn, now we're heading northwest, hugging the still-sparkling Charles River to our left, then a few minutes later Reilly points out my first glimpse of Harvard, says we're about to pass some of the big residential houses for undergraduates. I'm sitting forward against the right window, I press the button to roll it down now, I'm blocking everybody's view, but I don't care. First off is Dunster House, its big white bell tower and red dome soaring high above the dozens of tall chimneys, next is Leverett House, then Winthrop House. Just behind Winthrop, we can see the blue-domed bell tower of Lowell House, Reilly says the tower has Russian monastery bells, seventeen chimes, beautiful sound. Last along the river is Eliot House, one of the largest, its green-domed bell tower still bright in the lingering sunset. Wonder what it sounds like when they get all these bells around here ringing at the same time?

Chauffeur hangs a right, Reilly says we're now headed northeast on John F. Kennedy Street, he points out the Kennedy School of Government on the left, very modern architecture compared to the now-familiar Georgian of Kirkland House directly across the street. We continue straight for three blocks, past rows of little shops, stores, restaurants, narrow brick sidewalks relatively crowded, then we stop for a traffic light at a big intersection. "This is *it,*" Reilly announces, "Harvard Square, hub of the civilized world!" Me, I'm leaning out the window now, even I've heard of this spot. What it is, it's a large red-brick island in the middle of this intersection, big crowds of people hanging around in the warm twilight, young and old, swarms of them crossing with the light, traffic backed up for blocks, midtown Manhattan except for the buildings. Just across the square to our right, along Massachusetts Avenue, are the weathered buildings that enclose the southwest boundary of Harvard Yard, the oldest part of the university. When the light changes, we pass a few of those buildings, Lehman, Straus, and Massachusetts Hall, which is the oldest surviving structure on campus, 1720.

Now we pull over and park in front of an enormous black wrought-iron gate, the Johnston Gate, Reilly says, between Massachusetts Hall and Harvard Hall. Says the site of this gate has been the main entrance to the Yard since the seventeenth century. Takes you back. Chauffeur hops out, opens the doors, helps the ladies out, goes back, opens the trunk, starts to remove the luggage. Johnston Gate is closed, but there's a small gate on the right side that's open. A uniformed Harvard security guard steps from behind that gate and walks over to us.

"Sorry, gentlemen, ya can't pack heah."

Malloy steps over, shows his ID. "Good evening, officer. I'm Boston Police Commissioner Malloy. My friends have reservations in Weld Hall."

Guard glances at the ID. "Yes, sir, Commissioner Malloy, but I'm afraid this heah is a strict no packing zone."

"My chauffeur has to help carry in the luggage, there's just too much of it for us to handle. I'm sure you can under—"

"I got my orders, sir, I'm just doin' my job. If ya pack heah, I'm under orders to have ya cah towed away at ya own expense."

"What?!"

"Yes, sir. This heah is a tow-away zone. Strictly enforced."

Malloy's face starts to color. "Who do you report to?"

"Hahvid University Police, sir."

"Who, specifically?"

"Deputy Chief Jack Morse."

"Will you please call him? You can use the phone in my cah."

"Jack Morse ain't on duty tonight, sir. He works days."

"Well, call him at *home!* Y'got his home number?"

"Yes, sir, but that's strictly for emergencies."

Vadney knows his cue, steps over smiling, shows his ID, turns on the charm. "Good evening, officer, I'm Walt Vadney. Let me tell ya what's goin' on here, clear this thing up. See, my partner and me, we're providing dignitary protection for the gentleman over there, New York Police Commissioner Bill Reilly, and his wife. Bill's been invited to speak at a symposium at the Kennedy School of Government on Thursday. Now, all we're talking about here is a matter of a few minutes while we carry the ladies' bags in, okay? I don't think that's an unreasonable request, do you?"

"Yes, sir. Sorry, but ya just can't pack heah."

"Tell ya what, buddy. Ya bend the rules for a couple minutes, I'll personally put in a good word with your boss, huh?"

"No, sir. I don't bend no rules for nobody."

Now I take a good look at this guy. Middle-aged, short, heavyset, he's looking up at Vadney with his hands on his hips and his jaw set. Tough little bulldog-type guy, he's got his orders, he's sticking to 'em. Makes his money the old-fashioned way. Me, I'm pulling for him.

Vadney takes out his pad and gold pen. "What's your name?"

"Patrick, sir."

"Patrick? Patrick *what?*"

"Patrick. Dennis B. Patrick, Jr."

Chief jots it down carefully. "All right, Dennis B. Patrick, Jr., now I want you to listen up, because I'm only gonna say this once. New York Police Commissioner Reilly is an out-of-state dignitary and an officially invited guest of the university. As such, he's entitled to every courtesy and consideration that his authority demands."

"I'm givin' him courtesy," Patrick says calmly. "Consideration, too. We got dignitaries comin' in heah from all over the world. I give all of 'em all the courtesy and consideration they're entitled to. In return, I expect *them* to give *me* the courtesy and consideration *I'm* entitled to. Which means respect for my authority. Which means, when I tell 'em they can't pack their cahs heah, they can't pack their cahs heah."

Case closed. I mean, how can you top that? Jimmy Cagney playing a good cop. Here we are, eight of us in all, standing around this little guy, including more top brass than he's probably ever confronted in his life, and we wind up with collective laryngitis. This is the kind of stuff I love, this is straight from a 1940s movie, wish you could see each of these expressions in close-up. Bottom line, Malloy tells the chauffeur to drive around for half an hour, meet us back at the gate. Then Malloy, Reilly, and Vadney each grab one heavy case, the three ladies carry lighter stuff, and I'm told to stay and guard the remaining cases until they return.

Fine with me. I light up a cigar, shoot the breeze with Patrick. Taxi pulls up at the gate, out steps a distinguished-type guy, helps his lovely wife out, driver takes their luggage from the trunk, off they go into the Yard. Across the street is an old church with a tall spire and to the right of that is a fenced-in area that looks to me like a graveyard. Both are in heavy shadow now, the sun is setting behind them. I ask Patrick what church it is.

"First Church, Unitarian," he says. "This your first visit?"

"Yeah."

"That cemetery to the right is called the Old Burying Ground. Some gravestones in there date back to the early seventeenth century. Also, quite a few Revolutionary soldiers are buried in there. Just behind the church are the presidents' graves."

"Presidents?"

"Of the university, yeah. They go way back. But you wander through the Old Burying Ground, you get a perspective about this whole place, what it was like long back, when the college started. Three hundred and fifty years ago, this was all wilderness, just a few farms around. The first college building was a wooden farmhouse on a one-acre cow pasture. Over the next ninety years or so, all the original wooden classrooms and dormitories and chapels and like that all burned down. Replaced by brick buildings like Massachusetts Hall heah. And only one thing actually survived since the beginning. Intact, I mean, pretty much intact, the way it was. The Old Burying Ground." He pauses, nods to himself, then glances at me. "That's something you won't learn on any guided tour."

Next morning, I wake up about seven o'clock in 21 Weld Hall, big double room all to myself, overlooking what they call the

Old Yard. According to Reilly, this is *the* place to be—anywhere in the Old Yard—during the anniversary celebration, lots of good stuff going on around here. All of us are on the same floor, my room's right next to Reilly's, of course. Security in here is more than adequate, the two front doors are locked, manned by round-the-clock Harvard security guards (we have to show special ID cards to get in), and all the rooms have deadbolt locks. Weld is a solid old brick-and-stone structure, built in 1872, it's a freshman dorm (coed) during the regular school year. Nice place, I like it. Old stone fireplaces in all the rooms, they don't work, of course, but they give the place character. You look out the window, the Old Yard is crisscrossed with asphalt walks, the grass is trim and well watered, dominated by huge old elms, crowns full and deep green in the morning sun.

Picked up plenty of literature last night at the Information Center, booklets, brochures, maps, plus the Official Program of what's happening, September 3–7. Celebration kicks off today, but it's a very light schedule, Reilly says most of the alumni will be arriving in the morning and early afternoon. What Reilly says he wants to do, after breakfast, he just wants to stroll around, refresh his memory, show Sam everything (she's never toured it), and that sounds good to the Vadneys and me. Then, a leisurely lunch, they got a total of ninety-two restaurants in the immediate vicinity, so there's a twelve-page booklet, "Guide to Harvard Square Restaurants," to make sure you know what you're doing. Lunch, followed by more sightseeing at our own pace. Reilly stresses "at our own pace" because, you take one look at the map here, this place is absolutely gigantic, both sides of the river, it'd take you days to see all this stuff, and you gotta hoof it. No electric trams or Disneyland crap around here, folks, this is serious shit, this is Harvard.

Anyhow, according to the program, the schedule of events

shifts into high gear in the evening when most of the alumni are on hand:

7:00 P.M.–10:30 P.M.

Harvard's Floating Birthday Party *(No tickets required)*

A Birthday Celebration for the Harvard community and the University's neighbors and friends on both banks of the Charles between the Weeks and Anderson Bridges. There will be a 600-foot illuminated rainbow, laser projections on a water screen and appearances by The Cambridge Harmonica Orchestra, The Copley Brass, Stan Strickland, The Batucada Belles, Dario and Company, The Harvard Alumni Band, The Yale Russian Chorus, the clown Mme. Nose, the one-man riddle and rhyme show, "Electric Poetry," and Harvard student performers.

About 7:30 that morning, I take my towel, soap, and shaving kit to the big bathroom down the hall, have a nice hot shower, then shave, brush my teeth, comb my hair, the usual, but it's an effort. I've got a lulu of a hangover, as I knew I would, we had a relatively late night, hit at least half a dozen bars around the Square. Still, I figure I'll be back to normal after a Bloody Mary and a solid breakfast. Now I'm walking back down the hall, the door of Reilly's room opens a crack, then Bill steps out quickly in his pajamas, places a finger to his lips for silence, closes his door softly, motions for me to open mine. I unlock it, we go inside. He's holding an envelope. His face is very white.

"Close it quietly," he says. "Samantha's still asleep."

I close it carefully. "What's the matter?"

He sits on the bed near mine, looks at the envelope. His voice has a slight shake in it. "The security guard slipped this under my door about—I don't know—ten minutes ago. I was half awake, I heard him. As soon as I read it, I phoned down there. To confirm that he delivered it. Jesus Christ, I feel sick."

He hands it to me. Standard white business-size envelope, name and address typed: "Mr. William Reilly, 22 Weld Hall." Below that, to the left: "Urgent. Deliver Immediately." I open it, take out the letter. White bond paper, 8½ × 11, everything typed neatly:

"When I was a child, I spake as a child, I understood as a child, I thought as a child: but when I became a man, I put away childish things.

"For now we see through a glass, darkly; but then face to face: now I know in part; but then shall I know even as also I am known."

I Corinthians
13:11-12

Reilly:

The Gutenberg is gone. If you want to know why, stand in front of Lampy tonight, exactly 7:59.

Quickly, carefully, I hold the letter up to the light. Same watermark as the first one: Parchment Deed, Southworth Co., U.S.A., 100% Cotton Fiber. Typewriter face seems the same too: IBM Prestige Elite 72.

"What's the Gutenberg?" I ask.

"The Gutenberg Bible, it's a legendary—it's the most valuable book of Harvard's eleven million volumes, absolutely priceless."

"Where was it?"

"Widener Library. On display, it's been there for—decades."

"What's Lampy?"

"That's—the Lampoon Building. Home of the humor magazine, the *Harvard Lampoon.*"

"Okay. Now, Bill, first thing—"

"Jesus *Christ,* John. Do you realize—? I can't believe this is happening, it's *impossible!* Do you realize the *magnitude* of this?"

"Yeah. First things first, we've got to establish that it was actually stolen. Where's Widener Library?"

"In the Yard just behind us, easy walking distance."

"Okay, call the campus police, identify yourself, alert them to the possibility of a robbery at Widener. Ask them to meet us there with the keys."

By 7:45, we're dressed and hurrying down the wooden staircase, Vadney right behind us, still groggy, Sam and Sam standing at the top of the landing, hands clutched to the necks of their nighties. At the security desk, we speak to the guard who delivered the envelope, he's the only one on duty. Who gave it to him? Says it was slipped under one of the two front doors about 7:10 A.M., says that's not particularly unusual, happens with some frequency during the school year. Says he figured Reilly was probably still asleep, didn't want to ring his room, but noticed the "Deliver Immediately" instruction. So he just walked up the single flight of stairs and slipped it under the door.

We go out, walk quickly around the end of Weld Hall, and into this very big part of Harvard Yard. Just a handful of people strolling around in the early morning shade of dozens of graceful old elms; air is crisp, grass is still damp and smells freshly cut. Widener Library is a brick-and-stone structure off to our right, wide stone staircase leads up to about a dozen tall stone columns across the front, looks kind of majestic, like a courthouse, state supreme court. Reilly says it doesn't open until 8:45, but the Harvard Police should be here any minute now with the keys; their office is up in the northwest section, he figures it's less than a ten-minute drive.

When we walk up the stairs of Widener, I automatically go and check all the doors. Locked. Whole front looks like a fortress.

Vadney leans against one of the pillars, takes deep breaths after the climb, his face reflects the hangover in his thumping-bumping brain. Grecian Formula–darkened locks are matted on top, jut out at the sides, cowlick hangs over his tanned but deeply wrinkled brow, eyes are like cherries in a stubbled chocolate pud. Voice has traces of the Duke Wayne gravel-twang punctuated by sporadic hocks and no spit: "Now, Bill, can ya gimme some kinda details about the Gutenberg Bible and all? I mean, all I know is the name, I recognized the name, y'know?"

Reilly shrugs, looks more like a street kid than ever in his blue T-shirt and Levi's. "All I can tell you is what I remember from my student days, Walt, just basic stuff. The Gutenberg Bible is generally considered to be the most famous book, *printed* book, that is, in—I don't know—Western civilization. It was the very first book to be printed from movable type. I believe it dates from the fifteenth century. Fifteenth-century Germany."

"What's it worth today?" Chief asks.

"It's beyond monetary value, Walt. It's considered priceless, very few copies were made." He takes a crushed flip-top box of Marlboros from his back pocket, pulls out a bent one, straightens it, lights it, inhales deeply. "It's always been on display, public display, in a special glass case in here. I remember it was in the rear room of the two Widener Memorial Rooms. You go in the front door here, you go straight ahead, up the marble staircase to the first landing, through the first room, a display room with a high dome, then into the second room, which has the really rare stuff. The Gutenberg was always in the first display case to the right. Both rooms have very tall, thick double doors, which I assume are always locked when the library closes at ten every night. I also assume both rooms have sophisticated alarm systems."

"Are those the only doors?" I ask.

"Yes, absolutely, I've been in there many times. I used to study in the main reading room upstairs in the front of the building, so I had to climb those marble stairs to the first landing and pass by those rooms. This was practically every day. Occasionally, the doors were closed before ten. Normally, they were open, and a member of the library staff was always on duty in the second room. It was never left unattended. I remember, from the outside, as you passed by, you could look through both rooms and see a big lighted oil painting of Harry Elkins Widener on the far wall. He was a young man when he died, mid-twenties, he was lost at sea when the *Titanic* went down in nineteen-twelve. I think he'd just graduated about five years before. Interesting story. His mother had the library built as a memorial to him. Those two rooms contain his personal library, including the Gutenberg."

Exactly 7:57, three officers from the Harvard University Police walk up the steps toward us, two in uniform. Other man turns out to be Jack Morse, the guy Patrick mentioned, relatively tall, lean, mid-forties, intelligent-looking man, he asks for a quick rundown before we go in. Reilly shows him the letter, briefs him on the theft in New York, but doesn't mention any of the Satanic stuff.

Morse opens the main door, steps inside to the right, deactivates the burglar alarm first, then snaps on the bright overhead lights. Huge marble lobby, security checkout desk to our left. All five of us follow Morse straight ahead, up the flight of white marble steps to the first landing. Tall paneled double doors are highly polished wood, looks like oak, trimmed in bronze, plate-glass window in each, and we can see the room is lighted.

"Normally lighted all night?" I ask Morse.

"Yes, both rooms, we have closed-circuit television."

He unlocks the right-hand door, swings it open, steps in to the right to deactivate the alarm system. We follow him in. White marble floor and walls, tall vertical windows reaching to a white plaster dome surrounded by oval-shaped windows. TV cameras with red lights on are high up in all four corners. Room seems almost empty, only four glass display cases, individually lighted, one against each wall, holding various opened books and manuscripts.

"Who monitors the TV?" Reilly asks.

"Private security agency," Morse says. "We've alerted them."

Our footsteps echo as we approach the second set of double doors, identical to the first. I can see the oil painting of Widener through the windows and, as I get closer, several rows of individually lighted glass display cases. This room is paneled in a dark wood.

Morse unlocks the right-hand door, opens it, again goes to his right to deactivate the alarm.

"Oh, thank *God!*" he says.

Reilly's in next. "It's *here!* Oh, my God, it's *here!*"

I file in with Vadney and the two officers. There it is, in the first glass display case to the right, the beautiful Gutenberg Bible. Sight for sore eyes, I'll tell you. It's much bigger than I'd visualized, opened to the middle, bright white paper, two long columns of print to a page, and the first letter of every paragraph is huge and elaborate, in red or blue ink, sometimes both. When I take a closer look, I see it's in German, old-style shaded lettering. Looks very heavy, thick leather binding is a work of art, and the pages have gilt edges.

"Son of a bitch," Vadney says. "He suckered us this time."

Reilly turns to him quickly. "Wait a minute. *Wait* a minute, why would he—? Jesus Christ!" He walks quickly to the telephone on the librarian's desk, pulls a card from his wallet, squints at it, dials a number, drums his fingers on the desk as he waits. Then: "Sam! You all right? Okay, where's Samantha? Okay, I want both of you to stay in that room. Don't go out for anything. Make sure the deadbolt's locked. No, no, I just want—I'll explain later. We're finished up here, it's a false alarm. Yeah, it's safe and sound. We should be back in—say, ten minutes, fifteen tops. Right. Stay there. Right. Bye."

Me, I'm crouched down, I'm looking at the bronze sides of the display case. Now I find what I want, it's on the other side, just above one of the legs, an inconspicuous little silver-colored push button for the lights inside the case. I push it: *Click-click.*

Instantly, the Gutenberg vanishes.

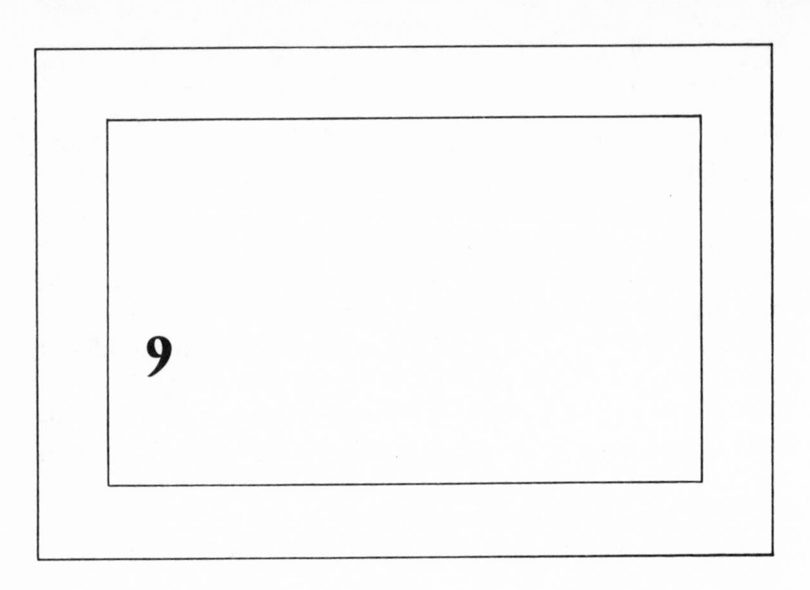

In its place is the now-familiar holographic plate of smoky glass with gray-green swirls. First few seconds, I glance from face to face: Jack Morse and his two officers have wide-eyed, shocked, frightened expressions, their sense of sight has been deceived; Reilly and Vadney take one look and turn away almost instantly with painful expressions, realizing what's happened. Hate to tell you what my first reaction is, I'm almost ashamed to admit it, I don't want you to get the wrong idea. Me, I feel a quick, vague spark of laughter deep inside, only lasts a couple of seconds, I manage to frown fast, look as agonized as I can. But I'm thinking: God *damn,* this is positively *ingenious,* this is far and away the most imaginative robbery I've confronted, personally, in thirty-one years as a cop. Because, just think about it, look at it logically, consider what was involved: Whoever did this had to get in and out of this room, and in and out of that special display case, at least *twice.* First, to physically steal the Gutenberg, get away with it, rush it to his or her fully equipped holography studio, shoot a large hologram with an appropriately powerful laser (probably many shots under various lighting conditions), develop, project, study all of them, then select one; second, rush back to the room and position the hologram within the lighted case in such a way as to project the most accurate three-dimensional illusion of reality possible.

And it's extraordinarily accurate, a highly professional job. I snap the lights on and off several more times for Morse and his men as I give them a brief rundown on the basics of holography. *Click-click,* now you see it. *Click-click,* now you don't. Exactly when was it stolen? Could've been last night, could've been last week or last month. Lights in the display case are on twenty-four hours a day. Virtually impossible to tell the real thing from the hologram.

Next fifteen, twenty minutes, Morse makes a series of phone calls to report the robbery, first to his chief, then to the curator of the Widener Collection at home, then to other appropriate university officials, most of whom are home, and finally to the chief of detectives of the Cambridge Police Department. Reilly calls Commissioner Malloy at home, explains the situation in some detail; Malloy speaks with Morse briefly, volunteers the services of the BPD Forensic Lab if needed, asks to be kept informed.

While we're waiting for people to arrive, Morse briefs us on the following facts: Both sets of double doors to the Memorial Rooms have special locks unlike those of any other rooms in the building; only three sets of keys exist and cannot be legally duplicated. There are two room-wide alarm systems in both rooms: Passive infrared and motion detectors. I'm familiar with both. Passive infrared systems measure the degree of infrared heat generated within a protected area; the body heat of an individual passing through this area will trigger the alarm. Motion detectors, called "ultrasonics" and "microwaves" in the trade, operate by filling an area with sound waves far above the audio-frequency range, or with electromagnetic waves of extremely high frequency, that are programmed in a specific pattern; anything entering that pattern in sustained motion changes the pattern and trips the alarm. Both systems are armed and disarmed by means of a wall-mounted display of numbered buttons on a small console; the six-number combination is known to only a few select people. Both alarms are "silent," wired to the same private security firm that monitors the closed-circuit TV, the Wackenhut Corporation, one of the most respected firms in the industry.

Who, specifically, has access to the three sets of keys to these rooms? Only four people: The curator of the Widener Collection, the foreman of the library's eleven-man maintenance staff, and the chief and deputy chief of the Harvard University Police Department. Period. Who knows the six-number combination to the electronic alarm systems? Seven people: The curator, the maintenance foreman, the chief and deputy chief of HUPD, and three executives of the Wackenhut Corporation. How long have these particular systems been in operation? Since September 1969, after the first attempt was made to steal the Gutenberg.

"*First* attempt?" I ask Morse.

"Yes, an attempt was made in August nineteen-sixty-nine. The man was caught, he never managed to get it out of the building. Before that time, we had no burglar alarms anywhere in the library. We just had two night watchmen, plus the maintenance staff."

"Still have the watchmen?" Vadney asks.

"Yes, but they don't go in the Memorial Rooms, of course, because of the alarm systems."

"Okay," Reilly says. "That attempt was made—let's see—that was seventeen years ago. So I assume the man's out of prison by now."

Morse winces at the memory. "He never actually went to prison, he was sent to a mental institution. This is—some psychiatrist convinced the judge that the guy was insane at the time he made the attempt. This is difficult to believe, but the man was released from the mental hospital about six weeks after he was committed. He walked away without a record, no rap sheet, nothing."

"Any idea of his whereabouts now?" Reilly asks.

"I'm afraid not."

"I'd like to read the case file," I tell him.

"Certainly." Morse glances at me, hesitates. "You might as well know this up front. Apparently, the investigation left a lot to be desired. For example, they were never able to positively establish his identity. He gave them several false names and addresses. They ran a make on his fingerprints, of course—federal, state, local—and came up empty. Anyhow, sure, you're welcome to see the file."

"Appreciate it."

He looks at his watch. "There's only one other thing that's not generally known. Back then, as a direct result of the robbery attempt, the acting curator made the decision that only one volume of the Gutenberg would be on display at any given time. The other—"

"There are *two* volumes?" Reilly asks.

"Yes. Not many people know this. At least, they didn't until a magazine article was published about it—about the robbery attempt—last spring. The fact is, because of its sheer size and weight, the Gutenberg was printed in two volumes. The first half has—I believe it's three hundred and twenty-four pages; the second half, I think it's three hundred nineteen, something like that. Today, the curator changes them periodically so that no single volume is exposed to the strong light for very long. The other volume is always kept in a safe."

"Good thinking," Vadney says. "So, bottom line, whoever stole this thing, he only got away with half the actual Bible."

"That's right."

"Detective Morse," I say, "you mentioned a magazine article about that robbery?"

"About the attempt, yes. Excellent article, it came out last spring sometime in *Harvard Magazine.*"

"How could I get a copy?"

"We had one at the office, it got passed around, I doubt if it's still there. You'd have to go to the magazine office, it's just over on Ware Street."

Now a funny thing happens, could've been a disaster. It's about 8:25, we're moving around, Reilly's calling his room again, one of the two night watchmen sees us through the windows of the double doors out on the stairway landing. Right-hand door is unlocked, of course, he tiptoes through the first room, we never hear a thing. Now he flings open the door to our room, steps in fast, revolver drawn, and he yells: *"Gitcher hands up!"* We freeze, look at this guy. Skinny Irishman, he's pushing sixty-five easy, face is sheet white, uniform's too big, even the cap, he's pointing this old .38 cannon at us, arms out straight—and his hands are shaking. Bad. Swear to God, shaking like he's got the palsy, scares the piss out of us. "Y'heard me, *gittemup!*" We gittemup fast. Now he looks us over, shaking, breathing hard, peak of his cap over his eyes and all, finally recognizes Jack Morse, lowers his arms slowly.

"Holy Jaysis, Jack," he says.

"Sorry, Mike."

"Holy Jaysis, y'shoulda—"

"Sorry, Mike, we didn't—"

"Y'shoulda called us ya was comin'!"

"I know, Mike, we didn't have time."

"Holy Jaysis, I took yez fer fuckin' *tea*ves!"

By 8:35, all kinds of people start to file in: Chief Tannen of HUPD, detectives and forensic technicians from the Cambridge police, university administrative types, library employees arriving for work, all like that, the word really spread fast. Every time somebody new comes in, I'm more or less expected to conduct another show-and-tell routine about holography. Why me? Seems I'm the only one who's got the spiel down pat, I listened to Louie so many times I know it by heart. All low-key, of course, soft-spoken, I even sound authoritative. Part I like best is the demonstration. Of course, the display case can't be touched, they've got the thing cordoned off now, chairs at its corners connected by a wide bright-orange tape that reads: CPD CRIME SCENE. They're getting set to dust for prints, which is probably a waste of time, but part of the routine of covering your ass upside down and backwards in a case of this magnitude. I'm the only one who's allowed to reach inside and push the button for the lights. *Click-click,* now you see it; *click-click,* now you don't. Feel like Blackstone, the magician, doing this stuff. You should see the bug-eyed eggheads taking in this show. You should get a load of Mike, the watchman, he's off-duty now, he's staying for all performances. Every time I make the Bible vanish, Mike makes the sign of the cross. Yeah. I mean, he's not obvious about it, but he does it every time. I can imagine what he's thinking now: Holy Jaysis, 'tis the work of the Divvil himself. Know what the irony is? Knew you would.

Curator of the Widener Collection arrives about 8:45, he had a long drive. Slim, scholarly, Oriental guy, Dr. V. R. Tas, probably mid-fifties, it's difficult to tell. He's quite familiar with holography, doesn't need any input, asks me to snap the lights on and off several times, studies the hologram carefully, then the glass plate. One thing I learn from this guy really gives me pause: Display case can't be opened with conventional keys or tools. Entire locking mechanism was changed following the robbery attempt in 1969. Today, the heavy Plexiglas top is deadbolt-locked to the bronze base on all four sides. It can only be opened by an electronically coded card inserted into a narrow slot in the bronze end facing the window. He shows me the slot; I didn't even notice it before. Seventeen years ago, this was considered space-age electronic wizardry, of course, but today the same type locking system has already started to replace conventional keys in an increasing number of security-conscious hotels. I've used them myself. When you check out, your coded key card can be thrown away, because the lock will be programmed to reject your code and accept a new one. Same deal here. Only one difference. Since Dr. Tas personally changes volumes of the Gutenberg every three months, the code is only changed four times a year. How many key cards to the display case at any given time? One. Who has it? Dr. Tas. Period. Now he shows me the card, it's no big deal, he'll have to open the case for the police anyway. It's the size of a standard credit card, only thinner, white plastic, nothing printed on it except the name of the manufacturer. Have to smile when I see the name: Yaletronic Lock System. Yeah. Yale! With a name like that, guarding Harvard's most valuable book, this system's got to be the best on the market, right? Democratic free enterprise system, nothing like it. Must stick in Harvard's craw though, know what I mean?

Okay, the forensic technicians are ready to go to work now, everybody's asked to clear the area. Wait a minute, hold everything. Here's this distinguished-looking man just walked in, relatively short, lean, well dressed, gray-white hair, bushy brows, probably mid-fifties. Whole atmosphere in here changes instantly. People stand back, lower their voices, they're all glancing at this guy. Dr. Tas walks over to him, shakes hands, speaks very softly. Now they walk toward the display case, toward me, with grave expressions. Where have I seen this guy before? Suddenly hits me. Cover of *Time.* Holy shit, it's him, it's Derek Bok, president of Harvard. Looks like a regular guy, too, nice tan, not many wrinkles for his age. Hologram happens to be lighted at this point, Gutenberg sitting there in three-dimensional splendor. Bok ducks under the bright-orange police cordon, stops in front of the case, leans over, hands behind his back, narrows his eyes, studies every inch of this beautiful Bible. Total silence in the room now, all eyes are on him. Close up, his neatly trimmed hair looks whiter than on the *Time* cover. Now he walks slowly around the case, clockwise, pausing, viewing the thing from every angle. Finally returns to the front, folds his arms over his chest, nods to Dr. Tas. Tas nods at me. I take a deep breath, reach down, push the button. *Click-click,* Gutenberg's gone.

Bok stands there motionless. Blinks several times. Leans forward, studies the holographic plate. Shakes his head slowly, negatively. Glances at Dr. Tas, speaks quietly: "Who discovered it?"

Dr. Tas nods at me. "Detective Rawlings."

"John Rawlings," I tell Bok. "New York Police Department."

"About what time?" he asks.

"Eight-oh-three."

"I understand there was a note delivered beforehand?"

"Yes, sir," Reilly says from the crowd. All eyes dart to him as he ducks under the cordon, pulls the envelope from the back pocket of his jeans, shakes hands with Bok. "Bill Reilly, police commissioner, New York. I'll have to ask you to use a handkerchief, Mr. Bok. We haven't dusted for prints yet."

Bok pulls a handkerchief from his pocket, shakes it open, drapes it over his right hand. Reilly opens the envelope, takes the letter out by the tip of its upper right corner, hands it to him. Bok reads it carefully, frowns when he gets to the message at the bottom. He hands it back, glances at his watch.

"I'd like to see you privately," he says. "Can you be in my office at—say, nine-fifteen?"

"Certainly."

We go back to our rooms in Weld, where Reilly and Vadney shower, shave, and change to dark, sincere, three-piece suits. Me, I don't happen to have a dark, sincere, three-piece suit with me, but even if I did, I wouldn't wear it, because I've always hated the idea of looking like I came from a corporate cookie cutter. I mean, I rented a tux and all, but that was different, I had no choice, it was a direct order. Me, I change to the stuff I feel comfortable in, my blue blazer and gray trousers. White shirt, conservative tie (four-in-hand knot, of course, I wouldn't be caught dead in a Windsor knot), knee-high black socks, and black shoes shined nicely on the backs of my trousers. I even check myself in the mirror, make sure I look presentable, don't want to embarrass any politicians I might know. Besides, you don't get invited to the office of the president of Harvard every day, right? Not that I was invited, I'm not saying that, but my job is to stick with Reilly all the way, I'm just doing my job. Still, it's not bad duty for a kid from the Lower East Side who never saw the inside of a college classroom, right? Highlight of my academic career, so to speak. Wish Cindy could be here, she'd love this stuff.

Sam and Sam love this stuff, it's written all over their faces when we meet down in the lobby at the appointed time, 9:10 sharp. No, they're not going to the meeting, but you can tell they approve of the company we're keeping. Sam Vadney, she looks like Snoopy running in the Boston Marathon, happily decked out in brand-spanking-new jogging duds, hair and makeup flawless. Sam Reilly, all I can tell you about this kid, even in jogging duds she's got a figure that'd stop a fast break by the Celtics. President's office is in Massachusetts Hall, diagonally across the Old Yard from Weld, so they walk us over there, then they're off for brunch in the Square.

Massachusetts Hall, you should see this old place in the morning, how the sun slants through the trees and makes patterns on the ivy-covered bricks and white window frames. It's four stories of straight and simple lines, the slanted slate roof has dormer windows and tall chimneys. Hard to believe, but this thing's been standing here since 1720, it's fifty-six years older than the country itself. Started out as a dormitory, Reilly says, but it was used as barracks for Continental troops during the siege of Boston in 1775. Only thing about it that doesn't look stately, they got a dumpy modern mailbox in front by the corner. If the original architect could see that mailbox squatting there in front of his masterpiece, he'd have a shit hemorrhage.

We follow Reilly inside. He says the executive offices occupy the first two floors, but the whole atmosphere in here seems more like an elegant home than an office. Bok's secretary greets us warmly, says he called from Widener, he'll be a couple of minutes late. Charming lady, nice smile, she shows us into his corner office, asks if we'd like some coffee. Sure would, we haven't had anything all morning. She says to sit down, make ourselves comfortable, she'll be right back.

Best way to describe this office, it's like a good-sized study in a tastefully modernized old house. Walls and ceiling are white, floorboards look original, darkly polished wide wood planks, mostly covered by a large and colorful Oriental rug, might even be Aubusson, what do I know? All four windows have white louvered shutters, closed now to the strong morning sun, and each has a cushioned window seat. Above the fireplace is a large oval oil painting of Ben Franklin, and to the left of that, in the corner, is a grandfather clock with exactly the right time. The president's desk is actually a simple table, obviously antique, holding just a telephone, a small appointment calendar, an ashtray, and a few knickknacks. There's a wicker wastebasket near his low-backed wooden chair, and Reilly says the two dark wood chairs flanking the desk are original nineteenth-century Harvard captain's chairs that are reproduced in quantity now and seen all over campus. He says the tall multidrawered cabinet against the wall to the left is the oldest piece of furniture in the room, dated 1681. Above and below it are modern rectangular ducts for heating and air conditioning. Overall first impression? Lean, hard, clean, severe. Of the nine chairs around the room, only the two upholstered ones near the fireplace look comfortable. Thought occurs to me, maybe this place isn't supposed to look comfortable. Maybe it's designed to have a specific psychological impact on visitors, the gut feel of lean, hard, clean, severe administration. Wouldn't surprise me. I mean, with an endowment of only $3.5 billion, you've got to look like you're running a tight ship, right?

We're finishing our coffee when Bok comes in at 9:19 with Chief Tannen of HUPD and Dr. Tas. Cursory introductions all around, then Bok gets right down to business, asks Reilly to lead off by briefing them on all basic intelligence about the case to date. Reilly starts at the beginning, August 23, when he received the first note just after the statue was stolen. He includes everything this time, all the weird shit that happened to me at St. Michael's, the reaction of the Bomb Squad dog, the Enochian writing, the holographic projection of the king cobra, all the way through to the discovery at Widener this morning.

Now Chief Tannen takes over, tall, muscular, soft-spoken guy, graying hair, late fifties. Briefs us quickly on what we need to know about his department: Total of sixty-five professionally trained police officers, all armed, all sworn deputy sheriffs in both Middlesex and Suffolk counties (Middlesex is north of the river, Suffolk is south). He's already assigned thirty-five detectives to work full time on the investigation. Twelve of these men are now beginning a thorough search of the Lampoon Building and are scheduled to report their progress by noon. In the meantime, the forensic unit of the Cambridge police is still at work in the library and the detective squad will work in consort with HUPD to the fullest extent possible.

"Commissioner Reilly," Tannen says, "my recommendation to you, of course, is to avoid the general area of the Lampoon Building entirely."

"I appreciate the advice," Reilly says. "I really do, and I understand your concerns. Unfortunately, I don't agree with you. I intend to be there."

Silence.

Dr. Tas looks astonished. "You can't be serious."

"I'm serious," Reilly says. "I have no intention of being intimidated by this guy. It didn't work in New York and it won't work here. I intend to stand in front of Lampy at seven-fifty-nine tonight."

Bok sits forward. "Commissioner, you know as well as we do that it's a potentially dangerous situation. In my judgment, you'd be placing yourself at unnecessary risk."

"Mr. Bok," Reilly says quietly, "let's get down to the real issue here. The Gutenberg has been stolen by an extremely intelligent individual. I don't know why I'm involved in all this, but obviously I am, and I feel a genuine sense of responsibility. The note read: 'If you want to know *why,* stand in front of Lampy tonight, exactly seven-fifty-nine.' *I* want to know *why.* So do you, so do all of us. I want to know what it's all about, what the man *wants.* I mean, we don't even—we haven't even established the *motive.* And we've got to know that, and know it cold, before we can deal with it. Now, I realize the university has a responsibility for my personal protection. I understand that and I appreciate it. But I want to point out something to you gentlemen that you don't know, that you had no way of knowing. Right this minute, I have two of the best detectives in the New York Police Department providing personal protection for me on a full-time basis: Chief of Detectives Vadney here and Detective Rawlings. They're both armed at all times. Their *sole* responsibility throughout this celebration is my personal protection. So, under these circumstances, I'm asking you to make an exception in jurisdictional authority, and I'll take full responsibility for my actions, in writing. I'm asking you to cooperate with me on this. I want to be there tonight and I think it's critical that I am. With your cooperation, we have a chance of getting some insights on this thing. If there's any hope of getting the Gutenberg back, we've got to play along with this guy—temporarily. And we've got to start tonight."

Permission granted. Next order of business, Chief Tannen drives Reilly, Vadney, and me to HUPD's office up in the northwest section. Big, modern, rectangular building at 29 Garden Street, corner of Chauncy. Reason for our visit is routine procedure. We were present at the discovery of a major crime and therefore must make a sworn statement, individually, concerning exactly what we saw, when, and under what circumstances. Time element is always important, so statements such as these should be made as soon after the event as practical while memories are still fresh. In this case, our individual statements will be tape-recorded in Chief Tannen's office, transcribed and typed by one of his staff, read by us, corrected if necessary, and signed.

Reilly goes in first. In addition to his statement about the Gutenberg, Chief Tannen wants him to repeat the chronology of events in New York leading up to this robbery, and to verify that although he was cautioned by Tannen not to appear at the Lampoon Building tonight, he will take full responsibility for doing so.

Vadney and I sit in the little waiting area across from the long desk in the lobby. Lots of activity, detectives and uniformed officers coming and going. I leaf through two stacks of magazines. Jack Morse mentioned that an article about the 1969 robbery attempt appeared in *Harvard Magazine,* a spring issue, and that it was passed around the office, so I look for issues of *Harvard,* find four of them. I pick up the issue dated March-April 1986, turn to the contents page. I'm in luck. Last article on the list is titled "The Gutenberg Caper," by W. H. Bond. I flip to page 42. On the left side of the opening spread there's a full-page color photo of a pleasant-looking middle-aged man in a tweed jacket and bow tie, leaning back against a display case. In the foreground is an opened volume of the Gutenberg. Caption reads: "W. H. Bond, professor of bibliography at Harvard, with half of the University's purloined Bible. Printed in two large folio volumes on heavy paper and stoutly bound, the Gutenberg proved to be a lot of literature to lift."

Long and fascinating article, I'm really enjoying this, W. H. Bond sure has a way with words. There's a high-angle cutaway drawing of Widener Library with a red line marking the thief's route, then an exterior photo of the same area as it appears today. Most interesting part for me begins on page 45. Professor Bond has set the stage superbly, and now he gets into the action:

On the morning of Wednesday, August 20, 1969, I was roused from my bed at about 5 A.M. by a phone call from a Widener Library colleague, Edwin E. Williams, who asked me to come to Cambridge as quickly as possible because an attempt had been made to steal the Gutenberg Bible. He gave me no other details. I pulled myself together as best I could and hurried in to town. (I was notified because I was temporarily acting curator of the Widener Collection.) In the headquarters of the police—they were still known as "Yard Cops," and had their offices in the basement of Grays Hall, only a few hundred yards from Widener—I learned what had happened.

At about 1 A.M. that morning, the maintenance crew coming on duty to clean Widener before it opened to readers at 8:45 went, as usual, to a room on Floor D (the lowest), opening on the west light court. There they were accustomed to change into their work clothes and pick up the implements they required. It was a warm night, and the windows were open. Groans could be heard, and they could see a dark shape on the pavement of the court outside. They called the Harvard police, who were there in a jiffy, as their headquarters were so close by. The Cambridge police were soon involved as well.

They found a man lying in the court, evidently seriously injured and very nearly unconscious. Under him was a knapsack, which proved to contain the two volumes of the Gutenberg Bible, a ball-peen hammer, a screwdriver, a pinch bar, and a roll of masking tape. He was wearing deerskin gloves. He was placed under arrest as a suspected burglar and taken by ambulance to the Cambridge City Hospital, where his condition was listed as critical. The Bible and the equipment found with him were taken to the Harvard police station for safekeeping, and there I had a chance to examine them.

I then went with the police to the Widener Rooms. The inner room was in a mess. There were fragments of glass all over the floor; the plate-glass case for the Bible had been smashed, and the inner and outer windows nearest it had been broken open. I learned that a stout piece of manila rope, knotted at intervals, which I had seen with the tools at the police station, had been found dangling outside the windows, the other end tied to a pipe on the Widener roof.

It was easy enough to guess what had happened. The thief had obviously cased the situation thoroughly in advance. It is simple to enter the Widener Rooms as a tourist and look long and hard at its arrangements; there are even display cases built in under its windows so one could study the fenestration while seeming to examine the displays in them. The top floor of Widener is also open to the public, and it has a corridor all around with windows looking out over the roof of the Widener Rooms and the whole façade of the inner part of the building.

It is not irrelevant that a popular movie of the late Sixties was *Topkapi,* a comedy thriller in which a gang of thieves sets out to steal the Turkish crown jewels, displayed (as they are now) in an elaborately guarded inner sanctum in the middle of the old harem complex in Istanbul. The *modus operandi* was to hide in the building with ropes and tools, cross the roof in the dark of night, and lower one of the crew on a rope through the skylight to effect the theft. Lots of people saw the movie, and at least one of them must have thought hard about the action; but he decided to operate by himself, without a backup crew.

Sometime during August 19 he walked into Widener with his rope and tools in a knapsack, not a sight to attract attention from anyone. People with knapsacks were as much a part of the ambience then as now, and knapsacks were inspected only on the way out, not on the way in. He drifted up to the top floor, and as 10 o'clock closing time approached, he locked himself in the lavatory conveniently located in the middle of the south side, the Massachusetts Avenue side. When the lights went out, he simply opened the window and easily stepped out on the roof of the Widener Rooms. He tied the rope to the pipe nearest the windows of the rooms, let himself down, covered a pane of glass on the bow window with masking tape to keep shards from falling, and broke in. Nobody could possibly see him doing this from outside the library; only one or two people remained in the building, and they were busy about their own concerns. And the well had no lights in it.

Once inside the bow window he had little need for more precautions. He broke a pane in the casement window, reached through, turned the latch, and stepped into the inner room. Whatever noise he made there could not be heard elsewhere, because of the protection given by the outer room. He smashed the plate-glass case containing the Bible. There was a plexiglass container inside designed to protect the book from ultraviolet light: we never expected it to furnish protection from sharp fragments of glass. The thief then put the two volumes in his knapsack along with his tools, swung out the window on his rope, and began to climb back up.

What he had not reckoned with was the weight of the books. They were in really massive bindings, commissioned for them by Robert Hoe, and weigh 30 or 35 pounds apiece. Despite the knots in his rope, the thief could not heave himself back up to the roof; and his rope was only long enough to reach the windows, six stories above the bottom of the light well. He evidently clung to the rope as long as he could, but when his strength failed he plunged to the concrete below. It was a ridiculous miscalculation: if the rope had reached to the bottom, he could have slid down, easily entered D level, and walked up four flights of stairs to a floor where casement windows would have let him out onto the wide ledge that circles the building. The iron cages over the windows below afford plenty of inconspicuous places to climb down to the ground. He could even have strolled nonchalantly down the grand front steps.

His one piece of good fortune was that he fell on top of the knapsack instead of under it; otherwise he surely would have been killed. But he was very badly injured, as we learned month by month as his preliminary hearing was put off for medical reasons. A representative of the library had to be present each time the case was called to testify to Harvard's ownership, and a good deal of time was spent in this pursuit. At last he did appear in court on crutches, but before formal proceedings started, lawyers and a psychiatrist approached the bench and the judge declared a finding of "no probable cause." The psychiatrist had persuaded him that the thief was insane when he attempted the theft, and the judge's finding was based on the thief's pledge to commit himself to an institution for mental therapy, so all those trips by librarians to East Cambridge proved a waste of time. Within a month or six weeks the doctors in the mental institution declared that he was cured, and out he limped without a record on this charge.

Despite intensive questioning while in custody, we never found out why he attempted the theft. The only answer he would give was that he wanted to study the Bible, believed that he would not be given a chance to examine it, and therefore decided to borrow it temporarily. Pure balderdash, of course; perhaps so pure that it is what persuaded the psychiatrist and the judge. Perhaps the thief had a client for it, one of those mysterious collectors we hear insubstantial tales about, who gloats like Fafnir over a hidden hoard. It would have to be hidden; the Hoe-Widener Bible is well enough known in all its physical aspects. Perhaps the thief or somebody else wanted to dissect it and feed it into the market leaf by leaf over many years; a single leaf now fetches $2,000 or so, and might be unrecognizable. Perhaps he thought he could hold it for ransom, believing that the Harvard Corporation would fork out a million or two to get it back, possibly a debatable proposition.

He gave his name in several styles, probably all aliases, so I will not list them here; the curious may consult contemporary newspaper accounts if they wish. Among several addresses given successively, Blue Hill Avenue, Dorchester, appears to have been correct. I don't know where he is now. About ten years ago someone told me he had been seen and recognized on Cape Cod. He was still walking with a decided limp. . . .

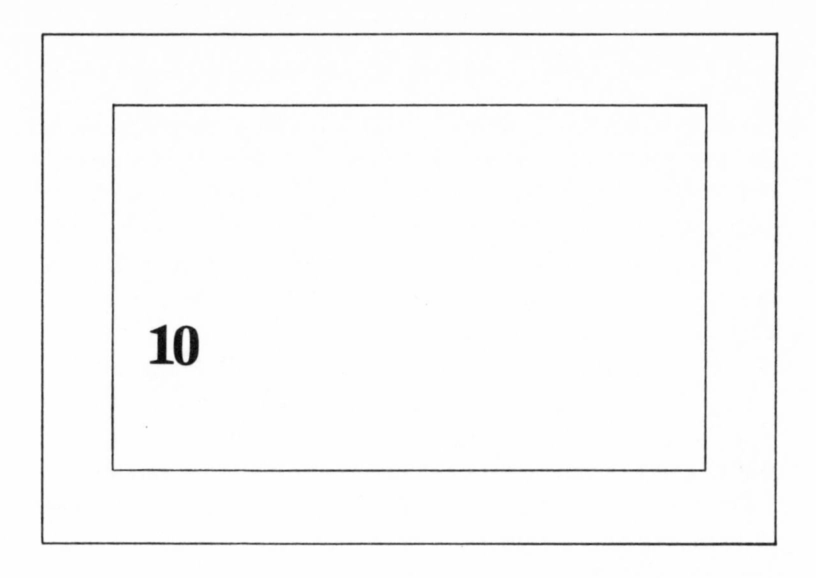

10

LATE THAT AFTERNOON, it's damp and cold when the "Floating Birthday Party" gets under way. Starts at six o'clock, we don't have to be at the Lampoon Building for almost two hours, so Reilly, Vadney, and the Sams, they say, what the hell, let's catch at least part of the show. Okay, by the time we buy all our picnic stuff and booze, it's 6:30 already, so now here we are, we're walking down Kennedy Street in this big crowd, we're wearing sweaters, jeans, and sneakers like everybody else, we're loaded down with picnic blankets, bags of sandwiches, potato chips, six-packs of beer for the guys, bottles of white wine for the coeds, cigarettes, cigars, cameras, binoculars, you'd have to see this shit, we look like kids, we feel like kids, we're out to have a blast despite everything. We get down there, it's 6:40 now, both banks of the Charles are jammed already, we can't even get close to the water—50,000 are expected—and the first thing that catches your attention is this rainbow Reilly told us about, this 600-foot, two-tiered, helium-filled Mylar rainbow arched across the river. Huge thing. Plus, they got this water pipe spanning the river too. What for? Get a load of this: Soon as it gets dark, Reilly says, they'll light up the rainbow, turn on the high-pressure water pipe (it's got holes in the top), out shoots a wide screen of water, which they light, then they present what's called a "laser mirage." What's that? Laser drawings projected on the screen of water. Yeah. I mean, we're talking high-tech entertainment here. But that's not all. While all this stuff is going on (we probably won't get to see it), and the crowds on both banks are getting bombed out of their skulls, they'll have barges with all kinds of orchestras and bands moving up and down the river. Right now they got yachts and sailboats cruising around, decks alive with cocktail parties, all like that. Pass the Grey Poupon.

Anyhow, we find a place on the grass, we spread our blankets, sit down, empty the grocery bags, and the Sam sisters start passing out the goodies. Me, I open a can of Bud, take a swallow, lean back, watch my politician companions get into the all-important social aspect. Sam Vadney, she's opening a bottle of wine, she's smiling, she's eating up the ambience, but she's your basic no-nonsense-type lady. Used to be a policewoman, that's how she met the Duke. He told me the story some years back. Seems they met at the old Academy shooting range. This is like twenty-five years ago, he's just a young buck, he's firing away, now he hears this fantastically fast rapid-fire sequence from the next booth. Thinks it must be a real hotshot gunslinger. Looks in there, here's this young broad still in the two-hand combat crouch. Says she had an ass on her like a couple of ripe watermelons. His words, not mine. She turns, sees him gawking, they're both wearing the regulation earmuffs, can't take 'em off in there, so he gives her a smart salute, a wink, and an all-out smile. What's she do? This lovely young dark-haired, dark-eyed damsel looks him up and down like he's a child molester, then she up and gives him the finger. Yeah. Not your conventional stationary finger, mind you, this kid gives him the up-and-down finger. Three or four energetic pumps right in front of his bug-eyed puss. Start of a beautiful romance. She's still quite attractive today, a bit heavier, of course, but I'm sure she still doesn't take much crap from him. Know how I know? Her eyes. If her eyes are the windows of her soul, I'm looking into a deep freezer. Eyes of Attila the *Hen,* know what I mean?

Now, Sam Reilly, she's got eyes that'd stop the Boston Symphony Orchestra in the finale of Ravel's *Bolero.* First time I met her just outside Reilly's office that Sunday afternoon, August 24, her eyes riveted my attention, remember that? Bright blue with savvy. Savvy beyond her years. I mean, she's got all the other equipment up the gazoo, she's loaded, but her eyes are the heavy artillery. Chestnut-brown hair thick and windblown over a high forehead, average cleavage, but a waist so thin Joan Collins would kill for it. She's poured into new Guess jeans, slim tanned ankles below the zippers, and she wears low white Keds rather than the kid-craze Reeboks. Before we left New York, I did some basic research on her, asked Reilly's secretary a few casual questions. Sharp kid, she knew the vitals: Born Samantha Smith in Bridgeport, Connecticut, where both parents were born; they still live in nearby Fairfield, that's where she grew up. Graduate of Katherine Gibbs in Boston. Executive secretary with Pan Am for around twelve years, New York, Miami, Los Angeles. Married Bill in 1977; two children now. Normal enough background, old Connecticut family, top secretarial school, solid airline experience, probably got to travel a lot when she was single. So what the hell bothers me about this kid, intrigues me enough to snoop around? What triggers these almost subliminal blips on my radar? What's my intuition trying to tell me? What do I see in those eyes? Beats the shit out of me, but I'm working on it.

We're finishing our sandwiches when the decorated barges start moving past on the river, slowly, one by one, with orchestras, big and small bands, singers, dancers, jugglers, all kinds of stuff going on, and the crowd hushes, then gives each one a loud ovation. Chief and I use binoculars, we're taking turns with the Sams; Reilly's taking pictures with his Nikon and a 200-millimeter lens. Band I like best, I look it up in the program, it's an outfit called the Batucada Belles, a twenty-three-piece all-girl samba band, they're something else, they got people dancing all over the place, terrific rhythm. Also, you look around now, groups of dancers and clowns and jugglers are moving through the crowd, good costumes, most of them look like students, and there's one you can't miss, it's a ten-foot-tall marionette of John Harvard, he's shaking people's hands, posing for pictures. Vadney gets one look at John Harvard, he asks Bill to get some shots of him and John, he bulls his way through the crowd, waits impatiently in line, finally shakes hands with the giant founder dressed in period costume. Once is not enough, he holds on for more shots, squinting in the low sun, forehead flat, ears back, all-out left-sided molar-shower, Duke Wayne meets John Harvard, Puritans, a sure-shot blowup for the office wall.

Time flies when you're having a floating birthday party. At 7:40, it's dusk, Reilly makes the command decision that Vadney will stay with the girls, I'll accompany him to the Lampoon Building, which is only a five-minute walk, then we'll come back and join them for the "laser mirage" and all, because the party's scheduled to go on until 10:30.

As we're wending our way through the picnics, heading north toward Memorial Drive, we have to stop and wait for this big group of student demonstrators, easily 125 or more, each holding a lighted candle, marching peacefully two-by-two, all chanting: "*Divest, divest—divest or face unrest.*" Over and over. Not shouting, just chanting in almost perfect unison.

Candles illuminate their serious young faces. They're holding a long white cloth banner with big black letters:

HARVARD PARTIES, S. AFRICA BURNS

Located on a narrow island between Mt. Auburn and Bow streets near Adams House, the Lampoon Building's official name is the Castle, according to Reilly, but known to most today as Lampy. Whatever you call it, let me tell you, this thing is totally weird. Built in 1909, its architect wanted to create a "standing joke," using the Sphinx as a structural base, Reilly says. Front part is cylindrical, made of brick and stone, designed to resemble the head of a man wearing a round helmet with a lamp in it that's actually a dormer window. His eyes are round windows, his nose a protruding old lamp that was once gaslit, and his vertical windowed mouth looks like it's wide open in astonishment, flagpole jutting out like a long panatela. Lampy's crowning glory, to me, is his "beard"—thick vines of ivy that cover much of his face now after a summer's growth. White stone entrance arch is his wing collar and the door is painted to resemble a black bow tie. Leading up to it, wide stone steps are flanked by stately brick sides to complete the Sphinx-like posture.

Dusk is obviously the best time to see Lampy, because his face is in shadow and, when all his windows are lighted, as they are now, his eyes, nose, and mouth have an eerie lifelike glow. Only his helmet still has fading traces of sunlight. Reilly tells me some basics about the magazine itself as we walk toward this thing, which is surrounded by cops now, I'm glad to see. It's the home of the *Harvard Lampoon,* the oldest continuously published humor magazine in the United States (110 years), now produced five times a year by a staff of about forty undergraduates. Over the years, he says, many of these kids went on to become famous authors, illustrators, and men of letters. He says one of its best-known traditions is the awarding of annual "Movie Worsts," and even I'm familiar with that, I remember Duke Wayne was a frequent winner, he loved that award. Last time he won it, they drove him around Cambridge in a U.S. Army tank, I saw pictures of that. Last year, Sly Stallone was the male winner, he showed up in a tux and all, humble as Rocky and Rambo, said he'd cherish the dishonor all his life. Mumbles to that effect.

Anyhow, we get to Lampy at 7:46, now I can see why its official name is the Castle. Cylinder front is deceiving, it's actually a long rectangular deal, looks like some weird medieval cathedral, elaborate stonework, stained-glass windows, even crazy spires. No squad cars in sight, but about two dozen cops are around, almost all detectives. We spot Chief Tannen and Deputy Chief Morse, go over there, they give us a brief rundown on security precautions. First, the building's been searched thoroughly by two separate twelve-man teams in the morning and afternoon, basement to roof, plus all surrounding areas, including the little bookstore in the rear, and the roofs and front rooms of Randolph and Westmorley halls, which are directly across Bow Street, the closest halls of Adams House. They even searched the big tree in front of Lampy. Now, since no actual death threat to Reilly was made or even implied, no heroics are being taken, which means no sharpshooters on roofs, stuff like that, but the building will be surrounded from a series of strategic positions across Mt. Auburn, Bow, and also Linden and Plympton, the cross streets. All surrounding roofs will be manned by at least two officers to preclude the possibility of anyone gaining access. All four floors of Lampy will be covered, plus both sides of the long cathedral roof. Also, Tannen asks Reilly and me to wear bulletproof vests and riot helmets as minimum protection, because we're the only ones who'll be standing directly in front here at the appointed time, 7:59. We agree without hesitation.

We've still got about twelve minutes, Reilly asks if we can take a quick look around inside, Tannen says sure, turns us over to Jack Morse. We follow him up the nine stone steps to the door with the big black bow tie. In we go through Lampy's larynx. First thing I notice, walls are completely covered with intricately painted tiles—"delft" tiles, Morse tells us, precious, furnished with the help of publisher William Randolph Hearst. Most ceilings are wainscotted in dark wood, windows are small and lead-framed, furniture and fixtures are obviously antique. One room we go in, Morse says it's supposed to be an almost perfect replica of a seventeenth-century fisherman's cottage. Others are examples of a variety of eras and styles, can't remember exactly, I think one was a nineteenth-century clerk's office, another was a modern circular library. Now, the upstairs floors are normally open to members only. See, Morse explains, in addition to being a humor magazine, Lampoon is also a club, among the most exclusive, and membership is permanent. How you get in, there's a creative competition held twice a year. Undergraduates submit humorous writing or artwork throughout a full semester. From an entering field of about 150, Morse says, between 5 and 15 new members are elected. That's when you get to go upstairs. Highly restrictive floors upstairs. Yeah, secret. But, yeah, we go up, sure. Official police business, okay? We meet the HUPD officers stationed on every floor, take a quick peek around. Naturally, I can't give away any secrets here, I wouldn't do that, it wouldn't be ethical. Right? I mean, I'm just not that type guy, I wouldn't cave in to revealing the ancient and honored secrets of the oldest continuously published humor magazine in the country, the magazine that spawned *National Lampoon* and all. No way. I mean, even if I *knew* any secrets, I wouldn't tell. Me, I'm a high school graduate, I wouldn't know a *Lampoon* secret from axle grease.

One thing I can't help noticing, these rooms up here haven't been cleaned in a long time. Real mess. Surprised the place doesn't have rats. Probably does. *Must.* Of course, there you are, there's the rub about secrecy. Ground floor is sparkling clean, that's obviously the showplace floor open to prospective members, visiting journalists, award winners like Stallone and them. Probably have it professionally cleaned on a scheduled basis during the school year. Upstairs? Forget it.

When we get outside, it's 7:54, much darker now, and from the top step we can't help but look due south to see the huge rainbow, finally lighted, multicolored, and the sparkling screen of water shooting high and silver against the sky. From our angle, we can't see any laser drawings on the screen, but the whole display is really quite spectacular. Chief Tannen is standing down by the tree in front talking with a couple of his detectives; obviously he's dispersed the rest of his men to their assigned positions around the building and up on the surrounding roofs. We go down and join him.

Next three or four minutes seem to go fast, we're helped into these heavy-duty black bulletproof vests, put 'em on right over our sweaters, then we adjust the headbands of the riot helmets, they have plastic visors that flip down, and chin straps.

"We'll be right across the street," Tannen says. "In front of Randolph Hall over there."

"You going to stand together?" Morse asks.

"No," Reilly tells him, then turns to me. "I want you back behind the tree, John. I'll stand right up there at the foot of the steps. Alone. I don't want anyone near me."

"Got your weapon?" Morse asks me.

"Sure do."

Tannen squints at his watch. "All right, gentlemen, synchronize with me, please. In—ten seconds, it'll be seven-fifty-seven." He waits, squinting. "Five, four, three, two, one. Mark. Seven-fifty-seven. Good luck."

Off they go, all four of them, heels clicking on the brick

sidewalk, then on the brick street. I turn and glance up at Lampy. This close, he looks enormous against the red-streaked clouds in the darkening sky. The bearded face is monstrous, eyes, nose, and mouth glowing bright yellow, with only the big vertical mouth casting pale reflections down the stone steps.

Reilly's looking up at it too, holding his helmet against his left hip. *Glaring* up at it, lips tight, chin set, hair windblown, dark eyes wide and unblinking. "Go ahead, John. Behind the tree. Let's see what this fucker's gonna pull here."

I walk back slowly, stand behind the dark silhouette of the tall tree, looks like an old elm. It's got a black wrought-iron fence around it, about four feet high, and the pointed bars at the top are curved outward to discourage climbers. I hang my helmet on one of those bars, reach back to lift up my vest and sweater, unsnap the hammer strap of my holster, draw my revolver carefully, hold it down at my side. Now I glance at my watch: 7:58.

Reilly walks up to the foot of the stone steps, helmet still held against his left hip. Looks small and chunky in the thick vest, but then he's only about five-nine to begin with. Stands there now, suddenly tosses his helmet aside; it hits the bricks with a hollow plastic sound, bounces once, rolls a little, stops. He checks his watch, then puts his hands on his hips, spreads his legs slightly, looks up at Lampy towering four stories above him. Posture of a street fighter: Go ahead, take your best shot. Man's got guts, I like his style. Distant red-streaked clouds are finally fading to black behind Lampy's glowing, progressively brighter eyes, nose, and wide-open mouth.

I'm chilly now, even with the heavy vest and sweater. I shiver as I look at the dark rooftops to my left. Can't see any officers up there. Silence is broken by the faint sound of Dixieland jazz drifting from another barge moving up the river. I glance to my right, I can't see any part of the rainbow or the water screen, they're blocked by the buildings, but there's a hazy reflection of colored light on the dark clouds over there. Breeze brings the smell of the river, it's probably much cleaner than our East River or the Hudson, but it smells almost the same, subtle traces of sewage. Reminds me of the night we waited across the street from St. Michael's. Didn't know what the hell to expect then, don't know what to expect now. Another holographic projection? Could be, but frankly I doubt it. *If you want to know why, stand in front of Lampy tonight, exactly 7:59.*

At 7:59, nothing happens. I knew it wouldn't. I stand there shivering. I know that in exactly one minute something dreadful and sickening will take place here. I know it, I feel it, I sense it, I see it in those eyes staring blankly.

It happens so fast and with such merciless impact that it's branded in my mind, burning, bizarre beyond belief: A human voice booms from Lampy's mouth screaming like a man totally engulfed in fire, every inch of his flesh burning, screaming in horrible pain, crying, wailing, screeching breathlessly, hopelessly, insane with agony, so tortured, so frightening, so loud, it's almost unbearable to hear. Reilly staggers back like he's been hit, crouches, claps his hands over his ears. It goes on and on, increasing in volume and intensity, hurting my eardrums now, I stick my fingers in my ears fast, even with the gun in my hand, I simply can't stand it. Lampy's door opens and a young detective runs out holding his ears, rushes down the steps, sprints across Bow Street. Another detective stumbles out, fingers in ears, bent at the waist as if in pain, hurries down the dark steps, falls, scrambles up, runs down Mt. Auburn Street. Last two detectives come out almost on top of each other, hands over ears, one races straight ahead past me, the other grabs Reilly by the vest and half drags him across Bow. Me, I run after them, I can see they're headed toward an open door in the hall over there.

The screaming stops. Abruptly, I think, it's hard to tell, I still have my fingers in both ears. I take them out as I run, just for a second, just to test. Silence. I stop, take a deep breath. My ears are ringing slightly. I turn, start to walk back, gun still in my hand. I'm almost in front of Lampy, headed for the door, when I hear the voice coming from his mouth, a man's voice, calm, relatively quiet, but obviously distorted, like it's coming from an echo chamber:

"Reilly, Reilly, Reilly. Did it hurt? Did it shock? Did it frighten? Reilly, is it possible, still possible, still? Is it still possible that your insensitive sensibilities have somehow retained the capability to be affected by pain, by shock, by fear? To be touched, reached, pricked by an emotion, by a cry, by human agony? Is it conceivable that your attention has been gained, earned, directed toward something even remotely commensurate with your capacity to recognize and react to human feelings, human suffering, human despair? Reilly, are you listening? Really listening? Finally, finally listening? After all these years?"

I turn, look back across the street. In the dim light, I can see Reilly standing with Tannen and Morse near the door to the hall. He starts to cross the street. I motion for him to stop, but he doesn't.

The calm, quiet, distorted voice continues: "My reasons for stealing the Gutenberg? Deceptively simple and logical. First, to humiliate you in full view of the distinguished faculty and alumni of the only institution you have ever loved in your life. Just as you did to me. Second, to humiliate the institution itself, for reasons that will become obvious. If you and your beloved institution want the volume returned safely, you must meet three demands, the first two of which are easy."

Reilly's standing next to me now, wide-eyed, hands on hips.

"Number one," the voice says, "you are to meet with Derek Bok tomorrow morning to explain what I'm telling you. Number two, Mr. Bok is to call an emergency meeting of the Harvard Corporation's seven-member board of directors for tomorrow afternoon. Number three, the corporation is to immediately vote for divestment of Harvard's complete financial holdings in firms presently conducting business with South Africa—an investment amounting to four hundred sixteen million dollars. Starting Friday, September fifth, for each day that passes in which the divestiture order has not been given, you, personally, will receive one page from the Gutenberg Bible that has been soaked in human blood. The volume I have, which happens to be volume one, contains exactly three hundred and twenty-four pages. Guide yourselves accordingly."

We stand there in silence, waiting, but the voice doesn't continue. Now we hear the footsteps of Tannen, Morse, and the two other detectives approaching. Without a word, Reilly walks quickly up the stone steps and enters the door. I follow him, holster my gun. When I open the door, Tannen and Morse are starting up the steps behind me.

Reilly's on the second floor, of course, near the tall window that's Lampy's mouth. The window's closed. There's an expensive-looking stereo console on the shelf of a cabinet that also holds a TV and VCR. He's already turned off the stereo and ejected the tape cassette. Now he slides it back in, turns on the set, presses the rewind button, waits a few seconds, then stops it, hits the play button.

Sound comes from two large stereo speakers on opposite sides of the circular room: "—for each day that passes in which the divestiture order has not been given, you, personally, will receive one page from the Gutenberg Bible that has been soaked in human blood."

I open the window quickly, lean out. Sound also comes from under the thick ivy on opposite sides of the window:

"The volume I have, which happens to be volume one, contains exactly three hundred and twenty-four pages. Guide yourselves accordingly."

Now I reach under the heavy layers of ivy on the left side, feel around, locate the speaker almost immediately, very close to the stone frame. It's a tall rectangular job, almost as high as the window itself, but narrow enough to be completely hidden by the dense growth of leaves. Bottom is braced by long nails drilled into the mortar between the rows of bricks. Exactly the same on the other side.

I duck inside. "Two speakers hidden in the ivy."

"I thought so," Reilly says. He's on his knees in front of the cabinet, reaching his right arm through the backless shelf between the TV set and the storage drawer at the bottom. "I'm trying to find the electrical outlet. He must have a timing device."

Tannen and Morse go to the window now. Morse leans out, reaches into the ivy; Tannen's searching for inside wires leading to the outside speakers.

Reilly pulls at something behind the cabinet, takes it out, holds it up. "Timing device. Jesus, this fucker's sure got a flair for the dramatic, I'll give him that." He hands it to me.

It's absolutely identical to the one we found in the basement of St. Michael's: Intermatic Time-All, plastic dial like the face of a clock, knob for automatic operation, two sliding tabs to set the "on" and "off" times you want. This one is set to switch on at exactly 8:00 P.M. and shut off at 8:04 P.M.

"One thing I can't figure," Reilly says, standing up. "How in hell did he get the volume so incredibly loud at first? In the screaming part, I mean, then low in the talking part?"

I go over to the stereo console, look at the volume knob. It's turned all the way to the right, maximum volume possible. "He had the thing turned up as loud as it'll go, so he had to record the speaking part at an extremely low volume.

Which means he's got relatively sophisticated recording equipment."

"Chief Tannen," Reilly says, "you have an emergency number for Mr. Bok?"

"Just his home number, but he wouldn't be there now. He's attending a private reception for Prince Charles."

Reilly looks at his watch. "Any way of reaching him tonight?"

"Yes, I think so," Tannen says. "According to my contact with Scotland Yard, Prince Charles is scheduled to arrive at the Floating Birthday Party between nine-fifteen and nine-thirty. Mr. Bok will be with him. Security for that particular limo is extremely tight, but I'm sure I can get a message through to him."

"Let's play it that way then," Reilly tells him. "Somehow, he's got to know what's going on as soon as possible. At the very least, he should know the demands and the timetable. Could you transcribe that part of the tape and get it to him with an urgent memo or something?"

"Certainly," Tannen says. "In fact, I'll take it right now and get it to headquarters."

Reilly flips the tape out, hands it to him. "Forget about fingerprints. This guy uses gloves on everything."

Now that we have a handle on the basic motive for the robbery, the surface motive anyway, I feel a definite sense of relief, along with Reilly, because now we can be reasonably sure that his life's not in danger, at least not for the present. Okay, that being the case, that frees me up a little, I ask Reilly and Tannen if it'd be all right for me to go over to Widener Library sometime tonight and speak with the maintenance foreman, I'd like to ask him a few questions. Tannen has no problem with it, he tells me that because of the Floating Birthday Party, all the libraries closed early tonight, Widener at seven o'clock, so the staff could join in the celebration. Therefore, the maintenance crew is already at work. Reilly has no objections at all, he helps me off with my vest, I help him with his, he says he's going back to join his wife and the Vadneys, there's nothing more he can do until the message gets through to Bok. He tells me to go ahead and join them later. Tannen asks Jack Morse to go along with me, get me in, introduce me, all like that.

Widener's not far away, Morse and I walk north on Linden Street, jaywalk across Massachusetts Avenue, enter a big gate between some dorms, and the back entrance of Widener is straight ahead. Morse says this is the door that's normally used by the maintenance crew anyway, so he goes up and rings the bell. We wait a while, I notice all the windows above are ablaze with light, then the door's opened by a middle-aged woman in work clothes. Morse shows his ID, asks for the foreman. She says she thinks he's up in the main reading room, second floor front. We have to walk around the hallways to the lobby, where we run into Mike, the shaky night watchman, who recognizes us, thank God; up the white marble stairway to the first landing (big double doors to the Memorial Rooms are closed), then up another flight, past the card catalog room to the right, and the main reading room is straight ahead, brightly lighted.

Tell you what, this room is positively enormous, looks like it stretches across the whole front of the building. Marble pillars reach up to a very high ceiling where dozens of chandeliers hang on long chains. Place is filled with rectangular wooden tables, each maybe fifteen feet long, and their wooden chairs are upside-down on the tables now because a crew of four men is washing the marble floor, working their way out from the tall front windows. Quite a job in a room this size. We walk around, Morse spots a guy he thinks might be the foreman in an adjoining room to the right. We go over there, the guy's wearing a gray jumpsuit like the others, but he's white-haired, sitting at a table, drinking coffee, reading the paper. Must be the foreman. Morse introduces himself, shows his ID, all that. Turns out he's right, it's the foreman, man by the name of Eddie Kazak. Thing that makes me smile, here we are, after-hours at the library, Morse and Kazak are speaking so softly, they're practically whispering. Now Morse introduces me, even *I'm* doing it, can't help myself.

Anyhow, I start off with routine questions to loosen him up, before long we're speaking in normal conversational tones. Of course, he's been questioned earlier in the day by both the Cambridge police and HUPD, but he's cooperative as they come, tough little guy, built like a fireplug, he sits there, sips his coffee, goes along with the gag. He's sixty-three, he's been working maintenance at the university for twenty-two years, eleven as Widener foreman; before that, he spent three years as a longshoreman on the Boston docks; before that, he spent exactly twenty years in the U.S. Navy, retired with the rank of chief warrant officer, full pension. Lives in neighboring Watertown now, married thirty-seven years, four grown children.

"Now, Mr. Kazak," I say, "as I understand it, the Memorial Rooms have special locks unlike any others in the library."

"Right."

"And only three sets of keys exist?"

"To our knowledge, yeah. I got a set, the curator's got one, and the HUPD. They can't be legally duplicated. It says right on 'em, 'Do Not Duplicate,' it's stamped right on both keys." He reaches back, pulls a huge ring of keys from a spring device on his belt, finds the two in question, points to the stamps. "See there? 'Medeco. Restricted. Do Not Duplicate.' No locksmith would do it, he could lose his license, he could be sent up for that."

"True. Okay, let's talk about the alarm systems. Now, as I understand it—"

"Passive infrared and ultrasonic. State-of-the-art electronic alarm systems. Know how they work?"

"Yeah, I'm familiar with both. As I understand it, the combination, the six-number combination, is known to only—is it seven people?"

"Seven. Me, the curator, the chief and deputy chief of HUPD here, and three guys at Wackenhut."

"Okay. Now, this morning I talked with the curator, Dr. Tas. He explained that the display case can't be opened with conventional keys or tools. That it can only be opened by an electronically coded card."

"That's right. That whole locking mechanism was installed in nineteen-sixty-nine after the first robbery attempt. Same with the alarm systems, same year. Up to then, they didn't have any alarms in here."

"Were you working in Widener back then?"

"No, I was working the freshmen dorms then, days, but I knew some of the guys who were here, who actually found the man on the court outside Floor D."

"Uh-huh. So you didn't get a look at him?"

"No, he was long gone by the time I found out."

"We've got his file," Morse tells me. "You're welcome to see it, as I said before."

"I appreciate it, Jack. Now, Mr. Kazak, I want to be sure on one other point. That electronically coded card, Dr. Tas has the only card, is that correct?"

"Yeah. Also, he changes the code itself from time to time, so the card has to be changed too."

"So I understand."

He sips his coffee, glances at Morse, shrugs. "You guys as baffled as it says in the paper?"

"I haven't read it yet."

"Extra edition." Kazak hands it to him.
It's the *Boston Herald.* Front-page headline reads:

Priceless Bible Stolen

Holography Used in Theft of Gutenberg at Harvard

As Morse reads the first few paragraphs, I glance at Kazak, notice that he's got a good tan that's accentuated by his white hair.

"When did you take your vacation?" I ask him.

"August, always August, it's one of the lightest months for us. Summer School runs from the last week in June to the middle of August. I get four weeks now. The wife and I go up to Marblehead, we've had a cottage up there for years."

"Hear it's great sailing up there."

"The best. Best spot in the state, in my opinion."

"And who replaces you as foreman?"

"Same man every year, guy by the name of Carr, Jimmy Carr. He's been doing it for—I guess it's six years now, counting this year. Excellent foreman, never had a complaint about him from anybody on the crew in six years now."

"You know him well?" I ask.

"Oh, sure, absolutely. I just saw him on Monday, my first night back, he gave me the usual briefing, everything that's been going on, all like that. Good man, I trust him completely. Bright man, too, he takes courses at the Summer School every year."

I turn to Morse. "I assume all maintenance people are carefully screened, is that right?"

"Yes, we run a standard check. Complete background check, plus they're required to take a polygraph. Boston runs 'em all through the computer for us, local, state, and FBI."

"As a temporary employee, would he have a personnel file?"

"Oh, sure," Morse says. "You could check it out in the Personnel Office tomorrow morning. No, wait a minute, not tomorrow. The Convocation's being held in the Tercentenary Theatre tomorrow morning—that's the main part of Harvard Yard, the big open area out in front of the library here. So the administrative offices are closed. They're in University Hall, right in the middle of everything that's happening."

"Can you get in touch with the personnel director?"

"You mean tonight?" Morse asks. "I doubt he'd be home."

"Tomorrow morning?"

"I think that's possible," he says. "In fact, I'm sure he'll be at the Convocation. Y'know, with Prince Charles making the keynote address and all? Hell, his wife wouldn't let him miss that."

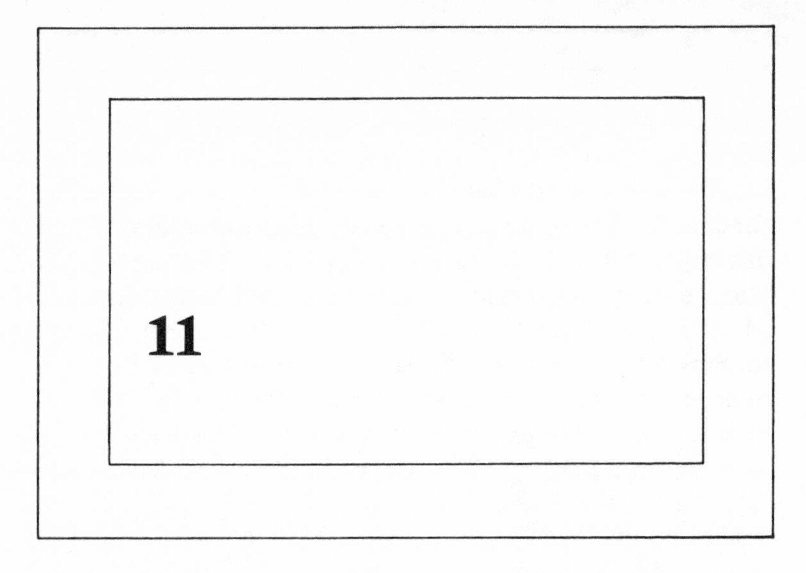

11

EARLY NEXT MORNING, Thursday, September 4, I get a call from Jack Morse. First thing, he briefs me on what we couldn't find out last night, that Chief Tannen finally managed to get his message through to Derek Bok, complete with a transcript of the last part of the tape, in which the suspect made his demands and gave the Friday deadline. According to Tannen, Bok was angry, but agreed to at least report the situation to the six other members of the board of the Harvard Corporation in a meeting at 1:30 this afternoon. Reilly's invited to attend, along with Tannen, but nobody else. Fine with me. I mean, I don't feel left out or anything like that, know what I mean? Already met the president, twice, no less, once in his office, don't forget. So it's all downhill from there, right? Not that I'd turn down an invitation to attend if one happened to be offered, don't get me wrong. Happen to like the guy's style, down-to-earth as they come, like to hear him pepper his remarks with a few choice expletives in front of his distinguished board of eggheads.

Anyhow, second reason for Morse's call, he just got off the

phone with Harvard's personnel director, man by the name of Hugh McCauley, who agreed to pull the file on temporary maintenance foreman Jimmy Carr. Says it's no big imposition for McCauley, he and his wife will be here for the Convocation anyway, just like he thought. I'm to meet the man at the north front door of University Hall at exactly 8:30 this morning. Morse can't be there, he's got his plate full today, it's the formal opening, Foundation Day, he's looking at a fifteen-hour shift. Warns me, says if I leave the Yard before breakfast, be sure to bring my Convocation ticket with me or the guards won't let me back in. I ask him where to go for breakfast, he says try the Harvard Faculty Club, just a short walk east past Widener, it's at 20 Quincy Street. He's a member, says he'll call and make a reservation for 7:30, says to sign his name on the bill.

Unfortunately, it's raining right now, 7:15, a steady drizzle, but it was predicted. Vadney was philosophical about it. "It's gonna be a clear-up shower," he tells me. "Clear up your ass!" I love brand-new original lines like that, restores my confidence in politicians.

I go down the hall to shower and shave, can't hear a peep from the rooms of my companions, none of whom were feeling any pain last night. When I come back, I hear loud snoring from Vadney's room, sounds masculine, but I wouldn't make book on it. At 7:45, when I go downstairs, I'm wearing a raincoat and carrying a fold-up umbrella, thanks to my wife, who always remembers to pack stuff like that. When I travel, which isn't often, Cindy makes a list of everything I'll need, then packs it all for me. Yeah. Even including my vitamin C tablets, which I take every day. I mean, she's wonderful, what can I tell you?

I open my umbrella and walk toward Widener in the cool drizzle. It's still fairly dark, but I can see that the whole big part of the Yard here is filled with endless rows of wooden chairs under the trees; Morse said 16,000 people are expected.

Also, they got flags all over, look like historical flags, I pass by some I recognize, including the Confederate and Union flags of the Civil War. Nice touch, takes you back. Rain-drenched front steps of Widener are almost completely covered with thousands of pots of red and white chrysanthemums; Cindy has them around the house, even taught me how to pronounce the name, only took a couple of years. Drizzle's not hard enough to damage them, they still look healthy. It's a shame though, a lot of people went to a lot of trouble and expense to make it look festive and all. Best laid plans of mice and millionaires, right?

Harvard Faculty Club's a stately three-story deal, ivy-covered brick in the recessed center, flanked by big white bay-windowed wings. I walk up the stone steps to a large patio filled with umbrellaed tables. Open the green door, close my umbrella in the little foyer, step inside. Nice warm clubby atmosphere. Table directly ahead holds crisp copies of the *Boston Globe,* the *New York Times,* the *Wall Street Journal.* I take a copy of the *Times,* turn left, hang my raincoat and umbrella in the cloakroom. Walk back through the living room to the main dining room, can't miss it, huge room, dwarfs the dozen or so early diners. Young lady at the desk has my reservation, guest of Mr. Morse, no problem. She shows me to a choice window table yet, Morse must have clout.

Bleak morning light slants in through the tall bay windows, I glance around before consulting the menu. Distinguished old gents in big oil paintings glance down at the quiet clientele sitting in black captain's chairs around neatly laid tables. It's a buffet breakfast, good selection, I opt for the basic New England nourishment of orange juice, scrambled eggs, muffins, and coffee. Up I go to the buffet table, I'm wearing a clean white button-down shirt, smart club-like tie, my impeccably correct blue blazer, of course, dark-gray trousers, I feel like a gentleman and a scholar.

Leisurely breakfast, I'm reading the *Times,* story about the robbery starts on the front page, little column at the bottom. Finish it, can't help thinking about the suspect. One thing's for sure, it's got to be somebody on the "inside," in the sense that he obviously knows Harvard. Knows it cold. Another thing, the speech rhythms on that tape intrigue the hell out of me. His voice was distorted, very cleverly I thought, but he couldn't disguise the natural patterns of his speech. Seems to me I've heard that cadence before. Can't remember where, when, or by whom. Who've I met recently who went to Harvard, other than Bill Reilly himself? Nobody I can think of. Thought flicks through my mind, Samantha Reilly went to Katherine Gibbs in Boston, probably dated a ton of Harvard guys. Then I recall something strange. That first night we arrived, we're all out drinking, Reilly says what he wants to do next morning is just stroll around, refresh his memory, show Sam everything because she's never toured it. That's right, that's the way he put it, she's never "toured" it. Seems strange to me, her living in Boston and all, but maybe not. Still, she wouldn't necessarily have to tour it to know it, being married to Reilly. If it's true he loves the place so much. What was it the suspect said about that? "Humiliate you in full view of the distinguished faculty and alumni of the only institution you have ever loved in your life. Just as you did to me." Okay, without pushing it, marriage is often referred to as an institution, right?

Finish breakfast about 8:20, walk over to University Hall in the rain. Church bell is ringing, beautiful sound, cheers up the whole atmosphere. Lots more people around now, umbrellas and raincoats, most of them are headed for the big church directly across the Yard from Widener, even I know its name, Memorial Church, that's where the bell is ringing, up in a very tall, tiered white tower. Front of the church has four thick white columns, then its wide wings are brick with graceful arched windows and white frames. Like to go in and take a peek later on, must be something, judging from the outside.

Off to the left, the back of University Hall is a real contrast. Three stories of ivy-covered stone, plus some dormer windows. Long, squat, rectangular job, looks quite old. I go around its south end, walk north toward the second flight of stairs where I'm supposed to meet this guy McCauley, north entrance. On the wide strip of grass between the two stairways, here's this big statue of John Harvard. You see pictures of it all over, it's famous, there's a good shot of it on the cover of my "Facts & Figures" booklet. I'm a little early, I stop and take a gander. Statue's on a relatively high granite pedestal, looks like it's cast in bronze, larger than life, John Harvard sitting in a chair, holding an open Bible on his right knee, staring straight ahead. Looks very young, no more than thirty, seems to be contemplating what he just read. Long hair, high forehead, straight nose, strong chin, wears a minister's outfit, long robe, knickers, high socks, heavy shoes. According to my booklets, not many facts are known about John Harvard. Kid had a short, tough life, that's for sure. His father and four of his five brothers and sisters died in the London plague of 1625. His mother died in 1635, the year he received his A.M. from Cambridge. In 1636, the famous date, he was still living in London when he married the sister of a classmate. They sailed to New England in 1637, where he was granted pastures near Charlestown for raising the cattle he brought with him. He died of tuberculosis in 1638, a year after the death of his remaining brother. How he got the place named after him, he left all his library and half his estate to the new institution, he was its first benefactor.

I'm standing there, I'm looking up at this kid's serious face in the gentle rain, church bell bonging in the distance, somehow it gives me a strange sensation. When he died, he didn't have a clue they'd name the school after him. Not a clue. Nobody did until the Great and General Court of the Massachusetts Bay Colony came up with the idea. When the statue was finally commissioned on Harvard's 250th anniversary, the sculptor didn't have the vaguest idea what the man looked like. They had no photos, of course, no paintings, not even a sketch of the guy. So it's called an "ideal" of his likeness. But it's not him. Wonder what he really looked like? Rain falls, bell tolls, I remember a fact I read that really sent a shiver up my ass. When a fire destroyed the entire college library in 1764, only one of John Harvard's original 400 books survived. It was out on loan, overdue. Title? John Downame's *The Christian Warfare Against the Devil, World and Flesh.*

I continue on now, climb the second flight of stone steps, wait just inside the tall stone archway over the double doors. Off to the west, many people are entering the Old Yard now through the small gates flanking the big Johnston Gate, which remains closed. Wonder if Dennis B. Patrick, Jr., is one of the guards? Probably. Sorry, gentlemen, ya can't pack heah. Tough little bulldog, I'm still pulling for him. Hugh McCauley and his wife arrive almost on the dot of 8:30, we go through quick introductions in the rain. He unlocks the door, snaps on the light, we go in the lobby. I show him my ID now, he glances at it and nods, good-looking Irishman, mid-fifties, five-ten, maybe 165, silver-gray hair, bright blue eyes behind silver-framed glasses. His wife's name is Fran, quite a bit younger, dark hair and eyes, classy-looking kid, doesn't need much makeup.

"We read about it in the paper," he tells me. "How come the New York police are involved?"

"I'm afraid that's classified, Mr. McCauley. I'm sorry."

"I understand. Now, the man's name is James Carr?"

"Right."

"That's C-a-double-r?"

"Correct."

"And he's a summer replacement for the maintenance foreman at Widener?"

"Right. Last six years, month of August only."

"No problem."

We follow him up the stairs, his corner office is on the third floor, spacious and modern. Take off our raincoats, he says to sit down, he'll be right back. Off he goes down the hall. Mrs. McCauley and I exchange small talk. Interesting lady, she works for the Cambridge Post Office, absolutely loves it. I ask if the postal rates will stay put for a while. She laughs, she says, "All I can tell you, the twenty-five-cent stamp could be a reality as early as next year."

McCauley comes back in no time flat with the file folder in his hand. Invites me to sit at his desk, go through it, take notes if I want, but he'd rather I didn't take the original file out of the building. Says there's a copying machine just down the hall and I'm welcome to use it.

I thank him kindly, sit at his desk, glance through it quickly at first, it's relatively thin. Harvard employment application dated July 2, 1981, routine security check by HUPD and BPD, polygraph test, three letters of recommendation, IRS W-4 Withholding Certificate, six-year salary history. That's about it. I take out my pad and pen, jot down the basic information:

Carr, James Morgan
16 Garden Street
Cambridge, MA 02138
(617) 547-4800
SS#: 104-25-6187
Height: 6'-3"
Weight: 164
Hair: Black
Eyes: Brown

Doesn't give his birthdate or ethnic code, that's strictly voluntary information on employment applications now. Still, I got what I came for. I close the file, get up, hand it back to McCauley.

"Thank you very much. It was very kind of you."

"Not at all. Find what you wanted?"

"Sure did. Wonder if you could tell me something. Is Sixteen Garden Street within walking distance from here?"

He adjusts his glasses. "Sixteen Garden? That'd be—that's up past the Common, the Cambridge Common. Let's see. Okay, I know the office of Harvard Extension is number Twenty Garden, so it's—sure, it's not that far, you could walk there."

"You'd never get a cab anyway," Fran says.

"That's right," he says, "not in this weather. Is that where he lives, James Carr?"

"According to the file, yeah."

"That's it then," he says. "If he changed addresses, he'd be required to notify us. Now, do you know how to get there?"

"No, sir."

"All right." He gestures with his hands. "Now, when you leave the building, go straight ahead to the main gate, cross the street, and you'll be at the fence of an old cemetery, it's called the Old Burying Ground. Follow that fence all the way to the end, it bends around to the northwest, it ends at an old church. Then you'll see the street signs, Garden Street, just keep going straight. Sixteen—I think it's on the left side of the street as you walk up."

"I appreciate it."

"Go ahead, don't wait for us, I've got to put this back and lock up."

I thank them again, shake hands, walk down the stairs, put on my raincoat before I open the door, then snap open my umbrella. It's still falling softly, but the sky seems somewhat brighter, it's about 8:45. Crowds are walking across the Old Yard now, hundreds of umbrellas in a rainbow of colors. I go out the little gate to the right of the big one, everybody else is going the other way, showing tickets to the guard. When I'm outside, I glance at the guard at the little gate to my left. Sure enough, it's Dennis B. Patrick, Jr. Looks good in his black poncho and rain hat. I wait for a break in the traffic, jaywalk to the island in the middle, wait again, jaywalk to the sidewalk in front of the Old Burying Ground.

As I walk north along the fence, I take a long look at the graveyard in the rain. Covers a very large area, goes way back from the street. Up ahead, the sidewalk and fence turn northwest, and I can see the whole scope of it. Fine mist hangs over it, seems to swirl like fog. Gravestones nearest the fence are simple slabs, so old they've sunk about halfway into the grass, so you can't see the dates, all you can make out are some of the names, and many have an angel's face chiseled into them. For some reason, I've always been intrigued with old graveyards, I used to walk through them when I was a kid, read the names and dates, stuff like that. New York has a real old one at Trinity Church on Broadway at the top of Wall Street, but the oldest gravestone in there only dates to 1681, guy by the name of William Churcher. Alexander Hamilton's buried there, Robert Fulton, lots of famous people, but most of them died in the eighteenth century. If what Dennis Patrick told me is true, and I'm sure it is, some of these stones go way back to the early seventeenth century, not only to 1636, but much earlier. I mean, I'm keeping in mind that the Pilgrims arrived at Plymouth in 1620, but still. What Patrick said sticks in my mind, gives me a haunting feeling as I look at this graveyard in the mist. He said this is the only place that survived pretty much intact, the way it actually was 350 years ago, across from a wooden farmhouse surrounded by a one-acre cow pasture. Where, this morning, 16,000 alumni and guests are gathering to hear Prince Charles speak. Wonder if the first college students wandered around in this graveyard? I'm sure they did. Wonder if any of them are buried in there? And I wonder what they'd think if they could see that cow pasture across the street now?

Sorry for the digression, happens frequently in old age.

Back to reality: I reach the old church McCauley mentioned, Christ Church, Episcopal, now I can see a street sign, Garden Street, I just continue straight. Cross Appian Way, cross Mason Street, pass the First Church, Congregational, on the corner, lots of churches around here, finally get to a big old hotel on the corner of Garden and St. John's Road. Large vertical sign reads: SHERATON-COMMANDER HOTEL. There's a deep courtyard enclosed by tall brick wings of maybe twelve, fourteen floors, tallest building around. I go in the courtyard, see the address: 16 Garden Street. Fold up my umbrella, go inside, my shoes are sopping wet by now, ditto the bottoms of my trousers. Lobby's almost empty, it's just past nine o'clock, everybody's gone to the Convocation. I go up to the desk clerk, fairly young kid, mid-twenties.

"Good morning."

"Good morning, sir."

"Nice day for the Convocation."

Gets a smile out of him. "What can I do for you?"

"Can you tell me what room Jimmy Carr is in?"

Kid doesn't hesitate. "I'm afraid you just missed him, sir. Mr. Carr checked out yesterday morning."

"Damn. I should've called. Know how long he was here?"

"He's a regular guest, he stays with us for about two months every summer, the last week in June through Labor Day. He attends the Summer School every year."

"I see."

"This year he stayed a few days longer."

"Did he leave a forwarding address?"

"Yes, sir, but—the thing is, Mr. Carr leaves instructions every year that we shouldn't give out that information. It's written in red ink right on his forwarding-address card."

I reach in my jacket pocket, take out my ID holder with the badge, let him take a good look. "I'm working with the Harvard police on an investigation. We'd appreciate your cooperation."

Kid nods. "Okay, I think—wait a minute, I think I'd have to get permission from the assistant manager."

"Certainly."

"I'll be right back." He goes off behind the desk. I keep my ID out, glance around the lobby. Looks like it was recently refurbished. Warm colors, attractive furniture, homey atmosphere. I'd guess they have plenty of permanent residents. Has that feel to it.

Desk clerk comes back with a short heavyset man, late-fifties, gray-white hair, gold-framed glasses. When he smiles at me, his teeth are pale yellow. "I'm Carl Madden, the assistant manager, may I help you?"

"Yes, Mr. Madden." I shake hands, show him the ID. "Detective John Rawlings, New York Police Department. As I told the gentleman here, I'm working with the Harvard police on an investigation. We'd like the forwarding address of a Mr. James Carr."

Madden glances at the photo on my ID, then at my face. "Forgive me, Detective Rawlings, but I'll have to call somebody at HUPD and verify this. Who are you working with over there?"

"Chief Tannen and Deputy Chief Morse."

"Excuse me just a minute, please." He steps over to the phone on his right, dials headquarters from memory (it's easy, 495-1212), asks for Deputy Chief Morse, gets through: "Jack, Carl Madden. Fine, how about you? Good. Jack, a New York detective by the name of John Rawlings is here with me now, he says he's working with you, is that correct? Uh-huh. Okay. Oh, God, the Gutenberg thing, I see. Yes. Yes, I read about it in the paper. Okay, sure, no problem, I'll cooperate in any way I can. You bet. Sure. Thanks, Jack. 'Bye." Hangs up, turns to the room clerk: "Get Carr's forwarding-address card." Then, to me: "May I ask you a question?"

"Surely."

"Is Mr. Carr—involved in all this?"

"No, sir. We're just conducting a routine investigation on a number of people. We need to ask him some questions, that's about it."

He nods, adjusts his glasses. "The man's been with us for years now, he stays two months every summer. Very courteous, pleasant, pays his bills on time, a real gentleman. When you speak to him, will you please explain that we honored his wishes about not revealing his address? I mean, until we checked and verified that it was official police business? Would you please emphasize that?"

"I'd be glad to."

Room clerk comes back with the card, gives it to Madden. He reads it before handing it to me.

SHERATON-COMMANDER HOTEL
Forwarding Address Card

Please print or type the address to which you want your mail forwarded and leave this card with the room clerk upon your departure.

Name James M. Carr
Address 534 West 68th St., Apt. 22-C
City New York State NY Zip 10023
Special Instructions Please do not release this address to any outside party.

Signature James M. Carr

He's typed the name and address part in black ink on a manual or portable typewriter with a cloth ribbon that's half black and half red. For the "Special Instructions" part, he typed the message in red. Everything's lined up neatly, no strikeovers or erasures. His signature is interesting. It's written with a very fine felt-tipped pen in dark-blue ink. The initial caps J, M, and C are relatively large and graceful; the other letters are small and meticulously formed, making the signature easily readable at a glance. Exactly the same thing on his Harvard employment application, the careful signature, the neat typing, the attention to fine detail. You don't have to be a shrink to know this guy's obviously a perfectionist. Probably has all the other baggage that goes along with it. It's not lost on me that the two notes to Reilly were neat as hell, written on a different typewriter, but I've been a cop far too long to draw any conclusions on something like that. Lots of people type neatly and pay attention to fine detail. But I keep the comparison in mind, sure.

"Do you have a copying machine?" I ask Madden.

"Yes, in the back office."

"Mind running off a copy?"

"Not at all. Just one?"

"That's all." I hand him the card. "Appreciate it. I'll be glad to pay for it."

"That's not necessary." He hands it to the room clerk, who takes it in back.

I glance around the lobby. "I'd like to use your public phone."

He slides the desk phone to me. "Go ahead. Local call?"

"No, it's to New York." I glance at my watch. "I was supposed to call headquarters at nine."

"Okay, we have booths just down the hall to your right. Do you need some change?"

"No, thanks, I use a credit card. Goes on the expense report."

Couple of minutes later, kid comes back with the single copy, I thank them both, shake hands, off I go to make the phone call. Who am I calling? Louie Diaz. Yeah. Figure I'll give him a shot at being a real street detective again. He'll eat it up, can't wait to tell him, can't wait to hear his reaction. But first, I want to have a little fun with him, pull some stuff from the old neighborhood. Now, I'm no David Frye, but I do a pretty fair imitation of Vadney on the phone. Guys from the Nineteenth know it, they've heard it, but I haven't worked with Louie for years until this case, there's no way he could know. Okay, I'm already getting my act together as I sit in the booth, I'm smiling as I get my AT&T credit card out, I get Louie's card out, drop a quarter, go through the numbers routine, I'm practicing the Duke's voice with the operator, sounds good to me. She finishes with the usual, "Thank you for using A, T, and T," and I say, "No, no, thank *you,* honey, for doin' such an outstanding job in such highly competitive circumstances." She pauses, she can't believe her ears, she goes, "Uh, thank you, sir." Click. Ring. Louie answers himself, humble CO that he is.

"Detective Diaz."

"Diaz, Vadney, got a job for the lab."

"Yes, sir."

"Some clown—now I'll be candid with ya, Diaz, I'm *angry,* I'm fuckin' *steamin'* at this point, buddy-boy, hope you can help me out."

"I'll do my best, sir. What's the problem?"

"Some sicko excuse for a human being dropped a—Jesus, I'm *incensed* about this, I'm lookin' at it right now. Some sick, sick man got into my office this morning, somehow, and dropped a giant turd right in the middle of my desk here."

"Dropped a—what, sir?"

"A *turd,* Diaz, a big, long, thick chunk a *shit!*"

"Holy Christ."

"I mean, I'm tellin' ya, this thing's gotta be—at least a *foot long,* Diaz. And it's no fake, it's no joke, that was my first reaction when I got in this morning, I thought it was one of them plastic or rubber fake turds ya can buy."

"No, huh?"

"No. Know how I know?"

"No, sir."

"I'll tell ya how I know. I know because I *touched* it!"

"Oh, my God."

"Yeah. Yeah, I know because I—Jesus, it makes me puke to even *think* about it. I thought it was a joke, I thought maybe Doris left it there, so I went over and tried to pick it up. It was—Christ!—it was still *damp!*"

"Oh, no."

"Damp, hell, it was *soggy.* I mean, I grabbed a *handful* of it, it got all over my *hand!* Stink? Ya wouldn't *believe* it, Diaz! Totally fuckin' unbelievable stench! I went to the bathroom, I washed it off, I nearly puked in the bowl it was so bad. Now, listen up, buddy-boy, here's what I want your guys to do. And this is strictly confidential, goes without sayin', I don't want *anybody* to know about this thing, y'read me?"

"Yes, sir, absolutely."

"I want one of your technicians to get down here immediately, fast as possible—I'm talkin' full siren now—get in here, scoop this sucker up, seal it in an evidence bag, rush it back to the lab, then go right to work on it."

Louie pauses. "Chief, I—what kind of work are we talking?"

"I want a chemical *analysis,* buddy! I want a positive identification on this thing—animal or *human!* Now, okay, if it's animal, that's one thing. If it's simply a piece of bullshit, which I suspect it is because of its sheer size, okay, that's one thing. I mean, I can take a joke as well as the next guy, huh? But now, wait a minute, if it turns out to be *human,* positive ID, that's an entirely different story. That's—I consider that a serious violation of my human rights, subjecting me to such physical discomfort and mental anguish here. And if that's the case, the proven fact that it's human excrement sittin' here, then I intend to launch a full-scale investigation into the matter. Because y'know what that *means,* Diaz? If it's human, I mean?"

"I'm not, uh, sure I do, sir."

"In simple language, it means some clown had the unmitigated balls to sneak in here this morning, climb up on my desk, squat like the vile dog he is, and drop this foot-long load—*in person!* That's right, in person, because ya can't pick it *up,* I *tried,* it's too *soggy,* right? Jesus! What kinda—what kinda sick, sick man would stoop that low to do such a—such an abominable, revolting, heinous crime like that?"

"Chief, I'll be honest with you, I'll tell you the blunt truth. Offhand, off the top of my head now, I can think of only one individual in the whole department who'd have the balls to pull a stunt that gross."

"Yeah? Gimme his name, buddy! Fast!"

"Little John Rawlings."

Breaks me up, I can't help it, he says it so softly, so seriously, sounds like Brando. I recover fast: "How y'doin', Louie?"

"How'm I doin'? I'm having a fuckin' heart attack here, that's how I'm doin'. Jesus Christ, John, you really had me going there, sounds exactly like the man, you got him down."

"How long did you know?"

"How long? Almost to the end. Yeah. I mean, I could picture that foot-long wiener sittin' on his polished desk, I'm having hot flashes, I'm wondering who the fuck I can send down there to scoop it up. Then it hits me, I remember Vadney's not even in town, he's up in Cambridge with you and the commissioner. You're bad, John. You're real bad to pull shit like that on an old buddy this early in the morning, you know that, right?"

"Couldn't help myself. What're you doing for excitement these days, what's happening?"

"What's happening? Nothing's happening, that's what, your call is the highlight of the week. I'm sitting behind a desk pushing fuckin' papers, as usual, what else? On the other hand, you guys must be having a ball up there on the Gutenberg robbery, right? Shit, it made the front pages here, it was the lead story on all the TV news shows. Tom Brokaw even had a guy give a demonstration of holography, how it works, all the basic stuff. I was thinking about you, John. Then they did a whole number on Harvard's holdings in firms doing business with South Africa. You guys must be up to your ass in eggheads. Got any leads?"

"Happen to have one I'd like *you* to check out."

"Yeah? Little John, you're a *prince!*"

"Got a pencil?"

"Go!"

"Name: James . . . M for Morgan . . . Carr. C-a-r-r. Address: Five-thirty-four West Sixty-eighth Street, apartment twenty-two-C for Charley. Manhattan. Basic stats: Height, six-three; weight, one-sixty-four. Black hair, brown eyes. Age, unknown. Ethnic origin, unknown. Social Security number, one-oh-four, two-five, six-one-eight-seven. That's all I got, Louie."

"Search warrant?"

"Right. Search warrant for the apartment, list all I gave you, state the reason as suspected burglary of the Gutenberg Bible, Widener Library, that's W-i-d-e-n-e-r, Harvard University. Date of burglary, on or about August thirty. Value of Bible? Okay, it's said to be priceless, but put, say, ten million, minimum."

"They said on TV fifty million."

"Okay, good, put that. Next, you know the routine, get down to Criminal Courts, try to get Judge Richard Roffman, he's supposed to be a personal friend of Vadney's, he'll sign it without any flack. If he's not available, grab any judge, tell him the warrant's on the authority of Commissioner Reilly himself. You shouldn't have any problem."

"Don't worry about a thing, John, I got it covered. If Carr's not home, I'll get the super to let me in. What'm I looking for other than the Bible? Holographic equipment, stuff like that?"

"Holographic equipment, books on holography, even holograms. Also, books on Satanism, Satanic cults, all like that. I'll level with you, Lou, it's a long shot. A very long shot. But it's all I got."

"It's always a crap shoot, John, what the hell?"

"Okay, take my phone number, huh? Area code, six-one-seven; number, four-nine-five, seven-nine-six-one. I'll be out all morning, probably most of the afternoon, I don't know. So make the call at—let's say four. I'll try to be there. If not, I'll call you before five."

"Check."

"Oh, and Louie?"

"Yeah?"

"This is just a suggestion, just to cover all possible contingencies, okay?"

"Absolutely."

"Just in case you run into Satan up there in the apartment, all alone, it couldn't hurt to carry a crucifix, know what I mean?"

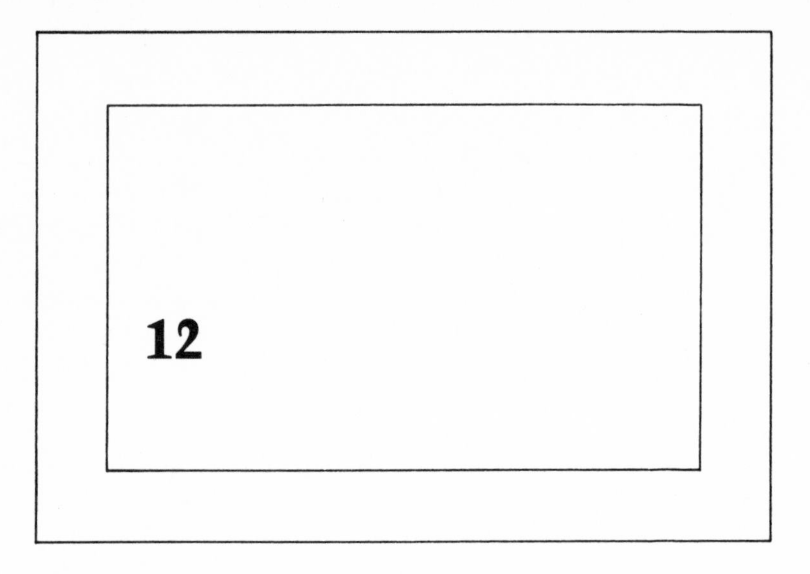

12

PRINCE CHARLES turns out to have a good lively sense of humor about this whole Convocation extravaganza here in Harvard Yard, what my program calls the Tercentenary Theatre. I'm sitting way in back with the Reillys and Vadneys, we're under our umbrellas, it's still cool and drizzling, and Charles's keynote speech is delayed about forty minutes by preliminary pomp that just gets out of hand. All 16,000 people are supposed to be in their seats by 9:30 sharp, which we are, more or less, then the music starts, now here comes a formal academic procession of the Harvard faculty, all dressed in caps and gowns, I'm talking thousands of them, all coming from the Sever Quadrangle, according to Reilly, that's way off to our right. Guess where the procession leads? To the front, of course, best seats in the joint, all roped off for them. Next we sit through songs, prayers, classical orations, speeches by university officials, all like that, ad infinitum. We're sitting there shivering, passing the binoculars, Vadney's growling that we should've watched it on TV. Charles is scheduled to speak about 10:30, he doesn't get the nod till 11:10. Receives a standing ovation, of course, strobes flash like fireworks; Princess Diana stayed home with the kids, so he's the main event for a change. Me, I can't even get a glimpse of him till everybody sits down. Once I focus the binoculars, he looks smashing in his cap and gown; Sam Reilly informs us he's wearing "the dragon-emblazoned gold silk robe of the University of Wales, where he's chancellor." Nice to know.

Charles starts off strictly ad lib, something nobody else had the balls to do: "Ladies and gentlemen, the suspense of this mammoth occasion has been killing me; you've devised an exquisite form of torture!" Gets an icebreaker belly laugh from the hoi polloi, I'm watching in the binoculars, the kid's trying hard to keep a straight face. Goes dramatic now, gestures with his robed arms: "I now realize that all the royal training which I have endured in the past has prepared me for this great occasion!" Brings the Yard down, he's got 'em in the palm of his royal mitts. Keeps ad-libbing, he's on a roll, throws away some lines about how the good people of Massachusetts regarded the English Crown during the Revolution, then he puts himself down with solid-gold panache: "Have no fear, ladies and gentlemen, I am used to being regarded as an anachronism. In fact, I am coming round to think it is rather grand!"

Grand-slam home run, bottom of the ninth, everybody's howling, applauding, kid's hit the egghead jackpot and he hasn't even started his speech. What's he do for an encore? Ready for this one? Okay, I know, I realize this might be difficult for the rational mind to accept, but it's no lie, it's just too totally bizarre for anybody to make it up, and the TV cameras have it all on tape for posterity anyway. The split second Charles starts his prepared speech—*the sun comes out!* Yeah! I'm talking *bright* sun. Drizzle stops, boom, over, gone, done. Bright sun breaks through the clouds, that's it, let there be light. Gives you pause. I mean, everybody's looking at each other, they're whispering, they're mumbling, they're giggling, what the hell's going *on* around here? What'd we just witness? Okay, I know there's a very logical explanation, all I'm saying, if something like this doesn't send a jagged icicle up your ass, you're not human, know what I mean? Two possibilities flick through my troubled brain: Either we witnessed the rare occurrence of a split-second atmospheric fluke that defies all known laws of mathematical probability, or (a far more realistic alternative for this august gathering) the real seat of all knowledge and power in the cosmos, The Harvard Corporation, just made a minor decision.

Tough act to follow, but Charles makes a serious and eloquent keynote address, calling for more emphasis on moral standards in education. Convocation finally ends at 12:25, which backs up the next event, originally scheduled for noon, "Luncheon Spreads in the Old Yard." Works out fine and dandy, because now that the sun's out, we can actually have luncheon spreads in the Old Yard.

Everybody migrates west past University Hall, carrying raincoats, umbrellas, even children. Reilly hurries us along, says every chair at every table will be filled within ten minutes flat. We manage to find a table for six right under a graceful old elm tree in front of Hollis Hall. There are long buffet tables spread out at strategic locations, and lines are beginning to form, so the girls go off immediately to make the selections while we guard the table. Around fifteen minutes later, the Sams return with trays of goodies, pass out paper plates with tunafish salad, coleslaw, potato salad, beer for us, white wine for them, paper napkins, plastic utensils. We're sitting there in the leafy shade, we got it made.

I look around, Reilly was right, Old Yard's almost completely filled already, 16,000 ticketholders. This yard is considerably longer than the other, but not quite as wide, it's like a long rectangle bordered by dorms and University Hall. Hollis faces east, it's just around the corner from Harvard Hall near the main gate. Big long dorm with simple lines, four stories of red brick, white window frames, the usual tall chimneys, and three front doors. Reilly tells us Hollis is the oldest dorm, built in 1763 at the expense of the Massachusetts Bay Colony. But that's not its only distinction. As he opens a bottle of white wine for the Sams, he tells us Hollis was occupied by the likes of Ralph Waldo Emerson, Henry David Thoreau, and John Updike, to mention just a few. Me, I never read anything by Emerson or Thoreau, too highbrow for me, but I read Updike's *Rabbit, Run.* Liked Rabbit a lot, identified with him because of the basketball stuff.

"These all freshman dorms?" Vadney asks.

"Right."

"Which one were you in?"

"None of 'em."

"Why was that?" Sam Vadney asks.

"I didn't live on campus." He pours the wine into two plastic cups, hands them to the girls. "See, these dorms are for Harvard *College* freshmen. I didn't go to the college, I went to the Harvard University Extension School, because I had to work during the day."

"What'd you do, Bill?" Chief asks.

"I drove a delivery truck for Elm Stationery Company down in Haymarket Square, Washington Street."

"Full-time job?"

Reilly opens his can of Bud. "Full-time job, nine to five. I had no choice, Walt, I was eighteen years old, I was on my own, I had to pay tuition, room, board, books, clothes, the works."

Sam Reilly holds up her cup. "Here's to Foundation Day."

Beer's not exactly cold, but it sure goes down smoothly. Conversation level around us is low and civilized, no transistor radios to be heard, grass smells fresh after the rain, who could ask for anything more? I take off my tie, put it in my jacket pocket, unbutton my collar.

Reilly sips his beer, looks off into space, smiles. "My first day here, about a week before classes started, I went in the Job Placement Center, I read all the little cards on the bulletin board, the job listings. The one for Elm Stationery, they wanted two students, they wanted to work them in four-hour shifts, and they stressed that you had to know the Greater Boston area absolutely cold. I'd never been to Boston before in my life. Okay, I removed the card from the bulletin board—something that was strictly forbidden—in effect taking the job off the market, at least until I checked it out. Next, I took the MTA down there, it was called the MTA back then. Asked directions and all, found Haymarket Square, found the store, went in and met the owner, man by the name of Vic Cohen, good man. He told me about the job, what it paid, that I'd split the day with somebody else, work a four-hour shift, depending on when my classes were. I said, 'Mr. Cohen, you don't need two guys to do this job, I can do it alone.' I said, 'I'm in Harvard Extension, all my classes will be at night.' Then I really leveled with him, I said, 'Listen, I need this job bad, I'll work eight hours straight every day, six days a week, and I'll never goof off, I swear to God, I'll give you your money's worth.' He said, 'When can you start?' I said, 'Tomorrow morning, nine sharp.' Bingo, got the job, didn't even have to lie, at least not out loud. Next morning, nine sharp, he and his helper already had the truck all loaded, set to go, nifty little pickup truck. All full of packages, big and small, all neatly labeled, separated by area. He gave me the keys, said to give him a call if I needed help. Okay, I took off, I pulled around the corner, I parked the truck, right?" He starts to laugh now, gestures with his hands. "I'd bought this big street map of the Greater Boston area, best I could find. Jesus, you wonder where you get the balls to do stuff like this when you're a kid. I whipped out the map, looked up where I *was,* right? Didn't even know *that.* Grabbed the first package, got the address, found it on the map, then I drew a line—actually drew a *line,* okay, from where I was to where I was going, the shortest route to get there. Nothing to it, I took off, no sweat at all, I had it made. About five minutes later, Jesus, I found out to my horror that most of the downtown streets were *one way!*"

Breaks us up, we can picture the kid going through all this, plus Reilly's voice and facial expressions make him look more like a street kid than ever.

"So what happened?" I ask.

Reilly shrugs. "I got the job done, I got everything delivered, came back with an empty truck before five. Sweated my ass off, didn't even have time to stop for lunch. I'll tell you one thing, I studied that map religiously from that day on. Religiously. Took me about two months to really know my way around, but I did it. Also I was delivering to a lot of regular clients, so that made it easier. Kids are amazing. Amazing resilience."

Sam Vadney sips her wine. "Where'd you wind up living?"

"A rooming house. They used to be called 'rat houses' by some of the kids, but mine wasn't bad at all. Just a bed, dresser, closet, common bathroom down the hall, but I had a nice landlady, she kept everything nice and clean, well heated when it got real cold. The address was Fourteen-A Eliot Street, the house is still there, I saw it yesterday. It's been converted into an office now, but it looks exactly the same on the outside." He sips his beer, looks off into space again. "It's just across the street from the Kennedy School of Government now, but when I lived there the school wasn't built yet, that whole area was the Boston Elevated Railway Yards. It was a huge area filled with trains, it extended all the way from Eliot Street down Boylston—Kennedy Street was called Boylston Street back then—all the way down to Memorial Drive along the river. And its west boundary was University Road. There was a fence around it, but I could see it from my window, I had a front room. I could see the old rattletrap trains snaking in and out of there. And hear them. Especially at night, the screeching of the wheels, the sharp slams of the couplings. It used to wake me up."

"Who called 'em rat houses?" Chief asks, then answers the question: "The rich kids in the college, the preppies, the elitists, right?"

Reilly starts to answer, hesitates, glances away, but I can see he's frowning and grinding his teeth. Sam Reilly gives Vadney a quick, sharp glance, hoping to get him to drop the subject fast, it's obviously a very sore point of some kind, but he doesn't see her.

"I mean, let's face it, Bill," he says, warming to the subject, "let's get it out on the table. I hate those type guys just as much as you do, always have, always will. Snooty, snobby, elitist sons of bitches, I've fought 'em all my life. It's a shame for guys like you, guys who came up the hard way, but that's the reputation Harvard's got, the reputation it's always had, that it's a flat-out elitist institution."

Reilly's reaction, I've never seen him like this before, he gets so angry so fast that when he finally looks at Vadney and points at him briefly, his hand shakes, and his voice shakes even though he speaks quietly: "Like most people who make that statement, you don't know the truth because you didn't go to school here. You heard it from people who didn't go to school here. You heard it from people who derive pleasure from criticizing institutions like Harvard because it makes them feel somehow morally superior. Labeling Harvard 'elitist' was fashionable in the past, it sounded so knowing and imposing to spit out profound value judgments like that. And maybe there was some truth to it back then, years ago, long before I got here, I wouldn't doubt it, I'll give you that in fairness. But every time you use that word to describe Harvard today, what you're doing, what you're really doing, is making a generalization that's so patently absurd, it makes *you* look absurd. Absurd and uninformed and dated."

Sam Reilly touches his arm, but he doesn't look at her.

Chief clears his throat, frowns. "Now, Bill, calm down, huh? I didn't mean it in that context. I mean, you're not—you're not accusing *me* of being absurd and uninformed, are you?"

"And dated, yeah. When you make statements like that." He sips his beer, glances away, then back. "When you make statements like that to people who know the truth. To people who know the truth firsthand because they've experienced it, or to people who've taken the time and effort to check the facts firsthand and find out the truth for themselves."

"Facts?" Chief says, smiling now. "Come on, Bill, I'm not talking about facts, I'm talking about *people.* I'm talking about snot-nosed, rich-boy preppies, that's what started this whole—conversation."

"Uh-huh. Let's just drop the subject."

"I mean, isn't it? Isn't that what started this whole—"

"That's right," Reilly snaps. "Okay, let me tell you something about snot-nosed, rich-boy preppies. Let me tell you some facts. Fact: Last year, in Harvard College alone, sixty-six percent of the whole student body received some form of financial aid. Sixty-six percent, okay? That's over four thousand three hundred undergraduates. Why? Because they had a demonstrated *need* for financial aid. They had to *prove* it, their parents had to prove it beyond any possible doubt. That's the plain, simple truth. I know it's the truth because I experienced it. I didn't even *apply* to the college, because I was ineligible for a scholarship. I was ineligible because my father's income was too high. They had to draw a line somewhere, just like they do today, and my father's income was over that line. What wasn't taken into account back then was the fact that my father had a big family to support and educate. He was up to his neck in debt because he had *five kids.* So I knew, and he knew, and my whole family knew that if I wanted a Harvard education, I'd have to go out and work for it. And I did. Elitism? You want to talk about elitism? The Harvard Extension School, where I went for four years, has a policy of *open enrollment.* That's a fact. Know what that means? It means no entrance requirements. It means no entrance examinations and no residence requirements. And that policy has been in effect for *seventy-six years.*"

"Okay, okay," Chief says. "Point well taken, Bill. No need to get upset about it, huh?"

"Seventy-six years of open enrollment. Does that sound like elitism? You're taught by Harvard faculty members in Harvard classrooms and given the opportunity to earn a Harvard degree, a four-year Bachelor of Liberal Arts degree, among others offered. Okay, it's not the Bachelor of Arts degree offered by the college, but it's a bona-fide Harvard bachelor's degree. And the tuition is a fraction of what it is in the college. Know why? Because the plain, simple *fact* is, Harvard's not interested in keeping people *out,* it's interested in offering a first-class education to anybody—*anybody!*—who's genuinely interested in learning. I was. That's why I went to the Extension School. That's why I went on to the Kennedy School of Government. And I'm still interested. That's why I'm here, that's why I'll speak at the symposium this afternoon. Because I'm interested in learning."

Chief spreads his arms. "Bill, calm down, huh? I mean, God, I wouldn't've brought it up if I'd known you felt so strongly about it. I mean, I'm sorry, okay?"

"Yeah, okay, I'll just give you the bottom line on this, then we'll drop it. Here's what really infuriates me: Early in this century Harvard got tagged with the label 'elitist,' which may have had some truth to it, but since then, this place has bent over *backwards* to go in the opposite direction. And, apparently, guys like you *still* haven't gotten the message. I mean, there's an office here, it's called the Office of Continuing Education, it's part of the Faculty of Arts and Sciences. Now, get this: It's responsible for three major programs, the Summer

School, the Extension School, and the Center for Lifelong Learning, which includes the Institute for Learning in Retirement. Now, today, the combined enrollment in these three programs alone is more than *twenty thousand* students a year. Twenty thousand students, ranging in age from—I don't know, late teens to nineties, I suppose. Call that elitism? I mean, the whole idea is totally inconsistent with the facts. The people who run these programs—I know some of them—they're probably the most down-to-earth administrators you'll find anywhere in the country, people like John Adams of Extension and David Campbell of Lifelong Learning. They genuinely *care* about people like me, they *care* about learning, they *care* about Harvard's reputation, they've dedicated most of their adult *lives* to it, what more can they possibly do? That's the bottom line on the subject, that's how strongly I feel about it."

Chief nods, shrugs, digs into his tunafish salad now, he's eating humble pie all the way. Me, I'm intrigued by Reilly's sudden anger, never saw that part of his personality before, gives me insights. If he feels that strongly about Harvard, which he obviously does, then whoever stole the Gutenberg must have known precisely how to reach the man, must have known the complicated chemistry that would make him bleed. Because, look at it this way, consider the Machiavellian machinations behind the demands: What the suspect is doing, in effect, is placing Harvard on trial before a world court that's almost unanimously opposed to apartheid. And apartheid, by definition, is *elitist.* Interesting philosophical dilemma here. Derek Bok has gone on record many times about strongly condemning apartheid, but he opposes total divestiture.

Clever suspect in more ways than one: He's elected to use the Bible as a symbol. Couldn't have picked a better symbol or a better Bible. *Starting Friday, September fifth, for each day that passes in which the divestiture order has not been given, you, personally, will receive one page from the Gutenberg Bible that has been soaked in human blood.* Even that kind of symbolism seems right on the money too, a lot of serious-minded people believe the apartheid situation in South Africa will result in a bloodbath sooner or later. So, all factors considered, it's quite a scenario the guy's drawn up here, got to give the Devil his due, as it were, no pun intended: Powerful contemporary theme wrapped in a high-tech holographic heist inside a labyrinth of Satanic deception and intrigue. We got a handle on the what, when, and where aspects of the drama, but we don't know who or exactly how, of course. And, most important to me, we don't know *why.*

Riddle wrapped in a mystery inside an enigma.

Most of the luncheon spreads in the Old Yard are still spread at 1:30, when the seven board members of the Harvard Corporation meet with Reilly and Chief Tannen in the Perkins Room of Massachusetts Hall, where the board normally meets once a month. We can see the east end of the hall from where we're sitting in front of Hollis; Reilly's going to rejoin us here right after the meeting, tell us what went down, what decision was made, then we're all going to accompany him to the symposium over at the Kennedy School of Government. Symposium is scheduled to start at two, so he's cutting it pretty thin. According to Reilly, after the board meeting Bok will hold a "brief" press conference in his office, no photographers or television cameras, and issue a release revealing the suspect's divestment demands publicly for the first time and the board's response to those demands. Of course, this place is absolutely loaded with media people from all over the world, assigned to cover the celebration, so they're getting a story of major international significance straight out of the blue. I noticed some out-of-town newspaper stands in the Square, I'll have to get the *News, Times,* and *Post* tomorrow, see how they react.

I check my Official Program here, see that dozens of events

are happening this afternoon. Other symposiums, of course, the serious part of the celebration, Prince Charles will attend one called "The Future of the City," but there are a lot of fun things too, special tours, library and museum exhibitions, classic films, open houses, music recitals, stuff like that. When I check the evening schedule, I see why Reilly wanted our rooms in Weld. We'll have the liveliest event of the night right in our own front yard from 6:30 to 10:30. It's called "Bandstand in the Old Yard" and it's right in front of Weld. Program says it'll be "an outdoor 'Pops' atmosphere with a wine and champagne bar." Eight groups will entertain, one every half hour, looks like a good variety of bands, singers, dancers. Tell you what, they haven't spared any expense on this birthday gig.

Now something surprising happens. At 1:42, we see Reilly wending his way back through the tables. I check my watch again, I can't believe this. Board meeting took only about ten minutes? Unlikely. They must have asked him and Chief Tannen to make their statements, then leave before they got down to the real business. In any event, we'll have plenty of time to make the symposium now. He finally reaches us, looks smart in his dark-blue sincere suit and dark polka-dot tie.

"Short and sweet," he says, sitting down.

"The meeting's over?" Vadney asks.

"Over. Started right on the dot, it took about—I think it was nine minutes flat. Strictly a formality, they'd had a private breakfast meeting this morning. Tannen and I were introduced, shook hands with everybody, we weren't asked to say boo. The press release was all typed up, ready to go." He takes a copy from his coat pocket, unfolds it, hands it to his wife. "One hundred copies were made, ready to pass out at the press conference. Apparently Bok drafted the thing before breakfast, submitted it to the other six guys, they approved it in principle, they just fooled around with the exact wording, that's all."

Sam Reilly nods, passes the release to the Vadneys. "Very well worded."

"No deal?" I ask.

"No deal," Reilly says. "I can't say it surprises me. Essentially, they had only two alternatives anyway. One, strict silence on the demands, no contact was ever made, don't tell the media anything at all. Because, let's face it, I'm sure mass-media coverage was a major part of this guy's motive, to embarrass the university about its stand. Okay, if they did that, they'd lose the Bible, sure, but the public would never know what was happening—unless the thief tipped the media himself, which would probably be the case, so the strategy would backfire. Number two, play it wide open, tell the media everything up front. Hold a low-key press conference, answer all questions, don't try to cover up anything. And play it down like they've done in the release. Play it down, don't give the slightest impression that this might be a hot news item. Treat it as just another extortion-like demand from an anti-apartheid extremist group; the university faces stunts like this—but less extreme—on a relatively frequent basis."

Vadneys finish reading the release, pass it to me.

News From
HARVARD UNIVERSITY

Office of News and Public Affairs · Peter Costa, Director · Holyoke Center 1060, Cambridge MA 02138 · (617) 495-1585

For Release:
Upon Receipt

Contact:
David Samson
495-1585
September 4, 1986

* * Media Advisory * *

Demands Made Known in Gutenberg Theft

At approximately 8:00 P.M., September 3, the thieves who burgled the Gutenberg Bible from Harvard University's Widener Library earlier this week contacted a third party and announced "demands" that would have to be satisfied to ensure the safe return of the bible.

The third-party contact, New York Police Commissioner William Reilly, here to speak at a symposium during the University's 350th Anniversary Celebration, was told to arrange a meeting with Harvard's president Derek Bok and tell him to call an emergency meeting of the seven-member board of directors of the Harvard Corporation today.

The major demand made of the Corporation was "to immediately vote for divestiture of Harvard's complete financial holdings in firms presently conducting business with South Africa." The penalty to be imposed for not agreeing to the demands was made explicit. Beginning tomorrow, September 5, for each day that passed in which the divestment order had not been given, Commissioner Reilly would receive one page of the Gutenberg Bible that had been soaked in human blood. The stolen volume (one of two volumes) contains 324 pages.

In a brief meeting early this afternoon, the Harvard Corporation's board of directors voted unanimously not to accede to this demand.

"It is a matter of public record that we strongly condemn apartheid," President Bok said. "That is why we will continue our responsible policy of selective divestment."

According to the most recent report of the Corporation Committee on Shareholder Responsibility (CCSR), Harvard's total investment in firms with South African operations dropped from $527 million in June 1986 to $416 million this month and is projected to continue the decline to $298 million by January 1987. In that six-month period, the University will have sold more than $130 million of holdings in seven international corporations that did not meet its investment standards for firms operating in South Africa.

CCSR revealed in its report that the seven corporations included four major oil companies (Chevron, Mobil, Royal Dutch/Shell Transport, and Texaco) and one automobile manufacturer (Ford) whose products were used by the government of South Africa to enforce apartheid. The University had also intended to sell more than $35 million of stocks and bonds in Exxon, but reversed the decision when Exxon announced plans to withdraw from South Africa.

-end-

Later that afternoon, following the symposium, I'm in my room in Weld when Louie Diaz calls from New York at the appointed time, four o'clock. His voice sounds disappointed.

"John, I think we struck out on this guy Carr."

"Yeah? Tell me about it."

"Okay, I did everything strictly by the book, I got the search warrant signed by Judge Roffman and all, I get up to the apartment on West Sixty-eighth about eleven-thirty. It's one of those big old West Side dumps, no doorman, nothing. I go in the little foyer there, first thing I notice, apartment twenty-two-C isn't listed under the name James Carr; I check the names on all the doorbells and mailboxes, no James Carr. Twenty-two-C is listed under the name T. Regnilas."

I grab my pen. "Say it again?"

"I think it's pronounced Reg-*neil*-as. T for Tom, R-e-g-n-i-l-a-s."

"Okay, go ahead."

"I ring the bell three, four times, no answer. I check his mailbox. Stuffed, John, crammed with mail. Now I look up the super, ring him, identify myself, he comes down and opens up. I show him gold, I show him the search warrant, da-da, he takes me up to apartment twenty-two-C, no questions asked. He rings, he knocks, he yells, 'Tony!' No answer. Uses his passkey, we go in, walk around, nobody home. Super says he don't want to get involved in nothing, he leaves me alone. I go to work. Okay, it's a fairly big old place, three bedrooms, two baths, but it looks to me like he lives alone. One bedroom's used as a study, another's converted into like a playroom, he's got a pool table set up in there. Single bed in the bedroom, the closet's filled with one man's clothes, I checked carefully on that. Same size jackets, same length pants, same size shoes. One man. Okay, I wander around, I start looking for holographic equipment, holograms, books on holography, books on Satanism. Spend about two hours looking for stuff like that, every room in the place. Come up empty. One thing I'll say for the guy, he's a hell of a good housekeeper, everything's all—"

"What?"

"—neat and clean. Place is shipshape, John, spick-and-span, everything. Surprised me for a guy living alone. Kitchen, bathrooms, you name it. Could that be something?"

"Possibly. I mean, it's grasping at straws, but the guy we're looking for happens to be a perfectionist. Tell me about his study, describe it."

"Okay, let's see. Desk in the corner near the window. Three large bookcases completely filled, mostly hard-cover books. Long sofa opposite the—"

"What kind of books, Lou? You looked at all the titles, right?"

"Right. What kind? I'd say—it's hard to say for sure, but most of 'em, most of the titles seemed like novels, y'know?"

"Any general category? Serious, mystery, romance?"

"Serious, mystery, yeah, lots of those. I saw some spy novels, let's see. Some Isaac Asimov science fiction, some historical stuff, some Stephen King horror novels, stuff like that."

"Nothing on the occult?"

"Nothing, John, not even close."

"Get in his desk?"

"Negative. That's one of the first things I tried. Locked."

"Anything *on* the desk?"

"Yeah. Let me think. Lamp, telephone, yellow legal pad, pencils, box of typing paper, all neatly placed."

"He's got a typewriter?"

"Yeah, off to the side, separate little table."

"Know what make?"

"What make? No. No, it had a cover on it."

"Happen to notice what brand typewriter paper?"

"No. No, I saw the label on the box, but I can't remember."

"Okay, Lou, I'm really reaching on this, but let me explain something. You didn't see the notes sent to Reilly, but they were both typed on the same brand of paper. I'm not absolutely certain the same typewriter was used because I haven't compared them; the first note is back in Reilly's office. But I want you to take down this information. Got a pencil?"

"Wait a sec. Okay."

"Where're you now, the office?"

"Right, just got back."

"Okay, take this down. On the paper, we're looking for a very high quality twenty-pound bond. It's got a watermark, three lines. It reads: Parchment Deed. Southworth Company, U.S.A. One hundred percent cotton fiber. That's it. Now, on the typewriter. It's an IBM Correcting Selectric Two, with a typeface element called Prestige Elite Seventy-two. That's all we got, that's everything. Again, it's a very long shot, but would you go back there and check it out?"

"Absolutely. Be glad to."

"Because here's the thing, here's my reasoning. The paper, the typewriter, and the typeface element are all very common, okay? They're popular products, they're sold all over the country. Now, I'm guessing, but I think probably millions of people use IBM Correcting Selectrics, and many thousands of those people use that typeface element, the Prestige Elite Seventy-two. But, according to Jim Mairs, who checked it out, a box of that particular Southworth paper sells for twenty-two bucks. That's for five hundred sheets. And that's a lot of money for typewriter paper. So—and this is strictly a gut feeling—if we found somebody using all three products in combination, the odds drop way down, they'd almost have to. The laws of probability would be in our favor."

"No question. Could be the key. That's it, I'm gone, John, I'm going back up there right now. Where you gonna be?"

"Right here. Waiting."

"I'll call you from the apartment. Collect."

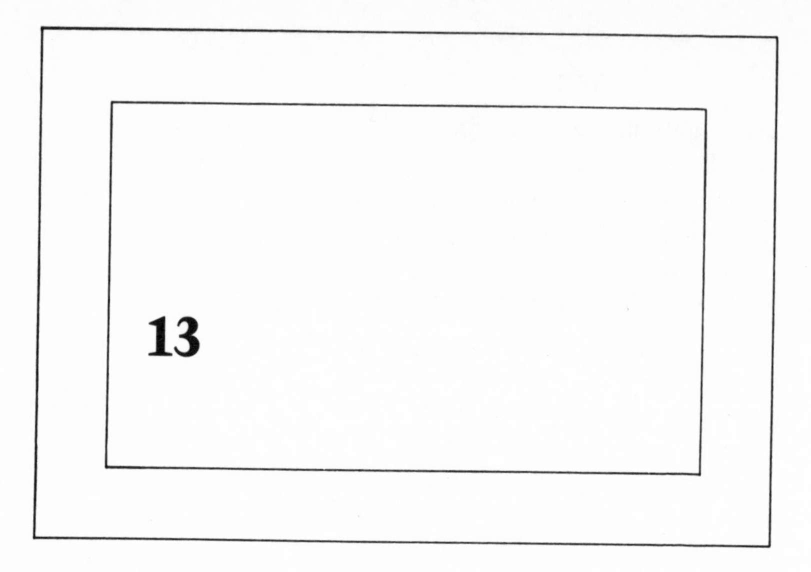

IN THE SHADE of the elms, the Old Yard outside my window is bustling with activity now at 4:20, workmen setting up long rows of wooden chairs, thousands of them, extending back from the steps of Weld, just below my room, all the way across the lawn to Matthews Hall, the freshman dorm on the west side. I'm sitting there with the window wide open, leaning against the windowsill, smoking a cigar, thinking, daydreaming, wondering. Know what I'm wondering? What it would've been like to go to school here as a kid. Yeah. Not the college, the Extension School, working during the day like Reilly did, going to classes at night, living in a rooming house close to the campus. Jesus, I mean, I actually could've done that, I could've gotten in, and I never even knew it until today. Never had a clue. Open enrollment, absolutely no admission requirements, not even an entrance examination. Tuition so low that even an eighteen-year-old kid driving a delivery truck could afford it. Wonder what four years here and a real shot at a Harvard bachelor's degree would've meant to me, to my life? Probably never would've been a cop, right? Hate to think of stuff like this, but I guess it's one of the things that happen to you when you reach my age, you can't help it, you start asking yourself questions, even the biggie: What might've been? Spooky question. Still, if I'm honest about it, I have to say I've enjoyed my career, most of it, it's been satisfying to me. Thirty-one years as a cop. Where'd the time go? Swear to God, it doesn't seem anywhere near that long. I don't feel anywhere near fifty-three, I really don't.

What might've been? Listen, wait a minute, that's *tame* compared to this next one that keeps flashing through my brain from time to time. How about: *Is it too late?* Now, there's a question to send a blizzard up the gazoo. *Is it too late?* Is fifty-three too old? Too old to do what? Lots of things, but try this one: Is that too old to enter college for the first time and start to enjoy learning for its own sake and maybe even get a degree of some kind in the bargain? Wonder how many people actually have the guts to do that? Plenty do, I know that. Wonder if *I* would? Me? A broken-down old cop who smokes cigars and drinks martinis and reads the *Daily News?* Forget it.

Is it too late? Looking out the window, that question keeps coming back for some reason, I can't seem to shake it. It's painful and pleasant at the same time. Painful because, like most people my age, I'm a creature of habit, I'm set in my ways, I'd never seriously consider anything like entering college now. Pleasant because there's this kid inside me somewhere, this kid who makes my life exciting, this little boy who's a dreamer, who's still creative because he hasn't been educated out of it, the real me inside myself, who's laughing now, deep down in his throat, the way only kids can laugh, and who's saying: Are you kidding? It's never too late, don't you know that? It's never too late until you're dead. That's when it's too late.

Telephone rings at 4:35. I glance at my watch; seems too

early for Louie. Collect call for anyone from Lieutenant Diaz in New York; will I accept the charges? Sure will.

"John. Bingo!"

"All three?"

"All three. I'm sitting here at his desk looking at 'em. IBM Correcting Selectric Two typewriter; Prestige Elite Seventy-two typeface element; Parchment Deed, Southworth Company, U.S.A., one hundred percent cotton fiber."

"Holy shit. Great work, Lou."

"Your idea all the way. But that's not all. I got something else for you that's gonna blow you out of that room. Second time around, I picked up on something I missed. In the little foyer downstairs, remember I told you about the names over the doorbells and mailboxes?"

"Yeah."

"Okay, I didn't notice before, I was too intent on finding the name James Carr, but this time I look at the name T. Regnilas, I notice the little slips of paper he typed his name on. Y'know, that you insert in the name holders? All the other names, the paper's—like faded and dirty from people putting their fingers on it. Now, the ink on his is smudged and all, just like the others, it's dirty, but the paper's not faded. That's something we look for in the lab—paper ages, it's affected by various elements, oxygen, carbon dioxide, heat, smoke, soot, all like that."

"Uh-huh. Phony name?"

"Believe it. So now, when the super takes me up in the elevator this time, I do a very simple thing. I know he didn't look at the name on the search warrant when I showed him the first time, he was listening to me talk, he just wanted the apartment number. So now we're going up in the elevator, I ask him, I go, 'Do you know the correct spelling of this guy's name?' He says, 'Yeah, I think it's—' John, you jotted down his name, right?"

"Yeah, got it right here: T. Regnilas."

"Okay. Now, spell the name backwards."

"Backwards? S-a-l-i-n—oh, my God."

"Salinger. Anthony Salinger."

Now he comes closer, you should see this, he's a white-haired old black man, he's got a white goatee, he's hunched over the handlebars, long thin legs riding high on the pedals, intense expression on his face, like his mind's on the 1988 Olympics, but the message never reached his body.

"John? You okay?"

"Yeah. Yeah, Louie, I—"

He keeps studying the wall and pedestal, dark eyes moving up and down, side to side, doesn't even glance at us when he speaks—suddenly, sharply, spitting out the words like he's known us for years: "Diaz, Rawlings, this is unconscionable, this is deliberate, reckless destruction of private property owned by the Archdiocese of New York."

"John, speak to me. You all right?"

"Yeah, I'm—I'm fine. Excellent work, Louie. First class all the way. Okay, let's see, let's figure the time element here. You said his mailbox is completely filled?"

"Crammed."

"New York schools start the first Monday after Labor Day, so that'd be—?"

"Next Monday, the eighth."

"Means he's probably still here. And he's probably got the Bible with him."

"But you don't know where, right?"

"No. He was staying at a hotel, but he checked out yesterday. He left the forwarding address I gave you."

"Get the Boston police to put out an APB. You can give 'em a good description now, everything. Tell 'em to concentrate on airports, train stations, bus stations, rent-a-car offices, the whole routine."

"Good idea. Will do."

"Tell you what. DMV's still open, I'll put in a call right

now, see what they've got. Also, I'll run him through NCIC soon as I get back, all three names."

"Okay. I think he's clean, but it's worth a shot, sure. And, Lou, call headquarters, speak to Matt Murphy, ask him to put the apartment house under twenty-four-hour surveillance, just in case, now through Sunday night."

"Done."

"Call me if you come up with anything at all. I've got to get together with Reilly and Vadney now, tell them what you found. Louie, I can't thank you enough, really, you broke it wide open."

"My pleasure. Hey, know something?"

"What's that?"

"I would've made a hell of a good street detective."

Now things start to get a little wild around here. We have a meeting in Reilly's room, the girls are out shopping, I bring Vadney and him up to date on everything. First time I mention Anthony Salinger, Reilly says he remembers the guy well, he was janitor at St. Michael's when Reilly was a student there, 1956–59, says they used to call him "J.D.," after J. D. Salinger, the famous novelist. I ask if he ever had any trouble with the man, he says no, not that he can recall. I ask if he ever humiliated the man in front of the faculty and students, he says absolutely not, at least he can't remember anything even remotely like that. Says he liked the guy, they got along fine. Anyhow, there's no time to lose now, Reilly calls Commissioner Malloy, gives him an update and a detailed description, Malloy says he'll order an APB on Salinger, effective immediately. Chief gets on the horn with Jack Morse, fills him in, Morse agrees to assign as many men as possible to check the hotels, motels, and rooming houses in the immediate vicinity, all three names, plus the description.

Telephone rings at 5:07. Reilly answers, goes, "Yes, speaking. Oh, my God. When? Did you see him? Okay, thanks, we'll be right down." Hangs up, sets his chin, turns to us. "The guard downstairs. An envelope was slipped under the door, addressed to me, marked 'Urgent. Deliver Immediately.' He didn't see the person."

"God damn," Chief says.

Reilly starts for the door. "You're right on the money, John, he's here all right. Come on, let's see what he's up to now."

We hurry down the flight of stairs, guard's got the envelope in his hand, standard business size, white, Reilly's name and address neatly typed.

Reilly holds it up to the light first, opens it, doesn't bother to handle it carefully, reads quickly. He frowns, shakes his head, reads it again. "This is absolutely—*weird.* This guy must be insane." Passes it to Vadney.

Chief reads slowly. "Holy shit. I don't *believe* this guy." Passes it to me.

> "Blessed are they which are persecuted for righteousness' sake: for theirs is the kingdom of heaven."
>
> Matthew
> 5:10
>
> Reilly:
>
> The Gutenberg is back. If you want to know why, be inside the Old Burying Ground tonight, exactly 7:59.

Typeface is definitely Prestige Elite 72, I know it at a glance by now. I hold the paper up to the light, check the three-line watermark, big and bold: PARCHMENT DEED, SOUTHWORTH CO., U.S.A., 100% COTTON FIBER.

"Why the hell would he put it *back?*" Chief asks.

"Because he never intended to keep it," I tell him.

"How do you know that?" Reilly asks.

I hand him the note. "Check the typeface and watermark against the second note. Both identical. Both typed in New York. My guess, they were both written long before he stole the Bible."

Reilly turns to the guard. "Please call Deputy Chief Jack Morse and ask him to meet us at Widener Library with his keys." He gets out his wallet, pulls Morse's card. "His personal number is four-nine-five, one-seven-eight-four. Tell him it's an emergency. We'll be at the rear door."

Off we go again, around the corner of Weld, asphalt walks are crowded with strollers, sun's still out, but it's cool. Those thousands of pots of red and white chrysanthemums still cover the front steps of Widener, now Reilly explains something that never occurred to me this morning: Widener was closed all day today and will be closed tomorrow for the next Convocation, he says it's called "The University in a Changing World," starts at ten. All 16,000 chairs are still in place, TV scaffolds are all there, everything's ready. If Widener was closed all day, that means Salinger had the place to himself, with the exception of the watchmen guards, probably round-the-clock, but they can't get into the Memorial Rooms. All he'd have to do is know their routines cold, which I'm sure he did. One thing he doesn't know—he couldn't know yet—is that we know his identity.

Okay, we go around to the rear entrance of Widener and wait for Jack Morse up by the door. It's now 5:14.

"Where's this Old Burying Ground?" Vadney asks.

"Across the street from the main gate," Reilly says. "It's one of the oldest cemeteries in the country."

"Any idea why he'd want you there?"

"Not a clue, Walt."

Chief nods, takes a deep breath. "In my opinion, you'd be well advised to stay away this time, Bill. I mean, an old graveyard at sunset? We're playing with a real psycho here, no question about it."

"Psycho or not, I'll be there," Reilly says. "I don't know what his game is, I haven't seen the man in—let's see, twenty-seven years now. But he's simply not gonna scare me or intimidate me. No way. Sooner or later, we're gonna collar this fucker."

"On what charge?" I ask him.

"What *charge?*"

"At this point, we don't even have prima facie evidence," I tell him. "Everything we've got to link him to the robbery is strictly circumstantial. None of it would hold up in a court of law. Think about it. We could nail him on lesser charges, sure. Obviously, he used falsified documents when he applied for the temporary job here six years ago."

"Either that," Reilly says, "or he used falsified documents to get the job at St. Michael's. But I doubt it, that was at least—hell, that was at least thirty years ago, he was there when I was a freshman in nineteen-fifty-six. No, Salinger's got to be his real name. But either way, he used a phony Social Security card, which is a federal offense, so we got him there."

Morse arrives at 5:18, Reilly shows him the note first thing, his reaction is the same as ours was, total astonishment. Says he simply can't believe it, he won't believe it until he sees the thing. We go inside, he deactivates the alarm system. As we walk around the halls to the lobby, I bring him up to date on Louie's work in New York and he's really pleased that we've come up with something solid. No guards in sight, we go up the white marble stairway to the first landing. First room is lighted, we can see it through the windows in the tall double doors. Same routine as before, he unlocks the right-hand door, steps to the right to deactivate the alarm. Tells us he didn't alert the Wackenhut Corporation, the firm that monitors the closed-circuit TV, so they should call almost immediately. We go to the second set of double doors, I glance up at the TV cameras in the four corners, the red lights are on, they're operating. Morse unlocks the right-hand door, opens it, steps to the right to deactivate the alarm.

"It's back!" he shouts. "Christ, it's back!"

And it is. Not *in* the special glass display case, but on *top* of it, opened to the middle. All of us just stand there in silence for a few seconds. I glance at my watch automatically. It's 5:21. Now I go over and touch the Bible, I can't help myself, I've got to be sure it's there. It is.

Telephone rings; Wackenhut's right on the job. Morse goes to the librarian's desk, answers it, identifies himself, then gives a special code, letters followed by numbers. He tells the guy to expect various people going in and out of here for at least several hours. Hangs up, comes back.

Now I know how Salinger got past the TV problem.

"Jack," I say, "you gave a special code, right?"

"Yes, that's a standard part of the system. You're supposed to call them beforehand, before you enter the rooms. If you don't, they call immediately to verify authority."

"Complicated code?"

"No, not really. WMR, four-nine-five, two-nine-seven-one. The WMR stands for Widener Memorial Rooms, the number is simply the telephone number for this room. It's not listed on the phone itself."

"How many people know that code?"

"The same people who have keys to the rooms and know the six-number combination to the alarm system: Chief Tannen and me, the curator of the Widener Collection, the maintenance fore—" He goes back to the phone fast, dials a number. "Deputy Chief Morse again, WMR, four-nine-five, two-nine-seven-one. Were you alerted with this code earlier today? I see. How about the nine-to-five shift? Uh-huh. Don't you maintain a *log* for those calls? Why *not?*" He listens carefully, sits on the edge of the desk, facing away from us. When he speaks again, his voice is relatively calm: "No, no,

I understand. I understand, it's perfectly logical. Right. Okay, many thanks." Hangs up, comes back again.

"They don't keep a *log?*" Reilly asks.

"No. Not unless they're specifically directed to do so. The rationale is simple, it's a more effective fail-safe system than most major corporations they monitor, because fewer individuals are involved. Knowledge of the code is restricted to those few people who also have the special keys and the alarm combination. Any of those three elements is worthless without the other two. So, logically, anyone who calls and uses the correct code has automatic authorization to enter the rooms."

"And Salinger had it all," Chief says.

Morse nods, glances at the Gutenberg. "Obviously, we'll have to change the code now, as soon as possible. He had everything this time except an updated key card to the display case. Dr. Tas changed the code right after the robbery, so the second volume wouldn't be at risk when he put it in. He hasn't even had time to put it in yet. The most puzzling part of this whole thing, for me at least, is how this guy managed to get the previous key card. Dr. Tas has the only updated, operable card at any given time. Normally, he changes the electronic code every three months, at the same time he changes the volumes."

"Was a card ever stolen?" I ask.

"No. No, in fact, I questioned Dr. Tas about that, that's one of the first questions I asked him. He keeps the card in a safe in his office, where he also keeps the other volume of the Gutenberg. When we called him at home, just after we discovered the theft, he went straight to his office first—before coming in here—and opened the safe. The card was still there, together with the second volume."

"Where's his office?" I ask.

"Widener, third floor." Morse looks at his watch. "Listen, I'll give you a brief rundown of the routine, then I'll have to start making telephone calls. Here's what happens. He receives a newly coded card from Yaletronic every three months, that's been the routine since nineteen-sixty-nine. The new card arrives on the fifteenth of the month every February, May, August, and November—unless the fifteenth happens to fall on a Sunday, in which case it's delivered Monday. The very same day the card arrives, Dr. Tas opens his safe, takes out the previous card, which is still operable at that point, takes out the other volume of the Gutenberg, and comes down to this room. He's never used an armed guard to do this, he just doesn't like the idea. Anyway, he opens the display case with the 'old' card, changes the electronic code in the locking mechanism of the case itself, and tests the new card to be sure it's compatible with the new code. Then he changes the volumes, closes the case, and tests to be sure it's locked. Finally, he simply goes back up to his office with the other volume, places it in the safe together with the new card, and cuts the old card in half. At this point, the old card is useless anyway, but he cuts it in half and discards it. He's gone through this routine for seventeen years now, every three months. He says there's never been a departure from his routine."

"How's the new card delivered?" Reilly asks.

"Registered mail, return receipt requested. He has to sign for it personally. Nobody else is authorized to accept it. So that eliminates any possibility that it was intercepted before reaching him."

"What kind of safe is it?" I ask.

"A large Mosler. It's fairly old, he had it installed in nineteen-sixty-nine, but it's adequate."

"Combination?" I ask.

"Yes." He glances at his watch again. "I'll have to start making phone calls now. But the key element, in my judgment, is that this guy simply *had* to get in that safe. I mean, there's just no other logical possibility."

I'm inclined to agree with him. A seventeen-year-old Mosler doesn't present an impossible task to a real pro, particularly with the kind of electronic tools I've seen over the past several years. Surprises me about Dr. Tas. Still, according to Morse, until that article appeared in *Harvard Magazine* last spring, very few people even knew the Gutenberg *has* two volumes. But here's an interesting question: Why didn't Salinger steal the second volume while he was at it? Probable answer: It would've complicated his timing and his strategy; he had no way of knowing how many times Dr. Tas opened that safe in the course of an average week. The theft had to take place between August 15 and August 31; my guess, it was last weekend, probably Saturday night, August 30. I think the hologram was in place in the case on Sunday, August 31, Salinger's last official day on the job. Makes sense. Seems logical.

Another thing that makes sense to me now: Salinger knew beyond any reasonable doubt that the Harvard Corporation wouldn't budge an inch on its selective divestment policy. He planned and executed a master strategy in which every move was meticulously calculated far in advance for maximum media impact. First, a theft that was theoretically impossible. Second, demands that would not only call attention to Harvard's divestment policy, but place the university on trial before a world court unanimously opposed to apartheid and emotionally incapable of considering other points of view. A vital contemporary issue sizzling in the glasshouse of public opinion. Press release went to the media about 1:45 this afternoon, probably too late to make the afternoon editions of the papers, but a shoo-in for local evening TV news here and in other major cities. I mean, let's face it, here's a juicy little moral dilemma of national interest stuck in the middle of a star-spangled historic egghead celebration, what could be better copy? Media people thrive on this kind of crap, they eat it up, somebody pointing the guilty finger at a great institution just as it pats itself on the back in a glitzy celebration. But now, wait a minute, talk about timing? Next news peg turns out to be a skyhook balloon headed for the cosmos of Golden Rule morality. When Derek Bok calls another press conference and gives the nod to another low-key "media advisory," this little item will explode into a fast-breaking hard-news bonanza, front-page and lead-story network news coast to coast. I can see the headlines in the *Daily News* now: IT'S BACK! Priceless Bible Returned!

But the question the media will run editorials and commentaries about is a serious issue: *Why?* Why did he return it? To prove a philosophical point? To say to the world, in effect, this was not a crime, this was a symbolic act; we lost a battle, but we'll win the war? If that's what he's saying, I don't buy it. The truth is, this was a no-win situation for Harvard. There was simply no way the board could back down on its policy and give in to such demands, particularly in the glare of world media attention. No way. It was never even an option. I'm no media expert, but my guess is that very few lines will be written to explain (much less defend) Harvard's position on selective divestment, which happens to be shared by quite a few prominent economists in this country. Okay, papers like the *Times* and the *Journal* will explain it and analyze it and all, but not the majority, and certainly not the tabloids. Why? That's not *news,* that's not entertainment, that's not what people want to read or see or hear. Salinger knows that. Here's a guy who understands mass-media psychology. He knows that if he went ahead with his threat and sent Reilly each page of the Gutenberg soaked in human blood, day after day for 324 days, that little gesture would be dropped by the media after day one. It wouldn't be dramatic after that, it wouldn't be news, it'd be a rerun, it'd be boring. But now, give the Bible back, undamaged, unscratched, undefiled, and you've created the stuff of drama, you've made a statement, you've made *news.*

But something's missing here, the part that intrigues me most: What's Reilly got to do with all this? That's an equation the media haven't even picked up on, at least not yet, thanks to Derek Bok's discretion. Boys and girls of the media still view Reilly's role as that of a necessary but unimportant third-party contact, a figurehead police liaison between the principals. But if he's not one of the principals, he sure has a lot of scenes. What the hell did he ever do to Anthony Salinger? If Reilly can't honestly recall anything even remotely resembling a public humiliation of the man, then what's going on, and what's Satanism got to do with it? Of course, we're talking about something that happened between twenty-seven and thirty years ago, when Reilly was between the ages of, say, fifteen and eighteen. Boys that age aren't noted for thoughtful behavior, especially street fighters, which Reilly obviously was. I know, because I was one; I'm not even guessing, I'd know the body language of a New York street fighter five alleys away. My opinion, he did something that hurt Salinger deeply, really made him bleed, cut into a terribly raw nerve of some kind, and the wound hasn't healed, it's still festering.

When we get back to Weld about 6:20, Salinger's still on my mind. I keep visualizing his face as he studied the damage to the wall, I keep hearing his voice as he spit out the words. Angry man. Bright man. Old man. Wonder what motivates a guy of that age to pull a stunt like this? I'm sitting there, looking out the window, people are starting to fill the front rows for "Bandstand in the Old Yard" that begins at 6:30. Most of them are drinking wine or champagne, they got a couple of long bars set up down there. I could use a drink myself, but I want to be sharp as possible for this thing in the Old Burying Ground at 7:59. Reilly wants to leave at 7:30, go over there and look around while there's still plenty of daylight. I'm looking through my pile of brochures and booklets, trying to find something that would give basic information on the Old Burying Ground, when I run across this article in a booklet called "350 Years: Historical Notes on Harvard." Article's titled "The Black Presence at Harvard," by Caldwell Titcomb, '47, A.M. '49, Ph.D. '52. Long and fascinating piece, well written, obviously well researched, the work of a scholar. I read the whole thing quickly, can't put it down, then I go back and reread the first part slowly.

The earliest reference to a black at Harvard was the admission by the wife of the College's first head that a slave had lain on a student's bed in 1639. As the 17th and 18th centuries rolled on, the list of leading slave-holding families in Massachusetts contained the names of numerous Harvard men, including Presidents Increase Mather (1685–1701) and Benjamin Wadsworth (1725–37). In the 18th century and later, blacks in and around Boston were encouraged to attend Harvard's Commencement, which became for them the most festive day of the year; in 1773 they could have heard two seniors debating the legal pros and cons of enslaving Africans.

For most of the 19th century, the well-to-do undergraduates each had a black servant called a "scout" (a term borrowed from Oxford). Blacks later served as janitors, laboratory custodians, and waiters in Memorial Hall, where students ate from 1874 to 1924.

If the low opinion of the black race held by Harvard's most famous 19th century scientist, Louis Agassiz, was echoed by science deans Henry Eustis '38 ("little above beasts") and Nathaniel Shaler '62 ("unfit for an independent place in a civilized state"), the faculty did have its outspoken Abolitionists, such as Henry Wadsworth Longfellow and James Russell Lowell '38. Divinity School professor Henry Ware Jr. '12 was the founding president of the Cambridge Anti-Slavery Society in 1834, and the first anti-slavery novel, *The Slave* (1836), was written by Richard Hildreth '26.

The 1650 Charter under which Harvard still operates spoke of "the education of the English & Indian Youth of this Country," and a few Indians were enrolled between 1653 and 1715, though only one completed his degree (Caleb Cheeshahteaumuck in 1665). But the Charter said nothing about the education of blacks, and none appeared on Harvard's roles until the middle of the 19th century.

The earliest baccalaureate degrees that American colleges

awarded to blacks went to Alexander Twilight (Middlebury, 1823), Edward Jones (Amherst, 1826), John Russwurm (Bowdoin, 1826), and Edward Mitchell (Dartmouth, 1828).

The first black student to enter Harvard College would have been Beverly G. Williams, in 1847. He was an outstanding scholar in a preparatory-school class that included President Edward Everett's own son. Everett himself proclaimed the lad to be the best Latinist in his class, and Williams' virtues were even debated in the U.S. Congress. When grumblings were voiced about accepting a black student, Everett stated that, "as he will be very well fitted, I know of no reason why he should not be admitted." Unfortunately, a few weeks before the academic year began, Williams died of tuberculosis two months short of the age of 18.

Consequently, the first blacks to begin studies at Harvard were not in the College but the Medical School. In 1850, the celebrated Martin R. Delany and two other blacks were enrolled. Their presence split the white student body into two camps, and the faculty voted that the trio would have to leave at the end of the term. So it was not until the 1869 Commencement that Harvard would have its first black degree recipients: Edwin C. J. T. Howard at the Medical School, George L. Ruffin at the Law School, and Robert T. Freeman at the Dental School (its first graduating class). Ruffin and Freeman were the first blacks in the country to receive their respective degrees. Ruffin became the first black judge in Massachusetts; and Freeman, though he died young, had a dental society named for him.

The first black student in the College was Richard T. Greener, who entered in 1865 and took his degree in 1870, winning the chief prizes in writing and speaking along the way. He became a philosophy professor, law school dean, and foreign diplomat, and was an acclaimed orator. Radcliffe, founded in 1879, had in 1898 its first black A.B. recipient, Alberta V. Scott, although a black alumna of Smith, Mary S. Locke, had already taken an A.M. in 1893.

For some time the number of black students in Harvard College remained small, though since the Class of 1899 there have been only three classes without black members. A marked surge in black enrollment occurred starting with the class of 1963, and an enormous leap to more than 100 students a year began with the Class of 1973, the first class to be admitted following the national trauma of Dr. Martin Luther King Jr.'s assassination (Harvard and Radcliffe admissions were merged in 1975). The cumulative number of black men and women enrolled as undergraduates at Harvard and Radcliffe through the Class of 1986 comes to about 2,600. . . .

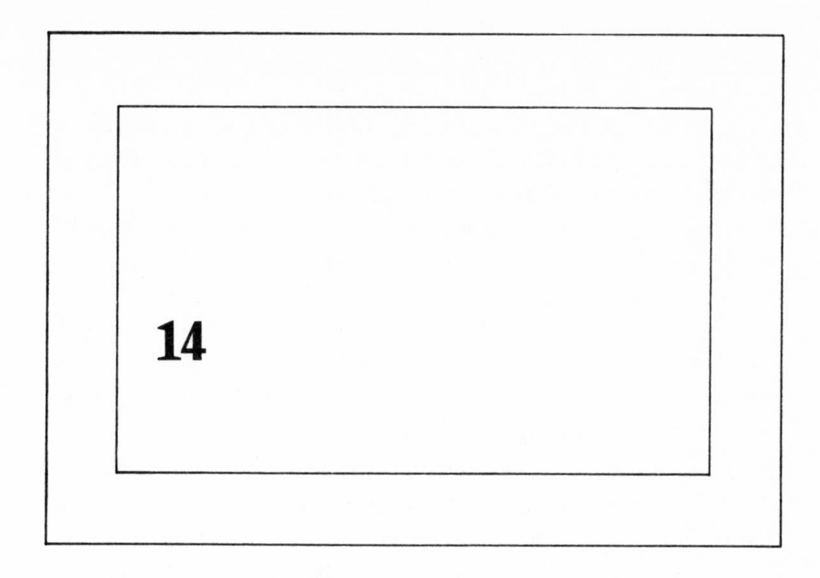

DEEP SHADOWS from the crowns of oak, maple, and elm trees slant east across the grass of the Old Burying Ground at 7:55, and only the half-sunken gravestones near the fence at Massachusetts Avenue are still touched by gold light. Morse, Reilly, Vadney, and I stand far back, north of the presidents' graves behind the First Church, Unitarian, and if a cemetery can be described as haunting and beautiful in the same breath, this is it, particularly at sunset. The air is chilly and the breeze carries a pleasant mixture of odors—trees, grass, earth, river—the sharp smells of oncoming night. I'm looking toward the Yard across the street and the spire of Memorial Church is still bright white, towering behind the white cupola of Harvard Hall. Off to the right, beyond Massachusetts Hall, the "Bandstand in the Old Yard" is in full swing now and we can hear the distant music above the rhythm of heavy traffic. We've had a chance to wander around, I've read many of the gravestones, and I like the place, it gives me a sense of history and perspective. More than that, if I'm honest with myself, much more. Somehow, in a way that's almost impossible to explain, or even understand, old graveyards give me a feeling of peacefulness and resignation about death.

Jack Morse, he's a stand-up guy, despite all the responsibilities he had to juggle this afternoon, he still had the foresight to send a team of six officers to the Old Burying Ground about 6:30 to search for incendiary devices. They searched with metal detectors for a full hour, covered every inch of ground, even climbed up in the trees. They were still here when we arrived. Came up empty, of course, but it sure gives us a secure feeling to know that we're working with a real pro like Morse. Talk about a busy man having time for everything, he even managed to get an arrest warrant drawn up on Anthony Salinger, a.k.a. James Carr, a.k.a. Tony Regnilas, charging him with a catch-all laundry list ranging from suspicion of grand theft to suspicion of falsifying local, state, and federal documents to obtain employment. It's all strictly by the book, signed by a judge. Next thing, he even thought to bring along bulletproof vests for all of us and, when Reilly politely declined, he absolutely *insisted* on it, said he wouldn't take responsibility for our security, said he wouldn't even go in with us. We're wearing vests. Like the man's style, he's every bit as stubborn as Reilly himself, which is saying something. Only one item he didn't think to bring along, a flashlight, but we didn't think of it either.

Still, at eight o'clock we'll have enough twilight to see by, I'm sure of it, judging by the last few nights. Starts to get really dark around here about 8:15 to 8:30. Now a horrible thought comes to mind. Imagine trying to get out of this place in the dark, tripping over half-sunken gravestones, walking into low-hanging tree branches and all? I mean, we'd have to literally feel our way out of here, and this is a very big field of daisies, let me tell you. Not that any of us would be scared or anything like that. Right? What's to be scared of? Only a weird Satanist psycho creeping up behind us in the dark, okay? Only a weird

Satanist psycho letting loose a gaggle of fast-and-dirty king cobras to slither around between the old gravestones. Sorry I brought it up.

Simple fact of the matter is, if Salinger runs true to form, he won't be here, he'll have some sort of high-tech surprise set up, although I don't understand what he's got to gain, he's already made his point loud and clear. I don't honestly think the man's dangerous, he hasn't hurt anybody so far, but I've been in this business too long to underestimate anybody. Can't help remembering what my old semipro baseball manager used to say, black guy by the name of Art Mitchell, played his whole pro career in the Negro National League. He used to tell us: "Never underestimate the hitter, no matter who he is. Anybody standing up there at the plate with a bat in his hands should be considered dangerous." How right he was. Expect the unexpected.

Clang. Wrought-iron gate next to the church slams shut, up ahead to our right. Figure of a tall, lean man appears, can't see him clearly in the shadows. I glance at my watch: 7:58. He doesn't hesitate at all, knows exactly where he's going, turns right, walks straight toward the fence along Massachusetts Avenue, carrying a fairly large object in his right hand. He walks with a limp. "*He gave his name in several styles, probably all aliases, so I will not list them here . . . I don't know where he is now. About ten years ago someone told me he had been seen and recognized on Cape Cod. He was still walking with a decided limp.*" His back is in silhouette against the distant headlights and streetlights until he reaches the row of gravestones nearest the fence, then his figure flashes into the patch of remaining sunlight. His hair is white, he wears a light-blue windbreaker and jeans. He stops in front of a gravestone now, stoops, places the large object on the grass; it's a bouquet of colorful flowers. Slowly, he kneels down, bows his head, and prays.

"Stay here," Reilly tells us quietly.

He walks straight toward the man, slowly, his silhouette seeming small as he passes under the branches of an old elm. Traffic noises are mingled with distant music and the voices of women singing. Breeze is much stronger now, cooler, swaying the heavy crowns of the trees, moving their long shadows, bringing the smell of rain. Reilly finally emerges into the patch of sunlight, his head appearing first, as if disembodied, then the light moves quickly down his yellow jacket, worn over the vest. He stops behind the kneeling figure, stands motionless, hands by his sides, waiting.

Almost involuntarily, I walk toward them. I don't like the idea of Reilly being alone with this guy, who's probably Salinger, although I'm still not sure, I haven't seen his face. I mean, it's always possible this guy could be a stranger, an old man bringing flowers to a grave, paying his respects. Doubtful, but possible. If it's Salinger and he wants to talk, that's fine, I won't interfere, I'll stand back. Let him have his say, he's not going anywhere. As I walk, I hear the soft footsteps of Morse and Vadney coming quickly behind me. I stop in the deep shadows about fifteen feet behind Reilly, unbutton my jacket, reach back, unsnap the hammer strap of my holster, grip the handle of my revolver. Morse and Vadney come up silently and spread out to my left; we're each about six to ten feet apart. Morse, who's next to me, opens his jacket, reaches back, and I hear him unsnap his hammer strap.

In the soft twilight, the old man finishes praying, makes the sign of the cross, holds his head erect. He speaks without turning: "Is that you, Reilly?"

"Yes."

"Do you know my name yet?"

"Yes."

"You must have good men."

"The best."

"I'm going to stand now."

"Keep your hands in plain sight."

Salinger uses both hands to help himself up from his knees, gradually, with difficulty. Now he holds his hands at his sides as he turns. Turns slowly, deliberately: His curly white hair, white eyebrows, and trim white goatee make his sharp facial features appear very black. His windbreaker is unzipped to his chest, revealing a blue workshirt, collar open. He's as tall as I remembered, at least six-three, but much leaner somehow, almost gaunt, and much older in this light, I'd guess mid-seventies. He's frowning, he looks angry, but he keeps his voice strangely calm. "It's been a long time."

"Twenty-seven years."

His dark eyes dart side to side now, narrowed against the sun, but I'm sure he can see us in the shadows. "Gentlemen, I'm not armed, I wouldn't be that stupid, so I urge you to relax as much as you can under the circumstances. I have no intention of causing bodily harm to this man. I have something to show him. I have something to say to him. Then I'll be at your disposal."

Reilly puts his hands on his hips now, spreads his legs, looks short and chunky in the heavy vest. Snaps his words like orders: "All right, let's cut the *crap* here. I don't know what kind of weird shit you're into now, but let's get *on* with it. I mean, frankly, if you want it flat-out, I'm sick of all this *garbage,* Salinger. I'm sick of *you.* You belong in a fuckin' *mental* hospital, you're a menace to society. But, sure, long as we're here, what the hell, go ahead. You got something to show me, *show* it. You got something to say to me, *say* it."

Salinger lets that sink in, folds his arms over his chest, speaks so quietly I can hardly catch all the words: "God, it's hard to believe, but it's true. You really haven't changed all that much over the years, have you? You're still essentially the same kid. The same arrogant, obnoxious, foulmouthed little wise guy you were as a teenager."

"I won't dignify that with a reply. You're obviously a sick man. We've got a warrant for your arrest. I suggest you come along with us quietly."

"There's no need for a warrant, Reilly. I'm giving myself up. Otherwise I wouldn't be here. I freely admit to borrowing the Gutenberg and returning it unharmed. I promised I'd tell—"

"*Borrowing* it?"

"That's correct. That's exactly what I did. I had no intention of keeping it. But, to continue, I promised I'd tell you why I returned it if you came here tonight. I keep my promises. The reason I returned it is that I happen to be a deeply religious man. I borrowed it for a specific purpose and that purpose has now been served successfully. I'd planned to do it for many years. And I researched every detail for the past six years. I planned it down to the exact time, day, and date: The most opportune moment of the past fifty years. It wasn't the first attempt. I attempted to borrow both volumes in nineteen-sixty-nine, but I failed, because I hadn't done my homework properly. I'm afraid I was less sophisticated back then. I needed to learn patience. I needed to do the required research. And I did. I'm proud of my accomplishment. I believe its ramifications will be felt for many years. If you define it as a crime, then it was clearly a victimless crime. In any event, I'll be proud to go to prison for it, if I must."

"You'll go to a mental hospital. That's where you belong."

"Yes, I suppose your logic is correct. A mental hospital is the appropriate place for anyone who had the audacity to make such an outrageous symbolic statement at such an inappropriate moment in the history of a great institution of higher education. Well, so be it. I'm seventy-three years old now. Almost all my friends are dead, my old friends, my real friends, the people I grew up with. I was born and raised right here in Cambridge, Reilly, did you know that?"

"No, I didn't."

"Right here in Cambridge. So were my father, my grandfather, and even my great-grandfather. That's as far back as I can trace my heritage. You're standing in the presence of part of my heritage now." He turns, steps up to the gravestone near the flowers, gets down on one knee, rubs his fingers over the face of the half-sunken stone. "It's a little difficult to read the inscription anymore, it's very worn, it was just a simple slab anyway. But when I was a kid, I discovered that sometimes, in late twilight, when the sun hits it at just the right angle, the shadows give just enough definition to read it. Can you see it from there, Reilly, can you read it?"

"No, I'm afraid not." He walks in much closer, gets down on one knee, narrows his eyes. "Yeah. I can read it now."

Salinger motions to Morse, Vadney, and me. "Please, gentlemen, come over and see this, it's important to me."

The three of us glance at each other, shrug, walk out of the shadows, into the narrowing band of gold light. Cool breeze is constant, carrying the distant music and voices of women singing, along with the smell of rain. Gravestone is in the first row near the fence and the sun hits it at a slight angle, creating sharp shadows in the weathered words and dates.

Here Lie the Remains of
JOHN JAY SALINGER
Born in the Year of Our Lord,
September 4, 1814,
Died June 9, 1862.
Overlooking Forever His Beloved
Harvard, to which He Devoted 33

Salinger looks up at us, still on one knee, right hand touching the top of the gravestone. "Gentlemen, John Jay Salinger was my great-grandfather. When I was a kid, some sixty-odd years ago, the next line of the epitaph was still showing above the ground. It read: 'Years in the Loyal Service of'; and my grandfather, Nathaniel, told me the last line: 'Mr. Jared Tolkin.'

John Jay Salinger was one of many slaves owned by Jared Tolkin, who ran a contract custodial service for the university. My great-grandfather started full-time work as a janitor when he was fifteen years old. He was born a slave, fathered seven slaves, and died a slave. Died of tuberculosis at the age of forty-eight, less than a year before Abolition. He told Jared Tolkin he wanted to be buried here, wanted it very much, right in this spot, which was one of the few east boundary gravesites left by that time. Not many people know this, but the Old Burying Ground is not owned by the First Church, Unitarian, here, or by Christ Church, Episcopal, up at the northwest boundary. It's owned by the city of Cambridge and it always has been. It was never an Indian burying ground. It was in use not too long after the town was officially 'settled' in sixteen-thirty. By the time the town became an incorporated city in eighteen-forty-six, there weren't many gravesites left. Harvard actually owns a small corner of the Old Burying Ground, just behind the church here, where the presidents' graves are. Henry Dunster, the first president, is buried back there, Charles Chauncy, Samuel Willard, Edward Holyoke. But all the rest of it is owned by the city. There aren't any other slaves buried here, they had their own 'separate but equal' burying ground, but Jared Tolkin honored the dying request of my great-grandfather, reserved this spot for him, bought the gravestone, and the epitaph you see here was actually dictated by John Jay Salinger. He was a proud man. A religious man. And he loved Harvard. He couldn't read or write, but he understood what was going on here, and how important it was, and he was terribly, terribly proud to be a small part of it. During his lifetime, three black students were admitted to the Medical School, the first black students at Harvard, in eighteen-fifty, and he used to talk about that with his children, especially Nathaniel, and what it might mean in the future. The black students were forced to leave after one term, but at least he was a witness to that piece of history. Anyway, gentlemen, if you'll note the birthdate on this stone, you'll see that today is the birthday of John Jay Salinger. For the past six years, I've come back here to honor his memory, to place flowers on his grave, and to promise that his gift was coming. Today, I made good on that promise. A symbolic gift to honor the life of a man who should not be forgotten on this day, the formal opening of Harvard's birthday celebration. In the interests of accuracy, Harvard's actual 'birthday' happens to be October eighteenth, sixteen-thirty-six, when the General Court of Massachusetts gave its official stamp of approval to the establishment of the school. But they couldn't celebrate it on that day, of course, because the university will be in session then. So, when I learned last year that September fourth was selected for the formal opening ceremonies, I laughed out loud. Laughed out loud at the wonderful, benignly indifferent ironies life seems to offer from time to time. Poetic justice, you might say. In any event, that's what I wanted to tell you and show you. My gift to this man on this day is, in cold, hard fact, the only significant achievement I've had in a long, troubled, insignificant life. I'm ready to go now, you can place me under arrest."

"Salinger," Reilly says. "Will you tell me one thing? What in the name of Christ have *I* got to do with any of this?"

"That's strictly personal. An angry, paranoid, personal vendetta. I'll tell you sometime when we're alone. I don't want that part of it to assume importance. It's not important. Except to me."

"For God's sake, man, *tell* me! Tell me what I *did!*"

Salinger stands slowly, turns, looks across the street at the tall white spire of Memorial Church. His long shadow extends across the grass, through the bars of the wrought-iron fence, and across the sidewalk. "You son of a bitch, you don't even remember. It's like chasing ghosts, I swear to God, it always has been. Exactly like that. For so many of us, from the time we're kids until the day we die. People hurt us long ago, hurt us badly, sometimes irreparably, and we want revenge. *Revenge,* pure and simple, nothing else will do, it's always in the back of our minds, the stuff of our daydreams. But we're chasing ghosts: Those people simply don't exist anymore. The people who hurt us back then, far in the past—in this case, thirty years—they're not the same people. They're gone, they're different people in a different time in a different place. They don't even *remember* how they were, who they were, what they did."

"Spit it *out!*" Reilly says. "Tell me what I *did!*"

He turns back now, glances at Reilly, then at the gravestone. "Back in my great-grandfather's time, blacks were generally considered to have the mentality of children, at best, all through their lives, and they were treated as children. When John Jay Salinger was born, he was named after a great statesman, the first Chief Justice of the Supreme Court. He was very proud of that name, but he was never called by that name, not by Jared Tolkin or any white man, ever, in his life. It was just too dignified for a fifteen-year-old nigger boy. Or a forty-eight-year-old nigger boy, for that matter. So, like all the other niggers, he was given a nickname. They called him 'J.J.' Yeah. Cute, huh? Childlike. Benevolent. 'Hey, J.J., haul yer ass over the shithouse there, somebody jes threw up on the flow.' Still, he was luckier than some; some of the nicknames were downright degrading. And they were *stuck* with those names. Stuck with them for *life.* I mean, it wasn't even considered racist or elitist back then, thoughts like that never even entered their skulls. Nicknames for niggers were taken for granted, they were meant to be *humorous.* Humorous? Humorous for *whom?* For the niggers who had to *live* with them, day after day, for the rest of their *lives?* Humorous? I'll tell you what it really is, Reilly: It's *humiliating,* it's *degrading,* it's *embarrassing,* and it's *elitist.* Don't you *know* that, don't you *understand* that?"

Reilly gazes off into space now, frowning, hands by his sides, and speaks just above a whisper. "Oh, no. Oh, my God, no."

"You think it went *away?*" Salinger snaps. "You think you give a humorous nickname to a black janitor in an elitist Catholic high school that's almost all white kids, and everybody gets a laugh out of it, and that's *it,* that's the *end* of it? You tagged me with it in your freshman year, nineteen-fifty-six, when you were a fifteen-year-old arrogant, obnoxious kid. You started it on your own, and nurtured it in front of the others, until the group mentality took over: 'Hey, J.D., how y'doin'?' Yeah. J. D. Salinger, our famous janitor-novelist. Cute, huh? And you think it just went *away?* Let me tell you the truth, let me tell you what hurts, let me tell you what makes me bleed: Every kid, black or white, boy or girl, who ever went to St. Michael's High School over the past *thirty years* has called me 'J.D.' Routinely. I'm talking about tens of thousands of them, generations of them, thirty years of them. From the time they enter as freshmen and get the word, until the day they graduate. Hell, the overwhelming majority have always taken it for granted that *is* my real name. For the past twenty years or so, even the *faculty* has taken it for granted, all the new members of the faculty, they come in and assume that's my real name."

"If you hated it so much, why didn't you fight it, why didn't you do something to stop it?"

"Reilly, come on, don't insult my intelligence. Over a period of—I don't know, the first ten, fifteen years, I tried everything in the book. At my request, various principals mentioned it in their public-address announcements to the classrooms, they included it in faculty bulletins, they asked teachers to give reminders in homerooms, they even had it in the school paper. But I'm sure you know how effective such commands are when you're dealing with high school kids, especially boys. As the years went by, I simply got tired of fighting it. I gave up. I gave up, but I didn't forget. Or forgive."

Reilly thinks about it, then nods. "I don't blame you. If it's any consolation, I never meant it as a racial slur. I really never meant it that way. And I don't think any of the other kids did, either, at least the guys in my class. It was just—a joke. We were just having fun, that's all."

"That's the real irony, Reilly. That's the rationale that's been used as the great panacea by racists for generations untold: It's all in fun, we don't really mean it *that* way; we call you guys Sambo, coon, jig, shine, crow, buck, nigger, uncle, jigaboo, pickaninny, jive-ass, jungle-bunny, all like that, but it's just a *joke.* In a way, I pity people like you, because you were inculcated with hardcore discrimination before you'd even reached the age of reason. By the time you were fifteen, it was far too late."

"That's just not true," Reilly says. "I'm not a racist, never have been, never will be. I never consciously intended that name to be a racial statement. That's the truth. I swear to God."

"You swear to God? *You,* Reilly? An avowed agnostic? I've followed your career closely over the years, the countless newspaper and magazine profiles, the radio and TV talk shows, you've always seemed so willing to admit that you happen to be of the agnostic persuasion. So, when you swear to God, I'm afraid it doesn't mean much to me."

"I resent the implication. For your information, Mr. Salinger, if I may call you that, the term agnostic is from the Greek *agnostos,* meaning unknown, unknowable, not knowing. I don't *deny* the existence of God, but I don't hold an orthodox religious position. I don't know, and I admit that I don't know."

For the first time, Salinger smiles. "Thank you for the enlightening definition. It seems we're divided in opinion on what's knowable and what's not. But then, that's only natural. As you know, throughout the pages of Samuel Eliot Morison's *Three Centuries of Harvard,* there's a phrase that's so true, it could've been used as the university's motto, right up there next to *Veritas,* and that phrase happens to be: 'Harvard men were divided in opinion.' I'm certain you're familiar with that phrase, aren't you, *Mr.* Reilly?"

"Yes." He hesitates, narrows his eyes.

"Yes, Mr. Reilly, it's true. Are you surprised? Are you flabbergasted that an old black high school janitor could possibly be a graduate of this magnificent institution? Gol-lee, Sassafras, wonders never cease, do dey? Harvard Extension, Class of 'Thirty-four. We received a degree called Adjunct in Arts back then, similar to the A.B. of the college, but it didn't make any difference what degree you had, because this country was in the depths of the Great Depression that would last for another six years. There were *no* jobs. *None.* I realize you weren't even born then, but nothing you've read about it or heard about it could possibly give you a realistic perspective about how bad it was. It was totally frightening. There were breadlines all over Cambridge, all over Boston, all over the country. If you were a kid straight out of college with no practical experience, you couldn't *buy* a job. FDR had to *create* jobs with the WPA. In fact, one of the WPA projects was to clean up and beautify this very graveyard we're standing in; I remember teams of men in here, that's when most of these trees were planted, in the early nineteen-thirties. I went to New York to live with relatives. In nineteen-thirty-six, when Harvard celebrated its Tricentennial, I got my first job, and I thanked God every day for it. I was hired as a janitor's apprentice at St. Michael's High School. I was twenty-three years old. With the exception of five years in the army during World War Two, I've been there ever since. That's a span of forty-five years at St. Michael's. They helped me when I needed it the most and I just decided to stay. It was good, honest, dependable work, and I've never been ashamed of it. It's an honorable profession. But it's time to retire now. I haven't told Sister Mary Garcia yet, but I'm going to start training somebody to take over. I'll be out on bail long before Monday, that's when school starts again, so I'll speak to her then. Oh, there's something else you don't know, Mr. Reilly. The statue is back, the statue of St. Michael and Satan." He squints at his watch. "Well, I don't know if he's got it all bolted in place yet, but I asked him to return it by eight o'clock. He's a close friend of mine, a young black man, we just borrowed it for a while. We wanted to play a joke on some agnostic honky I happen to know. We were just having fun, that's all. It was just—a joke."

"And a harbinger of things to come."

"That's correct, Mr. Reilly. A foreshadowing of the main event. A portent, an omen, a symbol, if you will, for those of us who need symbols. Tangible representations, like statues of St. Michael standing victorious over the ugly, cringing, defeated Lucifer, during the so-called war in heaven. An unfortunate symbol, in the judgment of some, because to believe it one must necessarily rely on the allegorical, mystical visions of St. John, telling us about an event that is clearly unknowable, given the limitations of finite intelligence, and therefore clearly unacceptable to people like you."

"If you want to know the truth," Reilly says softly, "your hologram of the serpent wasn't much better."

"Ah, but as long as we're telling each other the truth, Mr. Reilly, please answer this question truthfully, it's extremely important to me: When that coiled serpent suddenly appeared in the darkness, did you experience even a single *second* of belief that it existed?"

Reilly considers it carefully, then: "Yes. I think all of us experienced that, if we're honest about it. It was frightening, no question about it, I'll give you that. It's probably the closest

I've ever come to believing I'd experienced something supernatural."

"Thank you for being honest about it."

"Not at all. I suppose, being a deeply religious man, you believe Satan actually exists?"

"Yes, I believe that. I don't have to see him, or any symbol of him, to know he exists. His works are manifest, that's the only proof I need. But enough of this. I'm sure you gentlemen want to get this over with as soon as possible. I'm at your disposal. I'll give you a complete statement at headquarters, I'll try to make it as easy as I can."

Jack Morse steps over, identifies himself, shows him the warrant, formally places him under arrest. He turns the old man around, goes through the routine frisk as he reads him his rights in a quiet voice, then handcuffs him.

As the five of us walk toward the gate near the church, Salinger limping, the rain finally comes, a gentle rain, so light we can't see it in the shadows; we feel it on our faces. When I look back at the grave of John Jay Salinger, rain drifts like mist through the slender shaft of remaining sunlight and the flowers are still touched by that light. The breeze continues, bringing the distant music and voices.

Morse's car is parked across Massachusetts Avenue in an alcove near the subway entrance to the right of the main gate. People glance at us as we cross the street. Morse unlocks his back door, curb side, opens it wide, places his hand on top of Salinger's head as he eases him inside. I slide in next, on Salinger's right; Vadney gets in the other side. Reilly sits up front with Morse. After the doors are closed, nobody says a word. Only sounds are the engine starting, the headlights being snapped on, and the slow click of the windshield wipers.

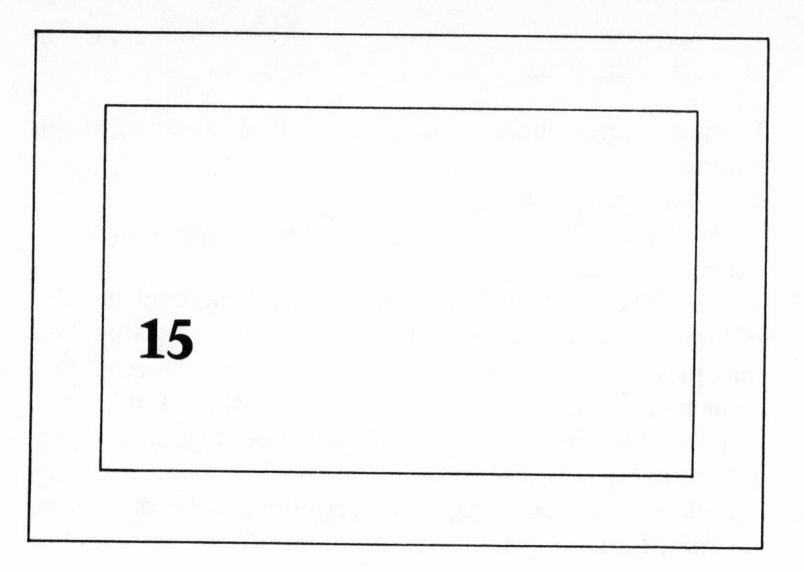

15

SILENCE CONTINUES as Morse maneuvers into the traffic on Massachusetts Avenue, passes the main gate, hits his directional signal, and turns left into Garden Street, heading northwest, with the huge, dark Cambridge Common off to our right.

"Mr. Salinger," I say quietly, "I'm curious about something."

"Yes, Rawlings."

"I mean, this is strictly off the record, just for my own personal information."

"Surely."

"Did you make the holograms yourself?"

"Oh, no, I couldn't afford that kind of equipment. But the art form has intrigued me for years. There are quite a few small studios around New York and Boston now. Holography's finally coming into its own, it's becoming relatively popular."

"That king cobra was really something."

"Yes, it was actually a hologram of a beautiful statuette. Unfortunately, you can't photograph living things—moving things—in holography, because you need almost total stillness for the plate to be successful. I bought that hologram at a little studio on Charles Street in the Village. It was on sale, I got a good bargain on it."

"Uh-huh. And you had the Gutenberg photographed locally?"

He nods, smiles at the memory. "The fact is, all professional holographers in large cities have to do their photographing very late at night. To avoid vibrations, primarily traffic vibrations, because the film is so sensitive. So that part of it worked perfectly for me. I found a little studio in downtown Boston, just off Berkeley Street, not far from police headquarters. I simply told the man I wanted a Bible photographed and I wanted to watch him do it. I made an appointment for three o'clock in the morning last Sunday. He had everything ready when I arrived, went straight to work, a real pro, fascinating to watch. It took him one hour and forty-five minutes to shoot, develop, and have three finished holograms for me to choose from. The man never had a clue what he was shooting. Never even asked a question about it, he was too intent on his work. I won't reveal his name, of course, but he's completely innocent."

Chief's taking all this in, frowning, nodding, shaking his head. Now he sits forward, clears his throat. "Anthony, one thing I still can't figure, it's been driving me nuts. I mean, you've agreed to make a complete confession and all, so it's no big deal. How'd you get hold of that electronic key card for the display case?"

Reflections of headlights move over the old man's face. "I simply hired a professional locksmith, a man who guaranteed me he could open the Mosler safe I described within fifteen minutes. As it turned out, he solved the combination in nine minutes flat. I'd been negotiating with him, on and off, for about two and a half years. Money was the only serious problem. He could never understand why I was going to return it instead of ransom it. I'm sure he thought I was senile or crazy. Anyway, since the risk factor was minimal, he finally settled for a flat fee, one thousand in cash. Not too bad for nine minutes' work."

Reilly's turned now, listening, studying the man's face. "How'd you get access to the Lampoon Building?"

"In the summer, there's very little activity in there, so janitorial service is reduced to once a week, the ground floor only. I've handled it during the month of August for the past two years. Did I manage to frighten you a little, Mr. Reilly?"

"You could've damaged my eardrums, you realize that? And you could've damaged the eardrums of four detectives who were inside at the time. That ever occur to you?"

"As a matter of fact, yes, it did. That's why I limited the high-frequency screams to thirty seconds, at an escalating volume. I reasoned that anyone inside the building would be long gone by then."

"How compassionate," Reilly says. "Who the hell was doing that screaming anyway?"

"An actor. An out-of-work young black actor. I had that recorded at a studio in New York about a year ago. I was quite pleased with the man's performance. I told him to imagine he was burning alive. To my ear, he sounded convincing. As I say, they recorded that segment at an escalating high-frequency volume, then I merely took the cassette home and recorded my message with my own tape recorder, speaking into a large glass container to distort my voice."

"What about the classroom tape?" I ask. "Recorded in a studio?"

He glances at me, smiles, nods. As the headlights of another car go past, I see tiny drops of rain on his face and at the edges of his white goatee. "Yes, Rawlings, you're absolutely right, I used a sound-effects tape. Afterward, when Sister Mary told me you suspected something like that, and even questioned her about it, I must say I was impressed. You combine good common sense with excellent intuition. The tape I used for the classroom was recorded in a studio, the same studio, as a matter of fact. Five minutes of chalk-on-blackboard sounds from stock sound effects, followed by five minutes of—they used stock effects of a growling Bengal tiger and recorded it at superhigh frequency, thirty gigahertz. That's far above the range of human hearing, but well within the range of most dogs. It causes some discomfort to dogs, but doesn't damage their eardrums. I planned that classroom scene about a year ago. I knew Reilly would show up after reading the note, and I knew he'd be advised to take the routine precaution of having the Bomb Squad search the entire school. And, of course, I knew it was standard procedure for the Bomb Squad to use a dog. So I thought the Enochian Key would be a nice touch, combined with a frightened dog."

"It certainly was," I tell him. "So you were—you *had* to be in the school that afternoon."

"Of course," he says, glancing at the brightly lighted Sheraton-Commander Hotel. "But I didn't know what time the Bomb Squad would arrive, so I had to play it safe. I went to the school about six o'clock that morning, printed the First Enochian Key on the blackboard, and rehearsed the scene quite a few times. I was concerned about the timing, about the exact number of seconds it would take the Bomb Squad officers, the dog, and Sister Mary Garcia to walk from the foyer to the lighted classroom, at which time the chalk sounds would stop and the superhigh-frequency growls would begin. So I walked through it all and timed it, trying to allow for an approximate error factor of plus or minus five to seven seconds."

"But then I showed up," I say. "I showed up alone and screwed up your whole show."

"Not really, Rawlings; I just had to make a few revisions.

I watched you arrive from a ground-floor window to the left of the front door. I took you for an advance man from headquarters or from the Bomb Squad. I watched you leaning against the pillar, smoking your cigar, I reasoned you were waiting for Sister Mary. Then, when you turned, said something, and walked up to the door, which I couldn't see from the window, I thought Sister Mary had arrived—she has access through the rectory. Who actually let you in, Sister Frances?"

"Sister—?"

"Sister Frances Barbella, the assistant principal?"

"No. I don't—"

It's over in seconds, but a sick, dizzy sensation lingers. I blink, use the pillar for support, clear my throat, try to smile at the dark figure in the doorway. "Sister Mary Garcia?"

Salinger studies my face. "It doesn't matter. Anyway, at that point, I went directly to the office and started the tape. It took about twenty seconds to get there. I reasoned that you'd talk in the foyer for a while, at least twenty seconds."

No answer. The silhouette is motionless. Now I squint, I see it's not a female figure at all, it's a man, relatively tall and lean, wearing a dark garment that looks like a priest's tunic. Before I have a chance to walk toward him, the heavy wooden door closes.

"Then," Salinger says, "when you heard the chalk sounds, you'd walk down to the classroom immediately. And I knew that would take seventeen to twenty seconds. Did the chalk sounds stop before you reached the room?"

It doesn't slam or anything dramatic, it just closes quietly and clicks, with the dark figure behind it. Strange thing is, the figure remained absolutely motionless. So how did the door close?

"Rawlings?" Salinger says.

"Yeah."

"I was just curious. Did the chalk sounds stop before you reached the classroom?"

"Yeah. Just before I went in. Mr. Salinger, forgive me, but I want to get something straight, it's important to me. Are you saying you didn't unlock the front door of the school, open it for me, and then stand there for a few seconds?"

"That's the last thing I would've done, Rawlings, let you get a look at me. In fact, later on, when I went back to the front window and saw you leave alone, I was surprised. Then, when Sister Mary Garcia arrived outside and met everybody, and you shook her hand, I just assumed Sister Frances had let you in. Do you remember what she looked like—about five-seven, a little overweight, quite attractive, mid-thirties?"

"It wasn't her," I tell him. "It was definitely a man. Tall, thin, wearing a priest's tunic."

The old man shakes his head slowly, negatively. "I can tell you this for certain. I was there from about six in the morning until—I think it was around three-fifty-five, when all of you were in the classroom with the Bomb Squad. I played all five minutes of the superhigh-frequency tape for the dog, then pulled it, replaced it with Sister Mary Garcia's cassette, and left by the rear door. In all that time, no priest was in that school."

At HUPD headquarters, Salinger is booked, fingerprinted, and has mug shots taken. He waives his right to call an attorney, says he'll take one appointed by the court. He wants to get the confession over with as soon as possible, so Morse takes him to his office, where he'll tape-record it. After it's transcribed and typed up, and Salinger reads and signs it, he'll be transported to the nearest precinct of the Cambridge Police Department for further processing, a night-court hearing, Legal Aid appointment, and bail procedures. Reilly's on the phone with his wife, giving a blow-by-blow report, Vadney's on the phone with the night city desk editor of the *Boston Globe,* gassing up a storm, telling him to get a reporter and photographer up here fast, it's an exclusive, hold the front page.

Me, I'm not feeling very well, I decide to go back to the room and lie down. I don't tell anybody where I'm going, I just go. I don't have an umbrella, I don't want one, the rain feels cool and soft on my face. I walk slowly down Garden Street, try to get my head together, try to put this thing in some kind of logical perspective.

And I say to myself: Come on, John, face up to the possibility, at least. Just the remote possibility, that's all. The possibility that you were in the presence of something that can't be explained by logic, that can't be understood, but that can't be *denied.* Admit to the possibility, that's all. Why not? Why should that be so painful, so frustrating, so totally unacceptable? Why can't you step over that line? Doctors do, scientists do, theologians do. They admit openly to the presence of weird phenomena that they don't understand, that they don't think anybody understands. Why can't you? Why can't you admit to the very real possibility that you may have been in the presence of Satan?

When I get all the way down to the Old Burying Ground and walk along near the wrought-iron fence, the crowns of the trees are in silhouette against the clouds to the west, and sometimes the reflections of headlights move over the gravestones near the fence. I stop for a while, just across the street from the main gate, where I can see the lighted buildings in the Old Yard and hear the distant band music, still playing in the rain. I cup my hands to light a cigar, lean back against the fence, and think: The son of a bitch *lied* to me. It's the one and only logical explanation. *That's the last thing I would've done, Rawlings, let you get a look at me.* Why would he lie to me, what possible reason would he have? The man's a psycho, that's why. Totally brilliant, but a psycho. *I can tell you this for certain. In all that time, no priest was in that school.* He's tall, he's lean, he had keys to the church, he had easy access to the vestry room, he could've taken a priest's tunic with no sweat at all. He knew I'd see him in silhouette with the lights behind him. But why would he do that to me, why would he lie, why would he want to cause me this kind of grief? Because he's a psycho, that's why. It *had* to be him. There's just no way I can believe anything else. That's it, that's the one and only logical explanation. Boom, over, finished, forget it.

I jaywalk to the center island, then jaywalk across to the main gate. It's closed, as usual, so I walk to the small gate at the right side. Guess who's the security guard? Right the first time, Dennis B. Patrick, Jr. Tough little Jimmy Cagney bulldog in his black poncho and rain hat, checking tickets, he don't bend no rules for nobody. I get my ticket out, give him a smile as I walk up.

"Good evening, Officer Patrick. Nice night for a band concert."

"Detective Rawlings!" He takes my elbow, ushers me off to the side, speaks confidentially. "I seen you guys across the street there. Comin' out the Old Burying Ground with Jack Morse."

"That's right."

"Who was the old black guy in cuffs?"

"Man who stole the Gutenberg."

"No!"

"Yeah."

"Rawlings, ya pullin' m'leg?"

"No. He confessed and all."

"*Confessed,* did he?"

"Yeah."

"Did yez recover the Bible?"

"Yeah. He returned it to Widener this afternoon."

"*Returned* it, did he?"

"Yeah. Says he just borrowed it."

"*Borrowed* it?"

"That's what the man said."

Patrick blinks, shakes his head. "Another crazy. Drugs?"

"No drugs. Just crazy."

"I'll tell you somethin', Rawlings. There's a lot of crazies out there these days. Dopers, terrorists, fanatics. Sometimes it seems to me the whole world's gone crazy."

"It's not like the old days, that's for sure."

He looks up at me, rain dripping from his hat. "I mean, it seems like nothin' is sacred anymore. Nothin'. Not even heah. Y'know, the people who founded this school were good, sober, God-fearin' men. Teachin' their students to be the same. That's how it was back then, that's how it started out." He holds my gaze, jerks a thumb toward the Old Yard, where we hear loud laughter and singing above the band music now, even a few catcalls. "Seems like it's all gone crazy."

"Hell, Patrick, they're just having fun."

"Fun? Half of 'em are bombed out of their skulls."

"Yeah, well, it's champagne, y'know?"

"Champagne, is it?"

"Yeah. Too highbrow for my tastes."

"Mine, too. Hate the stuff."

"What time you get off, Patrick?"

"Me? Ten-thirty, when it's over. I been on duty since eight-thirty this mornin'."

"You must be getting thirsty by now."

"Well, now, I just might be."

"You wouldn't happen to know any joints around here where they might happen to serve very, very dry Beefeater martinis, would you?"

He blinks, frowns. "Well, now, bejeez, I just might."

"You wouldn't happen to want an old New York cop to help you taste a few of those suckers, would you?"

"Well, now, bejeez, I just might."

I glance at my watch. "I gotta go in, grab a shower, lie down for a while. I'll be here ten-thirty sharp. We'll do some celebrating of our own. I figure, guys like us, we deserve it."

"Rawlings, now you're talkin'."

When I go in through the little gate, the music stops for a while. I walk slowly past Massachusetts Hall, and the ground-floor lamp hanging from the far corner, once gaslit, throws pale yellow patterns across the ivy-covered bricks and white window frames. Rain is like a very fine, drifting mist. It's a proud old building, four stories of simple and straight lines, strong and practical, the facade unchanged since 1720. Me, I love architecture like this, it's got charm and character, a personality all its own. Gives me a feeling of what it must've been like back then, long before this nation existed, when life was so different. Haunting, that's the only word for it. When I reach the end and glance back at it, I feel a sense of history, of a time and place that's difficult to imagine. But when I turn the corner and head toward Weld, the band music starts again, and I'm back in reality. All the lighted walkways are overflowing with people, young and old, a blur of colors, singing, laughing, shouting, drinking, and they're dancing in the Yard in the rain.

About the Author

John Minahan is the author of sixteen books, including the Doubleday Award–winning novel *A Sudden Silence,* the million-copy best-seller *Jeremy,* and the first five thrillers in this series. An alumnus of Cornell, Harvard, and Columbia, he is a former staff writer for *Time* magazine, and was editor and publisher of *American Way* magazine. Mr. Minahan and his wife, Verity, live in Miami, where he is writing the sixth novel in the series. He commutes to Cambridge every week to teach a novel-writing workshop at Harvard's Center for Lifelong Learning.